SKYING

SKYING

by

Peter Somerville-Large

HAMISH HAMILTON
London

HAMISH HAMILTON LTD

Published by the Penguin Group
27 Wrights Lane, London w8 5tz, England
Viking Penguin Inc, 40 West 23rd Street, New York, New York 10010, u.s.a.
Penguin Books Australia Ltd, Ringwood, Victoria, Australia
Penguin Books Canada Ltd, 2801 John Street, Markham, Ontario, Canada l3r 1b4
Penguin Books (N.Z.) Ltd, 182–190 Wairau Road, Auckland 10, New Zealand

Penguin Books Ltd, Registered Offices: Harmondsworth, Middlesex, England

First published in Great Britain 1989 by
Hamish Hamilton Ltd

Extract (p. 6) from 'Flying Crooked' by Robert Graves from *Collected Poems*
reprinted by permission of A. P. Watt Ltd on behalf of the executors of Robert
Graves. Extracts (pp. 38 and 44) from *Eugene Onegin* by Alexander Pushkin,
translated by Charles Johnston (Penguin Classics, 1979), copyright © Charles
Johnston, 1977, 1979, reprinted by permission of Penguin Books Ltd. 'Perfect'
(p. 134) by Hugh MacDiarmid from *The Islands of Scotland* reprinted by permission of
Mrs Valda Grieve and Martin Brian & O'Keefe Ltd. Extract (p. 144) from *Jonathan
Livingston Seagull* by Richard Bach reprinted by permission of Thorson Publishing
Group. 'Days' (p. 163) by Philip Larkin from *The Whitsun Weddings* reprinted by
permission of Faber & Faber Ltd. Extract (p. 180) from 'The Wind is Blind' by
Alice Meynell reprinted by permission of The Nonesuch Press.

Cataloguing in Publication Data is available from the British Library

ISBN 0241-12741-6

Printed in Great Britain by
Richard Clay Ltd, Bungay, Suffolk

Contents

CHAPTER ONE

Sandymount Strand and Carlow

As each new load was up-ended and tipped out over the dump, the cries of the seagulls became louder than the roar of the passing traffic. A covey settled on a patch of waste land and was excitedly jabbing with great yellow beaks. Here was one large bird moving away on a zigzag flight, carrying a piece of decomposing food, pursued by half a dozen others. A driver looked on from his cab as a forklift nudged more rubbish into this corner of Dublin Bay. I watched as well and, like any pilot, I was jealous of those wheeling, falling birds.

As a gull homed in, side-slipping its wings, seizing without touching ground something that was falling from the forklift, I remembered John Penrose's similar feelings to mine. 'I've always envied the seagull, he seems so free and uninhibited in his flying. In contrast with him I fuss and figure and clutter up the sky with noise just to stay in the air.' The gull is a daring aeronaut, capable of low-speed stalls, inverted spins and a miraculous ability to soar and dive to within a few inches of a wave before suddenly recovering its wasted flight. For formation flying the Red Arrows cannot beat him and his companions.

The cloud of birds was rising and falling against the stacks of the Pigeon House, shooting up like sparks, riding wind currents and then descending in a squadron on more dross thrown out by dear dirty Dublin. I was preparing to fly a microlight over Sandymount Strand, and they were only partly a distraction. Every flying novice is told by his instructor: 'Watch the birds!' Airmen should be bird-watchers like the psalmist. 'Oh that I had wings like a dove! for then would I fly away, and be at rest.'

Wilbur Wright was a bird-watcher before his brother flew their string-and-linen aeroplane. He left detailed notes.

'Hawks are better soarers than buzzards, but more often resort to flapping because they wish greater speed.'

'A damp day is unfavourable for soaring unless there is a high wind.'

'No bird soars in a calm.'

In 1900 Wilbur noted how 'a bird when soaring does not seem to alternately rise and fall as some observers have thought. Any rising or falling is irregular, and seems to be due to disturbances of fore-and-after equilibrium produced by gusts. In light winds the birds seem to rise constantly without any downward turns.'

Long after the Kitty Hawk had flown from Kill Devil Hill, his brother Orville wrote: 'Learning the secret of flight from a bird was a good deal like learning the secret of magic from a magician. After you know the trick and what to look for, you see things you didn't notice when you didn't know exactly what to look for.'

I found watching performing birds only made me feel discontented. I had so much to learn. I left them to their acrobatics over the garbage and went over to where pieces of metal tubing and Dacron, which looked as if they might be discards from the dump, were waiting to be assembled into a microlight.

The place we had chosen for our flying was Sandymount Strand which combines with Merrion Strand in a curving sweep of sand backed by the Wicklow hills. At low tide the sea retreats very far, leaving a shining plain where the sun gleams on water trapped in ridges of wet sand. Seaward the horizon, a melting combination of sand, sea and sky, is broken by the lump of Howth Head. Solitary walkers move beside the streams left by the ebbing tide which are attended by water-birds; men stop and dig for lugworms. You see the occasional pink-fleshed bather bravely wading into the cold polluted sea. The strands have been places of escape for generations of Dubliners. In the old days bathers wore nothing. 'The swarm of naked figures thus seen on the shore from Ringsend to Sandymount', a Victorian traveller noted, 'is as singular as it is surprising.'

Along the shore the first train in Ireland puffed its way to Kingstown on the same route the modern electric DART (Dublin Area Rapid Transit) takes today. Before the age of steam it had been a place of shipwrecks where sailing ships like the troopship *Prince of Wales* foundered after leaving the Pigeon House on a stormy night, and hundreds of soldiers' bodies were cast up on Merrion Strand.

Stephen Dedalus walked along here with his ashplant, contemplating. 'Do you see the tide flowing quickly in on all sides, sheeting the lows of sands quickly shell-cocoacoloured'? He called the sea 'that great quivering'. Dedalus was a good name for an aviator.

'Hold up the nose!'

'She's lifting.'

'I can't find the bolt nut and washer.'

'The petrol is dripping out of the can.'

The wind was blowing from the south-east and fleecy clouds drifted in from the sea. We were three elderly men who were spending our declining years participating in the rediscovery of flight. I was old enough to remember Alan Cobham's flying circus in Phoenix Park in the 1930s when I had watched fragile biplanes and goggled aviators doing stunts over the heads of a cheering crowd. Robin had flown many years ago on the North-West Frontier, while Tom was far more experienced than either of us. My own knowledge of flying had been limited to hang gliding, when all three of us had spent a period some years back hurling ourselves off the Sugarloaf and Mount Leinster.

Hang gliding is an inexpensive method of capturing the elemental thrill of pioneer flight, induced by the miraculous sensation of standing on the edge of a hill and jumping into the wind and the sky. The hang glider obeys the rules of aerodynamics like an eagle or a condor, and no other glider or flying machine offers such excitement. But it has its drawbacks, including the big inconvenience in this lazy age of having to be carried up a hill before take-off. As we got older, this exercise became less attractive. Hang gliding is also dangerous, or so our families thought. We sold our hang glider and acquired a micro-light.

During the past decade the microlight has developed as the motor bike of the sky, enabling pilots to fly cheaply in whatever direction they want. Basically microlights are motorized hang gliders with the same controls. Most average around fifty miles an hour; they take off and land within a comparatively small area – 400 to 450 yards; they weigh very little, and the majority have wings that fold up. Although they do not give you the pure thrill of hang gliding, they repeat some of the excitement of the early days of aviation. The joy of being in control of a very small flying machine is not what you feel as a passenger in a jumbo jet.

Our microlight was a second-hand Eagle bought by Tom, who had introduced microlight flying into Ireland. Although I found the idea of the noisy engine unattractive, I looked forward to being in control of my vehicle instead of always at the mercy of winds and thermals. Eventually I planned to travel around the British Isles at a leisurely pace, looking over England and Ireland.

Microlights are a very recent development in the history of aviation, having evolved quickly during the last decade from home-made string bags which used to be considered dangerous mechanical jokes. Now the latest models have enclosed cabins, and they are rapidly turning into little aeroplanes. Our Eagle was not only second-hand but second-generation. Generations of microlights have evolved with the speed of fruit-flies.

Slowly the bits and pieces lying on the sand were assembled into a stubby vehicle dominated by an outsized wing. The Eagle, a tiny machine powered by the sort of engine that runs a lawn mower, was a classic trike, the most popular form of microlight descended from the auto-giros devised by the Frenchman, Roland Magallon, in 1979. The body, containing a collapsible seat, a 450-cc engine and a wooden propeller fixed on behind, ran on three small wheels, and its appearance put you in mind of the side-car of an old motor bike. The immense wing hovering overhead was a thirty-foot boomerang of tubed metal covered in yellow and white striped Dacron.

I examined the trike, the wing bolted to it, and the propeller whose edges Tom had stuck all over with plastic repellent against any stones thrown up from the sand. Aids to flying were minimal, a foot throttle and an austere dashboard containing an altitude indicator, a rev counter and a small compass. Like the hang glider, it was guided by a steering bar which the pilot pushed in and out, or sideways if he wanted to initiate a turn. (They like that term 'initiate'.) There was no windshield to protect you from the wind and the rain and no cockpit, just a hollowed-out hole in the fibreglass body like a canoe.

People streamed over the sand to watch us as, trying to appear nonchalant, I tied a scarf round my neck and strapped on a bulbous helmet. The wind was bucketing up and down above the fragile body as Tom and I heaved our thirteen-stone frames into the hollow and arranged ourselves like mating frogs. My legs curled around Tom's back, and his helmet was an unyielding globe against my chest. The safety strap was reassuring.

'Hold the bar while I start the engine.'

That meant reaching past Tom and grabbing the thin horizontal wand that formed the only control. I could see a woman walking near the tide's edge exercising her dog, a train sweeping past inland, and more figures rushing over towards us kicking up sea-water.

'Clear prop!' Tom shouted as Robin tried to shoo away several children in danger of being dismembered. One small girl in particular, sucking an ice-lolly, kept advancing towards the propeller as if drawn by a magnet.

'All right, clear prop!'

The engine was started by pulling a cord. Nothing happened. Tom tried again.

'The carburettor has probably got flooded.'

Tom unbuckled and heaved himself out. Time passed before he was satisfied and clambered back, watched now by a considerable crowd. On these occasions a crowd willing you to go off can provide an element of danger, not only because any fool or child can interfere with the actual flight. The danger comes from its expectancy. You feel compelled to perform.

From the earliest days of flight pilots have flown in unsuitable conditions pushed into action by the urgency of staring eyes. Before the success of Kitty Hawk, the Scotsman, Percy Pilcher, one of the most intrepid of early gliding pilots, was killed by a desire not to disappoint. On 30 September 1899, he conducted a gliding demonstration for a group of aeronautical enthusiasts. His gliders had been left out in the rain overnight and were waterlogged, but he still went on with the show. Watched by an admiring audience, he took off in his Hawk, a glider with cambered wings and a tail unit that hinged upwards. Rocked in a high wind, soaked in water, it broke up in the air. A bamboo rod snapped, the tail assembly gave way and Pilcher plummeted to the ground.

Many similar tragedies took place after the discovery of powered flight, particularly in the years leading up to the First World War. The horrific casualty rate, with more than a hundred pilots killed, was in part due to the fact that flying was nothing more than a spectator sport where men were quite likely to die in front of audiences.

In contrast the Wright brothers had difficulty in getting anyone to come over and look at their flying experiments and had to hang out a flag to summon a few small boys and sparse beach-dwellers as witnesses to a new age.

The ignition switch was turned on again and the engine given a few sharp pulls. This time it responded with a fierce roar and began shaking and trembling with anxiety to be off. Tom shouted something I couldn't hear as Robin ran up pointing to the end of my scarf a few inches away from the propeller. After that Tom concentrated on the small rev counter, revving up the engine while Robin kept his foot on the front wheel. The propeller blades made a halo behind my head.

'All right?'

The Eagle faced into the wind with Sandymount stretching ahead, pools of water, drifts of bright green seaweed and bronze ripples of sand which glinted golden as the sun hit them under a big sky. Tom pushed down the throttle with his foot and, after a few sharp bumps, we rattled upwards, the machine giving a sense of effort like an old man climbing a hill. The pools of sea-water became mirrors reflecting the sun, the sand slipped into a new scratched pattern that seemed to undulate with our movement, the doughnut ring of spectators burst and scattered, and the woman and her dog were reduced to crumbs.

Tom turned his head and indicated that I should do the flying. In general terms the technique was simple — push up to go higher, and pull down to go low, while the throttle also affected altitude and height. I had not realized how much physical effort was required to keep the microlight going straight. In hang gliders the wind has to be tested and fought all the time, but I had though that a microlight, propelled by its engine, would be much easier to control. It wasn't. I had to contend with a certain amount of turbulence, and in my inexperienced hands the wings kept dipping and yawing above the sand like Robert Graves's cabbage-white:

> He lurches here and there by guess
> And God and hope and hopelessness.
> Even the aerobatic swift
> Has not his flying-crooked gift.

I learnt a number of things during that ten-minute flight between Merrion Gates and the stacks of the Pigeon House before Tom brought down the Eagle and we splashed across the sand as people began running towards us again to make up another crowd. I learnt how flying a microlight retained most of the thrill of hang gliding, although the measure of control was less than I had expected. I enjoyed having first-hand confirmation that it was possible to go on a journey in one, instead of merely moving through the sky on an aerial spree. I realized how much I lacked in skill. I was like Jonathan Livingston Seagull with his cry, 'I'm too dumb! I'm too stupid! I try and try but I'll never get it!' J.L.S. eventually acquired the skills of the birds I had seen soaring over the dump. I would need plenty of practice.

But the following weeks ushered in a terrible summer during which there were very few days offering good weather and the right opportunity to fly. I was condemned to endure the frustrations imposed by the weather that had marred my hang gliding interlude. Amazingly some of the world's best hang gliding and microlight pilots were British. Was it possible that the weather was better in England? Here it seemed that summer didn't exist, that the waves of wind and rain were controlled by monsoon forces, and that nowhere else in the world except perhaps in Patagonia were conditions more unsuitable for flying small aircraft than in Ireland. Moreover, there was another imponderable that impeded our progress – before we could fly, we had to wait for low tide at Sandymount.

Occasionally the sun shone, the wind was light, the tide was out, and the little Eagle became a part of beach life, taking its place with swimmers, exercise freaks, ponies, children digging sand-castles and ice-cream vendors. Tom made a number of people happy by giving them free rides. He took up members of my family, one of whom found the experience enduringly frightening, and now cannot watch Arabian fantasies about magic carpets without feelings of terror and cries of 'No one is wearing a seat belt!'

One day after we arrived on the beach and were beginning the laborious process of assembly, a German tourist drove up in a large van and proceeded to unload a shiny new single-seater microlight. His English was limited. Was it possible he was saying he had never flown in a microlight before? That appeared to be the case. He may not have understood the murmurs of three elderly gentlemen that it might be better to get some experience first, and as the ghost of the Red Baron peered through the haze we watched him buckle himself in and start up the engine. We looked on in fascinated horror as he put on full throttle which sent him skimming into the air like a frisbee. He shot above the sand this way and that and I didn't have to be an expert to see that he had only marginal control. After watching for a few agonizing minutes, Tom climbed into the Eagle and set off in pursuit. What he hoped to do was unclear. He could hardly shoot him down.

The German zigzagged like a blind bumble-bee, swerved, rose, initiated a turn as if he was on a parade ground, rocked, moved in some serpentine loops that had him brushing the seaweed, roared, dipped towards the horizon and finally went out of sight. That was the last we saw of him but, looking down from his height, Tom watched him landing in the sea. He was lucky because the tide at Sandymount goes out very far. A good crash is one where the pilot walks away, and this one waded away. Later, we learnt he put his waterlogged machine up for sale.

It would have been sad if he had hurt himself, since apart from injuries to his person, he would have put our flying routine, such as it was, into jeopardy. So far the authorities had been untroubled by the regular appearance of the Eagle on the strand, but a bad flying accident would have annoyed them.

Another week passed, and Robin took off from Sandymount on his first solo in the Eagle. Long ago he had flown planes over the North-West Frontier, dropping pamphlets on Waziris, urging them to surrender. (Our great age was a constant source of wonder to spectators and other pilots, but we become used to being addressed as Uncle or Grandad.) Now I watched enviously as he buzzed over the sand. A small man, he sat comfortably with his legs stretched in front of him, a pillow supporting his back, looking across Dublin Bay like a clubman after a good meal. He touched down as smoothly as sand ridges allowed, switched off the engine and unbuckled his seat belt. 'No problems.'

My own progress was unbearably slow and summer was well advanced before there came a Saturday when the tide was out by two o'clock and Tom said, 'This time you fly it, I'll sit in the back.'

As a back-seat flyer I had not yet undergone the essential training of combining foot throttle control and lift-off, while landing had been managed over Tom's back with only the frame bar under my supervision.

'She's all yours.'

I was suddenly sharply aware of how there was no cockpit or parachute, and the wing drooped overhead in a way that now seemed little more than ornamental. I held the bar tightly, switched on and pulled the cord, getting the encouragement of an instant start. Behind my back came the reassurance of the engine ticking over before I pushed down the throttle. Always keep on full throttle while taking off. When you are airborne, don't take off full power until you are well up, otherwise you invite the lethal danger of stalling.

The heartbeat note of the engine changed into a roar, continuing with the noise of a hundred tearing carpets as the wind rushed past and we were travelling faster and faster across the strand. Try now, there's all the room in the world. I pushed out. Nothing happened. Again. There was a pool of water ahead which was getting closer and figures that had been distant rapidly dominated the view, particularly a group of boys and a large dog. Collision with this dog became a distinct possibility, as the microlight continued to rush onward making dainty little bumps as it met the sand ridges. I pushed further out and we were flying. The boys below were looking up, while the dog leapt up and down, its mouth moving in barks I could not hear. I steadied out – down with the nose. A formation of birds was flying along the sea's edge. In the distance was the church spire of Dun Laoghaire and the crab claws of the harbour; Saturday's sailing races covered the blue sea with sails. Killiney Hill was beyond. Beneath us a road choked with traffic. She was slipping a little on the turn.

The distraction of the view, combined with my struggle to keep airborne, meant that I had pressed my foot too tightly against the throttle. A quick change of tempo, before we began coming down slowly on lines of houses and a green double-decker bus, as the pilot's intrusive eye peered into the gardens full of trees. I could see how the restless roads with their convoys of traffic deprived the urban landscape of tranquillity. Over the sand the Eagle, under my guidance, made a slow turn at the Pigeon House chimneys, giving me a glimpse of sprawling Ringsend. In order to land I switched off power and the Eagle come down like a hang glider as the engine roar changed into the shrill whistle of wind against the wire struts. The speed gauge read around forty-five, well above stalling speed, and I had to maintain it, knowing that a significant percentage of novice pilots crash because of immature stalls.

The few seconds coming in to land happen so quickly that your reactions have to be instinctive. You are safe in space, while the ground is a killer if you meet it the wrong way. Just when I was poised to land, I noticed two girls strolling unconcernedly, their backs to the silent machine. The wind was in their faces, and I was still coming down. They were deceived by the lack of sound, in the way I remembered walking along a deserted railway line, surprised and nearly caught by the swift approach of a silent train.

Tom's gloved hand pointed towards my unsuspecting victims. Quickly, more power, more throttle and we were airborne again. A few hundred feet up until once more we had the view of Dublin Bay that Gogarty described when he flew about in his small plane, one of the rewards of a lucrative medical practice (he also had a Rolls-Royce). 'On the right is the smooth outline of the Dublin mountains rising like cones and rippling into nipples like the Paps of Jura.' Again we came down silently, and on that first flight I didn't hit the two girls or the old man who had rolled up his trousers and was paddling on the edge of the sea.

I was hoping that Tom might say 'Take it up yourself', but he didn't. Some friends were waiting for a flight and by the time they had all finished, it was getting dark.

That day proved to be the end of our flying on Sandymount Strand. A problem arose unexpectedly when a newspaper photographer took a picture of the Eagle in mid-air, and through a trick of perspective his long-distance lens made out that we were skirting the rooftops of some adjoining houses. The photograph caught the attention of the authorities which had previously turned a blind eye to our flying and we could not convince them that they were deceived by an optical illusion. After being pronounced a danger to the public, we had to abandon the unique privilege of flying in the heart of a capital city with the gulls for company.

We had followed honourably in the eccentric tradition of other airmen who had used Dublin as a base. I thought of the first, Richard Crosbie, who ascended from Ranelagh Gardens, not far from here, in a balloon painted with the arms of Ireland. He was clad in an 'aerial dress' which he had designed himself, consisting of a robe of oiled silk lined with white fur, waistcoat and breeches combined in a garment of quilted white satin, morocco boots and a montero hat of leopard skin. He needed the quilting and the fur, since the date was 19 January 1785 when he attempted to cross the Irish Sea. He began well, rising and blowing eastward but he did not get far. The end of his journey was described in the *Freeman's Journal*:

from the most certain account we can inform the town that in about ten minutes after he became invisible on his ascent, he landed in perfect safety on the strand near the island of Clontarf.

Over a century later George Francis Fitzgerald, Professor of Physics at Trinity College, tried to fly a glider in College Park. He had purchased the glider, a monoplane of the No. 11 type, from Otto Lilienthal, who supplied ready-to-assemble kits to aspiring aviators all over the world. Percy Pilcher and William Randolph Hearst each possessed one. The monoplane, with radial willow ribs extending outwards to which cloth covering was attached like giant bats' wings, cost £25. The pilot controlled the glider by shifting his weight around, a manoeuvre which killed a number of good airmen who died at that momentous time when powered flight first appeared to be feasible. Lilienthal had written:

As yet strong winds are the terror of all aviators and to the whim of the wind has been added the whim of the motor . . . We have not yet succeeded in taming the wind and utilizing its wild forces. We have to continue our investigations . . . experiments guided by theoretical considerations will have to clear up many problems before we can claim victory from the air.

It may be that Professor Fitzgerald was more prepared to give a good show than solve the mysteries of flight. Although none of his attempts at flying was successful, apart from one episode of tethered flight, his experiments were extremely colourful. There are photographs of the occasion when the glider was launched in College Park on an April morning in 1896. 'Look out, Professor, there's bird-lime laid in the Park!' yelled a spectator. A slide was constructed which ran down from the cricket pavilion and it was hoped to pull the glider down this with rope fast enough to create the momentum that would get it airborne. Stalwart college lads dressed in cricket whites provided the muscle power and ladies and gents were there to watch and applaud the professor strapped inside, 'quite confident that, in a steady breeze, it would be quite feasible to soar with apparatus of this kind'. He weighed eleven and a half stone and he was almost raised in 'pretty strong gusts'. Almost, but not quite – the spectators dispersed.

Photographs show the bearded handsome half-length figure tucked into the flimsy glider wearing a top hat, the distinctive headwear for a Fellow of Trinity College. The hat did not necessarily denote a frivolous attitude towards the enterprise, since in those days flying-attire was often formal. Richard Crosbie's pioneering 'aerial dress' had not set a fashion. For his first powered flight Orville Wright wore a suit and a shirt with white collar and tie. He took off his bowler hat and put on a cap instead, which he secured with a safety pin, knowing already that, at a height of a hundred feet, 'if you did not take the precaution to fasten your hat before starting, you have probably lost it by this time'.

Professor Fitzgerald gave up his attempts to fly and his glider was suspended in the dome of the Museum Building in Trinity before a colleague acquired it and lent it to a friend who crashed it after a jump from the top of a hay-rick. The professor lacked the true obsession of an aviator pioneer. He was not impelled sufficiently by the passion described by W. H. Hudson as 'the desire we all have at times for wings, or at all events for the power of flight − the fact is, once we have got above the world, and have an unobstructed view all around, whether the height above the surrounding countryside is 500 or 5,000 feet, then we at once experience all that sense of freedom, triumph and elation which the mind is capable of'.

I often wondered why the professor did not choose Sandymount Strand and its wide spaces for lift-off. Exiled from its expanses, we missed it very much and finding an alternative location for flying proved difficult. The stony beach to the north of Dublin was unsuitable, while the ideal field below the Sugarloaf turned out to have dangerous turbulence. Other places were little better, until Tom found a farmer down in Carlow who was another microlight nut and was prepared to let us fly from his field.

Flying in Carlow, in the green heart of Ireland, a good hour's drive from Dublin, ruled out the spontaneous evening flights we had previously enjoyed. For the novice the restricted space was a worse problem. At Sandymount we had the whole beach to land on, while here was a thin strip of grass with no room for mistakes. New experiences were ahead of me, landing and taking off in a crosswind, which would teach me about accuracy. I could not always expect to have a beach below me every time the engine cut out.

The summer continued poorly and too often gusting winds blew away our plans. Tom had a new job which meant he had little time to spare and Robin and I sneaked down to Carlow on our own. When we motored down furtively and had a look at that narrow green runway, we decided it was too difficult for us. Just above it was a little hill and cross-currents coming down from there could provide difficulties for the Eagle's fragile stability. But half a mile away we found a large field belonging to a neighbouring farmer which, we agreed, looked fine. Never mind that it was thick with grass, and scattered with sheep, or that a number of trees stood on its boundaries and a wire fence ran down the middle.

By now Robin had flown quite a few times on his own and we decided that he should become my instructor. Would it be a case of the blind leading the blind? I didn't tell my family.

Diary:

25 August. Lovely day – slight north-westerly wind. Mr O'Brien and his family watched us unload and rig up. The batons kept sticking and for some reason when everything was put together the engine wouldn't start. After long investigation Robin thought he spotted what was wrong. Later another problem. We forgot to turn on the juice. I watched Robin take off and do a couple of circuits.

26 August. Back to the same field. The wings refuse to open and when they eventually do, we discover that one of the wires has got caught. Bolting the wing to the trike requires expertise which I seem incapable of acquiring. The washer keeps slipping and my fingers remain clumsy. With persistence the whole operation of rigging should take about half an hour.

27 August. I fly with Robin to Carlow on our first cross-country flight. The strand of Sandymount exchanged for green hills and barley fields. A few miles from our own field a ruined castle is a good landmark. We view the Blackstairs in the distance, dominated by Mount Leinster, from where we used to hang glide. We follow the road down to Carlow, flying at about 500 feet. From this height country life opens up page by page: a woman feeding hens in a back yard, a farmer on a tractor cutting silage, a lorry piled with grain. A car stops and two people get out and wave at us.

When we get back I decide to take her up on my own. I regret the decision immediately, but by then it is too late. Robin is only a crowd of one, but he has committed me to go ahead and the crowd increases when Mr O'Brien and his sons gather behind the ditch to watch. I check. Yes, I am safely buckled in, yes, the petrol is on and I am facing correctly into the wind. Switch on, check that no one is standing behind the propeller and give a good sharp pull.

I push my foot down hard and the Eagle begins to gallop across the grass as a hare scuttles for safety. The wind whips across my face, sheep scatter, the trees are coming nearer, also the wire fence. Now I push the bar up. At first nothing happens and I have a stab of fear that I will end up tangled in the wire. I push harder and then I am free of the ground.

A unique moment. All the anxious weeks and months fade as the trees come up and another slight push sends me climbing steeply over them. There is the familiar farmhouse and its outbuildings and a grain lorry driving on the distant road.

The marvellous realization that I am flying on my own is a different feeling from the exhilaration induced by hang gliding, when keeping airborne had been constant hard physical work tinged with fear which offered little time to examine one's finer feelings. Now, propelled along by machinery, I have leisure to examine this new short-lived happiness.

Why do some people feel a frenzy for flying? Why do they wish to do anything that jogs them from the comfortable tenure of their lives and sends them spinning through the air? I have always felt that the French pilot and philosopher, Antoine de Saint-Exupéry, went over the top with his metaphysical musings – 'A pilot finds that he has slipped beyond the confines of this world', 'One of the miracles of the aeroplane is that it plunges a man directly into the heart of the mystery' – and so forth. But it was true that flying on one's own promoted a particular sense of lyric intoxication.

In *England Have My Bones*, T. H. White, who took to the air in middle age, discussed the irrational impulse that made him seek out what he saw to be danger. 'One is surrounded ... with the depravity of the modern world. If for my whole life I were to redeliver the same lectures, nag at the same people, prattle the same scandal, what else would there be for it except to take earnestly to the drink?' In flying 'one would forget the sourness of the world and give oneself the illusion of happiness at any rate. Even sitting in the same chair rots one's soul. Decent men ought to break all their furniture every six months. Failing that, they ought to fly.'

Like White, when he took his initial solo, I was discovering that 'flying is the easiest and the most amusing thing in the world. You don't fly by rules or numbers, but by instinct and by feeling the pressure of the wind on your wings.' I was still climbing, and over to my left I could see the block of the Blackstairs with layers of cloud behind. I did my first turn, a gentle, surging glide that brought me parallel to the field, and it was trouble-free. I could see Robin and his blue car, Mr O'Brien and his boys and the farmhouse where I would have tea if I ever got down among those white specks of sheep.

Something was wrong – I was using too much throttle. Forget ecstasies. I had to get down, which was more difficult than taking off. Another slow turn over the field and I was too high. With trees and field rushing at me, however hard I pulled at the bar, I was still going to land in the middle of the sheep with no room to stop before I hit the far trees.

Quickly, power and height, up again. I pushed down the throttle making the little engine break into life once more. Why are so many fields bisected by electric wires, telephone wires, pylons, or simple strips of wire creating boundaries? I had forgotten about the fence below me and clipped it with a couple of feet to spare.

Always pick spot and try to hold the nose down to that. I aimed for a place slap in the middle of the field. Here we go. Turn, take off power, keep her flying at about forty-five miles an hour. One eye on the speed, another on a rushing green river of grass. Down a bit more. For a few seconds nothing happened as I held her off. I had it right, the blue car, the telephone lines, the gap in the trees and the clean whistle of wind. Push out a little, keep her flying, bump . . . then a second bump, slightly harder, and the wheels touched the ground.

I felt cheated that it had been too easy, pressed down on the throttle again and had another flight.

CHAPTER TWO

Marlborough

I sat in Polly's Tea Rooms eating muesli scones served with a basin of cream and strawberry jam. Opposite me an American couple in tartan hats attacked ice-creams described on the menu as concealing within them liberal fragments of chocolate. Could they find anything more luscious back home than Polly's Knickerbocker Glory, Jamaica Sun, or Strawberry Delight? At the next table an Arab schoolboy was gobbling something he described as fried toad. It was interesting to observe how boys from Asian and African countries slipped so easily into the mould of public school life. A master sipped his tea, ate a doughnut and read a newspaper.

'Did you know that there are three cases of AIDS in Marlborough?'

Good God! In a place that boasted, so I had been told, more retired military men than anywhere else in England. Through the window I watched an old stereotype of a colonel leading a Labrador. A thesis is to be written about the role of the Labrador in English middle-class life.

I was in a market town in Wiltshire on the former stage-coach route to Bath, a place which harboured a famous school and a lot of pubs with names like the Green Dragon, Ye Ripe Butcher and the Duke of Wellington. I tried to think of an equivalent town on the Dublin-Limerick Road – Nenagh, Roscrea. They do things differently in England.

I had come here not only to take a long and expensive course in flying, but ultimately to acquire a new Pegasus XL microlight which was made and sold by a firm called Solar Wings.

The factory, situated on the outskirts of Marlborough, wedged between a public garden and an old people's home, consisted of a number of large sheds where fibreglass microlight bodies were being assembled in lines of policeman blue, livened up by the occasional tomato red. The Eagle I had flown back in Ireland seemed a shabby old thing compared to the glossy little aircraft taking shape here. Another generation of microlights had arrived. The Pegasus XL had a larger, more powerful engine; the pilot sat with his legs protected by a fibreglass pod, there was a proper instrument panel and the moment when microlights were turning into aeroplanes was not far off. Those manufactured by Solar Wings were considered relatively cheap and I would be acquiring a flying machine for the price of an average family car. (Forget that the old hang glider had cost £300.) In Ireland there might have been a score of microlights in the entire country, but here the lines of red and blue shells seemed to indicate that the English were taking to the air in droves.

Solar Wings was prepared to help me in my plans to travel around England and Ireland and supply me with a new machine in three weeks' time, registered, tested and having full aeronautical approval. English microlights weighing over seventy kilos have to pass stringent standards which have given them an international reputation for excellence. (Oddly enough, even in 1987 ultra-lightweight machines were still not covered by airworthiness regulations.)

I would pay something over £5,000 for my tried and tested aircraft and running costs would be around £7 an hour. I could choose a combination of different instruments and select the colour of the wing. I would be supplied with a warm flying-suit, a helmet and other extras.

If only I could fly!

Since 1982 microlight pilots in England have had to obtain a licence which requires at least eight hours' dual flying and seven hours' solo. They must pass written tests of navigation, air law and meteorology, and even then they will get only a limited licence restricting flying to within eight nautical miles of the take-off site. To be able to fly where you please you have to take further cross-country tests covering at least forty nautical miles.

In Ireland I hadn't needed a licence to fly a microlight any more than a bird needed one to flap its wings. They will catch up over there, the way they caught up with driving tests, which were not introduced until the 1960s. My driving licence, obtained long before that time, merely requires me to state that I am not suffering from any mental instability. We still have no equivalent MOT tests for cars.

In England the pioneer days of microlight flying are long over. There is a group of pilots who consider themselves ageing, who remember the wild period of a decade ago with a fierce nostalgia. In that rough and ready era any amateur built his own machine, stuck on a little engine and threw himself off hills. Accidents arising from structural failure and piloting incompetence became unacceptable.

Microlights and ultra-light aircraft have had an odd history. Something very similar to an auto-giro was built in 1907, just four years after the Kitty Hawk Flyer first became airborne, by a Brazilian, Alberto Santos-Dumont. His Demoiselle, made out of bamboo and silk, made no headway in the history of flight and was soon forgotten. Nothing similar followed for more than sixty years. Meanwhile conventional aircraft got bulkier and turned into passenger carriers and weapons of war. But the idea of flying for Everyman remained at the back of men's minds.

In the 1970s the hang glider developed after its wing, an airfoil shaped like an obtuse V, had been patented by a space technician named Francis Rogallo. Dacron and tubing aided the flying obsession of the decade. But pilots wanted more – they wanted to buzz along. Seventy-five years after the Wrights had taught men how to fly, the flying machine was reinvented. The invention of ultra-light flying is generally credited to an American named John Moody who, in 1975, strapped a ten-hp engine and propeller to his glider to produce a powered hang glider that weighed less than a hundred pounds.

Reluctantly I accepted the inevitable, that the licensing system in England was extended not only to microlights, but to their pilots, with a subsequent reduction in the accident rate. If I wanted to fly in England, I would have to work hard. I would take flying lessons which Solar Wings would provide, since not only did the firm make microlights, but it gave lessons on how to fly them. However, during this spring the weather was turning out worse than it had been last summer on Sandymount Strand. The first day the rain poured down, squelching through Marlborough's gutters, while outside the town the Downs were coated in mist. The next day there was a pale blue sky, but a ferocious wind. And after that, one or the other, or a combination of the two, would keep me from experiencing the pleasure to be derived from that ugly phrase, fun-flying. Yeats summoned up its joys more elegantly when he wrote about a lonely impulse of delight.

Swallows were dashing around, brushing the ground with their bellies, and leaves were twisting and turning in the wind. We were on Clench Common in the Wiltshire Downs, based at a former wartime airfield where Canadian women pilots had flown in from across the Atlantic. Traces of war lingered, rusty Nissen huts, water-towers and enclosures marked in faded red paint, PWD. Microlights, mainly blue ones, were crammed into a hay barn beside the field, both dual-seaters and a few single-seaters. There was just enough room in the corner for some erected wings to be pushed together. The interior smelt of mud, straw and old diesel.

Rain drummed down on the corrugated roof, while inside the microlights were pinned down like a butterfly collection. David's job as instructor required not only patience to deal with the weather, but tact to soothe macho men and would-be pilots. He had experienced the far frontiers of fun-flying by taking a microlight on an Everest expedition and crashing it. Now he had nothing to do but wait for the rain to go away.

Meanwhile he helped to deliver a lamb. The birth was difficult; one foot came out, but he couldn't find the other and had to feel about inside. The ewe and the hay shed where the microlights were parked belonged to Simon and Diana Faux, whose farm was suffering from the recession in agriculture and feeling the pinch because of EEC cutbacks. A few years ago the Fauxs had got out of cattle after the Common Agricultural Policy demanded less milk and now they concentrated on sheep. Microlights were a new crop. They had the advantage of an airfield in the middle of their farm and they were making the most of their resources. Another resource was their spare room where I stayed and waited for the opportunity to fly.

28 April. Here I am sitting in the kitchen of the old red brick farmhouse beside a marmalade cat lying on top of the Aga and a Jack Russell curled in a basket. Outside the new Connemara foal runs after its mother, propelled by the wind. No flying today. Still, it is a consolation to view at close quarters a life-style envied by the middle classes, bolstered by its advertising images echoed in those magazines that Gillian persists in buying which are full of achievers stencilling their cottages or standing in herb gardens. But Diana will be the first to tell you that country life has become a luxury. Her family has been farming in this area for generations.

Simon, who is bearded and resembles an Elizabethan, Drake or someone, is also country bred. He possesses an amazing skill and ingenuity in dealing with machines. The most antique tractor, the most venerable piece of agricultural machinery, is transformed in his skilled hands. I would buy a used car from this man. A lot of rusty stuff awaits resurrection, and all round the barn housing the produce of Solar Wings I have seen bits and pieces lying in nettles which have nothing to do with flight. Simon hates microlights.

I have already looked at the sky. I am obsessed by wind. The Chinese called it the envoy of heaven on earth. The old vivid ways of personification, Boreas, the North Wind, Eurus, the grizzled East Wind holding up his cloak to bluff the storm, Notus, the virile South Wind, Zephyrus, the beautiful West Wind, are all taken over by depressing expressions of knots and directions from the Met. Office. De Maupassant mused on the force 'which knocks down men, blows down buildings, uproots trees, whips up the sea into watery mountains, destroys cliffs and hurls great ships on the reefs, the wind which kills, whistles, groans and roars – have you seen it?' De Maupassant was comparing the wind to God. David was talking about the Met. Office. 'I rang them. It's gusting thirty knots. There's a depression over Scotland. Flying is out.' High winds, rain, low cloud-levels, spiralling depressions continue to put flying out of the question.

I walk in the rain over the Wiltshire Downs, so much of them ploughed up. Clench Farm is exceptional; there the Faux farm their stretch of chalkland in the old way, not all that different from the methods of ancient herdsmen guarding tiny skinny long-horned animals. From time to time Simon picks up a flint tool worked into its arrowhead shape 3,000 years ago.

I visit villages with ancient names, West Overton, Fyfield, Wootton Rivers. Past a field of mustard grass I come upon a hamlet called Cuckoo's Knob. England's tranquil heritage is beautiful, enhanced by thatched cottages, old-fashioned inns, ancient churches and handsome manor houses. Everywhere I see a rural paradise and it takes time to learn that all these pretty places are part of a vast dispersed suburbia, and the old herdsmen and W. H. Hudson's shepherds have been replaced by Aga People and Volvo Folk. With the M4 and the train this part of Wiltshire is linked to London, and in what appears to be a farming community no one is talking about agriculture.

'How much do you think that cottage went for?' A nasty rotten hovel on the main Pewsey road. The equivalent in Ireland would scarcely make five figures. 'Ninety thousand!'

The affluent urbanites everywhere are strange to an Irishman and so are the beaming careful old people retired comfortably on pensions and savings, brushing and combing their gardens. Gentrification comes in all forms. There is the American who has bought two cottages down the road and thrown them into one, the Dutchman who has rethatched Mrs G.'s barn, the London solicitor who has bought the manor house, the commercial artist converting a mill, and every now and again a large curtained car goes by with rich Arabs inside.

The chestnuts in the village lanes are in bloom. Just above the farm is an escarpment which is regarded as the highest in Wiltshire from where you can look across the great quilted plain; on a clear day (not today) you can see the spire of Salisbury Cathedral more than twenty miles away. The country has an Augustan look of prosperity and contentment. Here is a place where generations have lived quietly going about their business. The trees are moving and spilling out gusts of air and the grass and young corn bow as the wind sweeps over them. The lilac is in bloom. From where I stand the only sounds to disturb the peace are the sighs of the wind, the hoarse chuckle of a pheasant and the sharp drone of a low-flying Hercules aircraft on a NATO exercise flying back to base at Brize Norton.

Pewsey is a few miles down the hill. In recent years the village with its thatched cottages and old shop-fronts has been transformed, 800 sleepy years changed out of recognition by the InterCity train. Life will never be the same again. There's the usual estate agent where some weekends people queue to buy. A remarkable number of the properties he displays in his window didn't start off as dwelling-places and he offers Wiltshire barns, mill-houses, gate-houses, follies, converted churches, converted pubs and converted shops, all stamped with the seal of approval, 'Pewsey–Paddington One Hour'. Every morning the small station courtyard is crammed with cars. The people who used to live in the pretty cottages are herded into housing estates to contemplate the changes in their lives, the overturn of the rural economy, the introduction of outsiders, the reduction of shops and the vanishing goods and services. Less than 10 per cent of the rural population here now works in agriculture and, apart from employment with the local builder, alternative work is hard to find. Gift shops, tea shops, delicatessens and bed and breakfast will not employ everyone.

In the evenings I go to pubs with picturesque names, knocked-down walls and exposed beams where they ask for vodka and tonic instead of beer. Used to the glum mysteries of Irish country pubs, I half expect to listen to people discussing the price of sheep in a soft Wiltshire burr (' 'Tis zummat vur I to do when I be comin' these ways . . .', etc.). Every time I am confounded. Missing the clue of the big cars spilling on to the narrow pavements outside, I am always unprepared for the blazers and silk chokers and the talk about investments and the other theme that is constantly drummed into my ears. In the old days when two or three middle-class people gathered together they talked about their children's education. Now it always works around to house property, even though the general election is imminent. The local contest is mentioned in passing.

'A pity about the Labour fellow.' 'Nice chap, but doesn't stand a chance.' Even the enormous advantage of having attended Marlborough College will not help him. All day from every bush and hoarding I have come upon the smiling face of the aspiring Tory candidate.

Landlords, who in Ireland have mostly vanished, leaving legends of ogres, flourish in these parts. Some like Lord Moyne and Lord Lansdowne have strong Irish connections. The ownership of the big estates has changed since this part of Wiltshire, including Savernake Forest, belonged to the Ailesbury and Brudenell families. In the heart of the forest is a column erected in 1798 by Lord Ailesbury commemorating George III's recovery to health, 'a signal instance of Heaven's protecting providence'. Lord Ailesbury gave acknowledgement in stone 'first to his uncle who gave him these lands, secondly to the King who created him Earl, but above all of piety to God, highest, best'.

Lord Ailesbury's family fell on hard times and now much of their land and much of the land round about is Crown property. Simon and Diana farm 350 acres of Crown land, for which they pay a hefty rent to the Queen. Not only that, but once a year one of Her Majesty's Inspectors comes down to inspect the books and see that things are done correctly. An almighty clean-up takes place. Farming is difficult enough without Ma'am constantly looking over your shoulder.

Diana is a local magistrate, very much aware of the dreadful conditions of English prisons, dealing with good sense, discipline and honesty with the medley of cases that come up before her. A child is taken into care, a car has been broken into, and endless soldiers face charges usually connected with drunkenness because the Army is planted on Salisbury Plain. Once again a private is drunk in charge, another has committed a nuisance. A couple of months ago another stole a tank and drove it home one weekend to show his Mum.

Diana brings the same disciplines she uses on the bench to farming. The farm with its large fields and woodlands tinged with bluebells seems luxurious to my eyes, but in fact is composed of second-grade land, difficult to cultivate. This had always been sheep country. The Wiltshire Downs used to have their own special type of sheep, last bred in 1840, the largest of the fine-wooled sheep in England, an ungainly animal according to Hudson, with a big clumsy head, 'a round nose, its legs . . . long and thick, its belly without wool, and both sexes . . . horned'. That ugly old thing has long been replaced by modern breeds like black-faced Suffolks.

The amount of work Diana and Simon put into their flock amazes me. I have arrived in the lambing season when, given the weather, the bleat of lambs is louder than the buzz of flying machines. There's the day-to-day business of looking after recalcitrant flocks and pregnant ewes. Every evening they walk around the fields looking for casualties, a ewe lying on its back, a sickly lamb, a sheep with a hole pecked in its flesh by a crow. A paddock contains the lambs that have lost their mothers and with constant human contact have become playful and tame.

There is the business of shows. Almost every day an announcement of some vitally important sheep show will drop through the letter-box, heralding another shampoo and clipping for the prize rams. The Empress of Blandings never got more attention and love than these rams, endlessly clipped and combed all over, their broad woolly backs flat as a runway, their faces stippled to impress judges. I learn about rivalry among competitors. A few are suspected of going beyond the permitted rules of blackening up these sleek trim wool carriers. It is whispered that some exhibitors will actually blacken a ram's leg or anoint him with eucalyptus oil to make the wool more attractive to judges and beguile them by make-up and medication to hand over the rosettes.

The Fauxs can remember stories of the old shepherds' lives when huge flocks were driven across the Downs to the great sales at Wilton. One or two old men of the Hudson mould are still living, but his shepherd is a ghost. 'That solitary cloaked figure on the vast round hill standing motionless, crook in hand and rough-haired dog at heel, sharply seen against the clear pale sky, is one of those rare human forms in this land which do not ever seem out of place in the landscape.'

The landscape itself has been transformed and most of the Downs are ploughed up, strewn with fertilizer and planted with barley and bilious rape. The Fauxs struggle to keep up an old tradition, at the same time obeying directives from city-bred civil servants about the need for diversification. Already aware of the nuisance value of microlights, they feel guilty as if their barn was full of Trojan horses.

CHAPTER THREE

Clench Common

The postman battled through the driving rain to bring me a brochure. 'Learn to fly where the warm winds softly blow. In the warmth of the Portuguese climate the smooth coastal flying conditions allow for the greatest amount of flying experience in the shortest time. Think how quickly you would learn and progress if you could fly more often.' I should have gone to the Algarve instead of relying on the English spring.

Every morning I pulled back the curtains and looked out. Were the leaves and branches shaking, what about the clouds, what was the direction of the wind? Was this one more day when the forecast would mention lows over Iceland? It took three weeks before I looked out of the window and felt that the morning sky was a sight worth more than a morning's sleep. Instead of the low grey cloud-cover I had seen over the Downs ever since I arrived, the sky was blue. There was a nice little breeze and, later on, even David was optimistic about the chances of flying.

'I've slotted you in for 10.30.'

He made me understand how fortunate I was, since there was an instant scramble for places in the sun. People would be coming here to learn flying from all over Wiltshire and others would be travelling from farther afield, even from London. There were young city gents literally aspiring to be upwardly mobile. There was the couple who had saved and saved to buy a microlight between them; the girl would do the navigation, while her husband did the flying. There was the engineer who had thrown up his job and put all his savings into a Pegasus, and the doctor who wanted to recover the old thrills of flight after fifteen years' absence from piloting an aircraft. There was Leslie, a man of my age, who had been flying for three months and still hadn't gone solo.

'Do you remember the Flying Flea?' he asked as he waited around to be fitted into whatever time slot the instructors allowed. Indeed, I could recall that early attempt to bring flying to the masses. We had been small boys when a Frenchman introduced the *Puce de Ciel* to the world, and for a short time it had seemed that the skies of Europe would be filled with his tiny machines. You bought a kit for £50 and built it yourself. The heavens would be transformed in the same way that the roads had been transformed by Model-T Fords. Now half a century later we were taking part in another aerial revolution.

Diana came down from the farmhouse to watch the line of cars going down the long avenue and the burst of activity around the barn and field. As long as the weather held, streams of visitors would invade her farm. Soon the neighbours would begin complaining again, some angry woman on her knees with a trug basket, a colonel going outside on a spring evening with his G and T and finding his peace being disturbed by a sharp wail overhead.

I had been made aware of how many people resented the new noise in the skies. A microlight travels relatively slowly, and if it is flying against a steady wind it may seem immovable up there. It is no use expecting a pilot to take notice of little white faces glaring upwards, or tiny fists shaking at the high-pitched buzzing which will not go away. But he is not supposed to fly at less than 1,000 feet and he should avoid built-up areas.

Both instructors at Clench Common were at pains to do a good PR job and appease the great British public.

'If you see a microlight flying too low, just take down the registration number and let us know. We don't want cowboys.'

Diana said, 'I don't like the way none of the pilots seem to have wives or steady girlfriends.' Obsessive dedication to flying machines does not seem to go with being good family men. Someone has yet to compile statistics of broken relationships among birdmen. Julie was one of those who had suffered, having lost her boyfriend to his flexiwing. She did not fly, but hung around the barn. There were plenty of women on Clench Common, none of them learning to fly, although one or two were learning navigation in order to help their men. The rest seemed to be merely flying groupies. Julie talked about the way pilots cultivated their macho image, were slightly deranged and all running away from reality. 'They're a weird lot. They are just not interested in anything else.' Their obsession with flying was close to clinical madness, they left wives, children and jobs, they went berserk when they couldn't get in the air. A day without flying was a day wasted, a day without a fix.

A group of aspiring pilots sat in the office where David propounded elementary theory about thrust and turbulence, how a wing flies, the angle of attack. Outside someone shouted, 'No bloody wind!' and pointed to the sagging sock at the end of the fields. After the bad weather the stillness was miraculous. Diana went back to her lambs. 'Much more interesting than microlights'.

I was given gloves, flying-suit and a helmet with an interconnecting-speaking tube. In Ireland we had flown without such adornments. The plastic front to the helmet slid down over my face.

'I don't want you to touch the throttle. I'm looking after that . . .'

David took the front seat, while I squeezed in the back. I was in the nursery once again. David gathered speed, bumped over the grass, kept the machine straight and lifted her above the Downs. In the sunny morning air I made the best of the circuit, downwind, crosswind and upwind. The controls were extremely responsive and it seemed that this microlight had no bad habits. How quickly you forget the anguish and frustration of hanging around, all the days when nothing happened.

Here we were, suspended a thousand feet above Marlborough hidden in its valley. Doubtless there were plenty of people in the Red Lion and the Wellington and in Polly's Tea Rooms who hated us. For the first time I was conscious of the stirring crowds below and I realized that I would have to work at assuming that part of the pilot's image which involves a studied indifference to complaints about disturbance of the peace. It was noise which did not affect me. The white helmet with the perspex visor clamped down across my chin might make me look like a jackass, but it shut out most of the sound behind my back.

We hovered over the college which John Betjeman had hated. Here was the quadrangle and cluster of buildings and, clear as a map, the town's broad main street with its churches at either end. Beyond I made out Westwood where I had walked in the rain, the long stretch of the Avon Canal, the dark green of Savernake Forest and the gently swelling Downs whose silence we were setting out to destroy. Before the days of microlights, and of other aircraft for that matter, Peter Gurney wrote of the shepherd living in the silence of the Downs 'so dead that it can almost be heard, every sound comes to him magnified. If it is only the soft scratch of a mole a few inches below the surface, he will hear it. The music of his bells, the bleat of the sheep, the distant barking of dogs, the whisper of the wind in the herbage.'

A haze was forming, obscuring the ground and the trees whose leafy patterns changed as we flew overhead. David took over the controls and did some sharp turns, quickly losing height before Clench came into view, the bright yellow and blue wings of microlights vivid on the grass. We circled the woods and the farmhouse, and landed.

Some students from the Royal Agricultural College at Cirencester had arrived, visibly excited and impressed.

'How long have you been flying?'

'What's she like to handle?'

'If you fly to Norfolk, you must call in at our place.'

The hearty accents of these country gentlemen emphasized a feeling of having stepped back into the past. Quilted flying-suits and perspex helmets may have replaced leather coats and goggles, but I felt like Biggles having descended from a sunlit heaven over an ancient English landscape. Except that the queue of people waiting wistfully to fly was a queue of the 1980s.

'You can't just walk into it and fly it' I was told over and over again. Since the training here followed a rigid set of rules and rituals, I had to forget altogether about flying in Ireland, an episode regarded with disapproval, as a remnant of the outdated flying-cowboy image. I was constantly reminded of how microlights had become faster, stronger and safer. No one around here told stories about them folding their wings or disintegrating in mid-air. Similarly pilots had to be improved. I was a novice again. Training was carefully tabulated and done in stages, taking off and landing, incipient stalls, forced landings without power, navigation, one thing to be learned at a time. The problem was that so little could be learnt in a twenty-minute flight, when all the time you were conscious of all the other would-be flyers down below waiting their turn to train.

To pass the time between flights we were given two fat books, as essential to our ambition as Grey's *Anatomy* is essential to medical students. R. D. Campbell's *Microlight Flying Manual* and Brian Cosgrove's *Microlight Aircraft and the Air* contained all the information on flight training, engines, airspace, safety and everything else a pilot needed to know. 'The minimum flying experience required by student pilots is 25 hours – of this at least 10 must be in solo flight.' 'If engine backfires or runs roughly, the throttle should be closed and take-off abandoned.' 'Safe airspeed is one of the most vital points to watch in flying, because keeping sufficient airspeed keeps the angle of attack below the stalling speed.' 'Most airborne collisions occur in the vicinity of the aerodrome and take-off sites.'

From the moment the wings were unzipped out of their long cigar-shaped holders, every movement the student made was watched minutely by the instructors. The checks and counter-checks sung out in a litany were more rigorous than anything I had previously experienced. Batons and kingpost had to be pushed into position, all the wires straightened, the edge of the wing checked in case of hidden dents by running one's hands along it. Erecting the microlight took about twenty minutes, although experienced operators could do it in far less time. There was always something magical about the trans-formation of a number of hollow tubes and a length of Dacron into something with a life of its own, sturdy and airworthy.

The engine and its parts had to be given the same scrutiny as the wing. This part of the routine still meant little to me and I was preparing to take it on trust – the mounting, the various important bolts, the air filter and carburettor, the stylish wooden propeller, all the cables and wires and the engine itself. It was an effort to get beyond the first golden rule: 'Never turn the engine off.' A microlight pilot must be a competent mechanic, and the thought was deeply de-pressing.

In spite of the advanced technology there were omissions to the design which surprised me. The Pegasus XL had no brake and the only way to stop it rolling along the ground was to put a foot out. There was no fuel gauge – I was told they were unreliable. The only method of discovering if you were going to run out of juice while you were flying was to crick your neck by looking back over your shoulder at the little plastic tube that fed the engine. If there was a bubble it means an immediate descent before the engine cut out.

Fifty years ago David Garnett published *A Rabbit in the Air* and I read it for comfort. 'I do not think [these notes] will be any help to other beginners, but I hope they may encourage a few middle-aged persons to learn to fly and be a consolation to the pupil who is slow to learn.' Indeed they were. After Garnett took up flying in mid-life, he thought he would never get it right, and it took him twenty-eight hours to go solo. The speed with which a person learns to fly varies very much, and it does not get easier with age.

My diary recorded the progress of essential skills. 'Wednesday 6 May: Power and incipient stalls. Thursday 7 May: Taking off and landing. Increasing speed without height. Monday 11 May: Engine failure and gliding in.' Often I returned to Garnett to read about another ageing pilot who 'did atrociously badly' and 'came away in profound gloom'.

The best moment of every flight came early after all the tedious preliminary rites – fuel check, harness check, feet evenly on pedals controlling the front wheel, all clear and then the sharp pull on the engine cord. I would head into wind, the Faux sheep would be safely to one side of the straight course ahead and everything seemed to be working. The throttle was pulled down and the little machine ran over the grass as clumsily as one of those heavy birds who are not at ease until they are in the air.

Suddenly the microlight left the ground and the engine stirred it from a sluggish earthbound vehicle into a creature of flight. Perhaps geese and swans feel something of the same joy. Part of the pleasure was the transformation of the land below into a map. Hills and fields were swinging below, so was the sprawling line of the river, the straight sweep of the M4 and the railway lines.

The microlight was shaken with fierce jolts, one wing dipped and then, more violently, the other.

'Inversion . . . take her up to 3,000 feet.'

Below us a haze obscured the ground and the trees whose leafy patterns changed as we flew overhead. Descending air, warming up as it went, had spread over the cold air layer below and covered it like fat on Irish stew. It was warm above and cool below, the opposite of over-thermal conditions, and the situation was therefore known as inversion. Endless stirring and movements over the ground, thermal currents, air exchanges and summer highs go to form the skyscapes where the shapes of the clouds are signals as definite as columns of flags on sailing ships.

I could just hear the metallic crackle of David's voice on the intercom. 'We'll initiate a left-hand turn at a steady 30 degrees against the horizon. You're pushing out too hard . . . relax, look right, look left . . . damn!' An RAF Buccaneer fighter screamed overhead. 'I told them we intended flying today.' Crossing the Wiltshire skies was like crossing the motorway. Soon the silhouette of a more stately Hercules could be seen low over the Downs and a minute later a marauding jet swept by. For the time being we were spared the nuisance of the RAF helicopters which flew over Clench Common like hornets, their rotor blades causing dangerous currents of air.

Our own tortoise ambled along at about forty-five miles an hour, constantly interrupted by flying exercises. There were stalls to be practised, and endless landings, which invariably gave the feeling of an obstacle to be overcome. David would point out a narrow rectangular field which always looked small. The right approach was essential and also the right speed in order to avoid the disgrace of the stall. Keep at the right height and distance, checking and counter-checking. Is the small nose-wheel held straight? Check the direction of wind, speed, altitude, harness and then on the final leg glide in without the engine. You are conscious that the world is concentrated in a corridor of wind and sky and a line of grass is approaching like a weapon.

The ordinary course of practice and tuition took us far from the Wiltshire Downs. In the process of practising stalls we reached Berkshire and were forced down on the Lambourn gallops. Raising the nose and taking off power or throttle produced waves of move-ment comparable to being tossed around in a violent sea. At one moment we were flying nice and level, then suddenly we had dropped a hundred feet, as a steep movement that went with gravity sent us reeling downwards gasping for breath. When we landed I got out and was sick.

Those stalls produced moments when I was not only imbued with nausea. At last I could understand the fears of airline passengers like my mother-in-law who sits tense in her seat throughout a flight watching other passengers go to the lavatory, convinced that their movements will tip the plane over. I understood anyone with mad eyes and quaking heart crying out for a drink or wrapping their heads in a towel.

Back to the microlight. Remount after you have taken a toss. I strapped myself in and tried to renew those feelings of exhilaration. All clear, ignition, full throttle and we were bumping across the gallops. Did the moment of flight impart its usual orgasmic thrill? Up to a point. I still felt sick. Under us racehorses were moving across the grass, while in the hazy distance the Didcot cooling-towers rose among bright green fields of young barley. Green took on the colour of life and humanity, while the blue of the sky was the colour of the infinite. And the clouds . . . I recalled a purple passage in my flight book. 'If the wind is the spirit of the sky's oceans, the clouds are its texture. They are embodied imagination.' And the birds: 'The crows and choughs that wing the midway air show scarce so gross as beetles.'

The voice crackled in my ear. 'I want you to imagine an engine failure. What do you do?'

David could devise plenty of other tortures known as exercises.

'I want you to try to land, but just before the wheels touch down, hold them off the ground and then fly away again.' Keeping the wheels a few inches off the grass, jumping the occasional stone wall or tree, then a sharp climbing turn and back to the same circuit.

More stalling as we stumbled back towards Clench Common. From all around I could see microlights coming in across the strips of Savernake Forest, winging their way from Marlborough and from the direction of Salisbury Plain. I could recognize some pilots by the colour of their wings – that red and white must be Eric, all the yellow ones were the uniform used for training by Solar Wings. Nearer, I could glimpse pilots sprawling in their seats. It was the best time to fly when the wind had dropped and turbulence from rising air had dissipated so that the magical return in the smooth silky sky made the microlight float like a becalmed schooner waiting for the merest puff of wind to set it in motion. Streaks from the setting sun gilded the Downs.

But clear days like that when I learned a good deal about flying and navigation were exceptional. Too often the weather returned to its spring gloom and my 'D' licence moved farther off. I had been at Clench Common long enough to see the bluebells shrivel; nettle-beds were thrown up around the trees, and lanes and hedges were patterned with cow parsley. Rain sluiced down on barns and sheds as I watched a rat scuttle across the yard through the downpour to the barn where the microlights were stored, while once again I cursed the vagaries of the English climate. It seemed that every day the clouds were sending up negative signals and time, patience and money were running out. At this rate of progress, acquiring the essential licence would take many more months than I could afford. After looking at my sums, David agreed.

'If you want to hop around England, your finances are not strong enough. You haven't any reserves. What happens if your propeller breaks? A replacement costs £200. Even a minor fault or breakage costs money. And what would happen, God forbid, if you had an accident?'

It was June. The lambs had grown sturdy, the Fauxs' son was sitting his O-levels and the Conservatives were winning the election. A prize lamb had won second prize in a top show. The way I was making progress I wouldn't be qualified to fly alone until the 1990s. If I wanted to fly around England in a microlight during the summer of 1987, I would have to get someone to fly with me. With great reluctance I decided I would not be able to do the journey on my own. I would have to look for a qualified pilot who would accompany me on the English part of the trip. When we got to Ireland, I would take over.

For the time being I decided to abandon my flying lessons and save on the expense. If I sat around waiting, while feelers were put out for someone to fly with me, I was improving my budget. I saved £40 a time just watching other people taking off and landing. From the side of the field I could see they were a new lot – the man in the army microlight with its khaki camouflaged wings, the rich Norfolk farmer who had bought an expensive Australian machine and was planning to fly it home. I met Norman who had lost his job in Swindon and had put his redundancy money into flying. Did he have a wife and family? Even the girl groupies were different. Had the others qualified, or had most of them given up?

They were testing the new 'Q' wing from the factory, when a little Cessna landed in the field to be regarded with admiration and suspicion. The plane with its enclosed cockpit and comfortable seats was considered over-comfortable and a little corrupt. Plutocrats with cigars flew planes like that. The Cessna pilot, on the other hand, disapproved of fringe flying and regarded the microlight as absurd and dangerous, a flying bedstead that gave aviation a bad name. Two concepts of flying were in confrontation – the open air, wind-in-the-face brigade, in touch with nature, versus the sophisticate enclosed in his comfortable bubble. The microlight clung to the spirit of adventure, which it was in danger of losing as it became more elaborate and comfortable. There was still a faint whiff of danger, a throwback to the old days which attracted a certain breed. I remembered the

Triumph motorbike which became less popular when crash helmets were made compulsory.

After a week I couldn't stay around listening to microlights without feeling depressed. To escape the incessant buzz I went back to walking, making my way to Millshill, the lump of chalk crowned with trees looking over all the Downs which have been described as resembling 'in their flowing forms . . . vast pale green waves'. Under the trees I couldn't see the microlights, even if I could hear their distinctive dominating drone.

The process of finding a co-pilot was much less easy than I supposed it would be. I had imagined that there would be copious frustrated pilots without a machine willing to fly with me to Ireland. I followed up recommendations – so-and-so was experienced, had been made redundant and had abundant free time. The man from Lancashire whose exploits had left everyone gasping. What about the Canadian drop-out? Finally David announced that he had nailed down one of the best microlight pilots in England.

'You'll like Graham.'

It appeared that Graham had been working for a small firm established somewhere in a barn that had been making microlights and had gone bankrupt. There were plenty of concerns like that all over the place, enterprising small firms manufacturing light aircraft, which had come and gone. He had been forced to sell his machine, and now he liked the idea of flying with me. He had never been to Ireland. We met briefly, exchanged telephone numbers and made tentative plans. He had to fix up things at home, while I had to wait for Solar Wings to deliver me a new microlight the following week. They would throw in a compass and a couple of flying-suits.

My flight didn't get them very excited. Not a week passed without someone doing something much more enterprising with a microlight, flying over glaciers in Iceland, penetrating the South American jungle, crossing Africa or Australia, or wandering around the foot of Everest as David had done. A trip to Ireland was not the thing to make Solar Wings sit up and take notice.

In addition to a fee, for the duration of the flight I would pay for Graham's food and lodging wherever we happened to find ourselves. There would be the running costs and essential accessories which he listed, charts, gearbox oil, an adequate tool kit, spare plugs, warm clothing. When and if we broke down, spares would have to be sent to any part of England where we happened to be. I would be a passenger, he would be chauffeur.

He wrote:

As discussed between us on Saturday, I have outlined the areas of attention which must be all completed before we can undertake the proposed trip. By the time you receive this, we will have probably spoken over the telephone regarding my personal requirements. I'm sure that the proposed project can be completed within 21 days of setting out from Clench Common. However, it is possible that the weather could delay our progress and that the destination is not reached. Any further involvement after 21 days by myself will have to be agreed between us, as I will possibly have commitments here.

All too easily I imagined being stuck on a Yorkshire moor or beside a Scottish loch, mist and rain for company, and day after day passing as succeeding meteorological disasters.

CHAPTER FOUR

Across the Severn

At last my microlight, registration number G-MTHK, arrived from the factory. In theory there is nothing to stop an owner parading his colours in the skies as if he had a racehorse. I could have chosen a wing covered with shamrocks, or painted with the name of a sponsor, if I had been lucky enough to obtain one. I could have ordered it spotted mauve or black, striped or chequer-boarded. I could have had a message written along its underside – I LOVE DUBLIN, or one of those pointlessly obscene slogans beginning MICROLIGHTERS DO IT . . . In election time I could have stamped it with a message: VOTE CON-SERVATIVE. In fact, the upper surface of the wing was true blue, the lower SDP yellow, just like most of the other microlights on Clench Common. It was immense, and in comparison the body underneath was like a rabbit in an eagle's claws.

These are the measurements of the Pegasus XL wing:

Span: 34 feet
Nose Angle: 121 degrees – which gave it a boomerang shape
Weight: 48.3 kilograms

The microlight came with an altimeter, a speedometer, a compass and a rev counter, a smart blue protective zip cover, and Dacron mittens to protect the wooden blades of the propeller. I had also acquired a quilted flying-suit and a Pegasus full-face helmet with inter-com system.

I felt pride of ownership, affection and great vulnerability. This was my little trike sitting in the barn among the other trikes and lines of folded wings perched between bales of straw. Although it was no smaller or more fragile than the rest, the fact of possession made it seem so. The canoe-shaped body and wheels covered with fibreglass spats to protect them from mud, the long blue and yellow boomerang wing, suddenly seemed a combination unequal to the challenge of flight.

Soon I would be a thousand or more feet up, bucketing around treacherous English skies. (Pity I had to take Graham along.) Saint-Exupéry compared the sky to an ocean. 'There is a poetry of sailing as old as the world. There have always been seamen in recorded time. The man who assumes that there is an essential difference between the sloop and the aeroplane lacks historical perspective.' The craft that sail in the sky are regarded as feminine in the same way as sailors think of ships, microlights are considered to have a coquettish mode of behaviour and a way of knowing their own minds. I should have thought of G-MTHK as 'she'. In fact I never did; if I personified my microlight at all, it was as a dour peasant, a man with a task to do.

It had to be tested before getting the essential Certificate of Airworthiness. David obligingly put it through its paces. First the trike was tied by a rope to a post and tortured. For an hour the sheep on Clench Common listened to the scream of the revved-up engine. A microlight heard from the air is bad enough, but at ground level the shriek was terrible, shaking the countryside for an hour of non-stop noise before the engine was deemed to be correctly run in. The model was a Rotax 447 power unit with integral gear reduction. The fuel tank capacity was 24.4 litres of filtered fuel whose petrol/oil mix ratio was 50 to 1.

David took it up and put it through a complicated series of exercises. Soaring, dipping and stalling, it wavered across the Wiltshire skies showing off its paces like a plump dancer until he was satisfied that the wing would not fall off or the engine seize up.

These are details of its performance:

Wing level stall speed at maximum auw (all-up weight):	31 mph
Height loss during recovery at max. auw:	50 feet
Wing level stall speed at min. auw:	24 mph
Height loss during recovery at min. auw:	20 feet
20 degree banked stalls at max. auw:	31 mph
Height loss during recovery at max. auw:	70 feet
30 degree banked stalls at min. auw:	29 mph
Height loss during recovery at min. auw:	20 feet
Descent rate power off at max. auw:	457 fpm

The take-off distance needed at maximum all-up weight was 566 feet. Its all-out speed was 67 miles an hour, which must never be exceeded. I had a vision of it breaking up in the air. Ideal cruising speed was 52 miles an hour, but the wind made all the difference to that.

Graham arrived with another list. We needed a four-gallon can for carrying extra petrol, a radio, thick woollen socks and gloves and adequate maps. There was very little extra room in a space the size of a bathtub for anything else besides two people weighing thirteen and eleven stone. I had long dropped the idea of strapping on a small bicycle under the wheels. (I was unaware that another manufacturer had designed a microlight which could be used as a motor bike once the wing was taken off.)

Graham looked grim at the sight of my Himalayan tent and bag of equipment. 'Where do you think that junk will fit?' Nearly everything I had planned to take had to be jettisoned.

These are the dimensions of the Pegasus XL trike whose main feature consists of a twin-seater fibreglass body.

Length (erect):	102 inches
Length (folded down):	102 inches
Width:	69 inches
Track:	63 inches
Height (erect):	100 inches
Height (folded down):	70 inches
Weight (dry):	200 lb
Maximum hang point load:	664 lb
Minimum payload:	121 lb

Behind the seat beside the engine was a space that would take a sponge bag and not much more. We pared down our essentials to suit it. I chose a couple of paperbacks. *Anna Karenina*? Not again. Dickens? Hardy, perhaps since we would be flying over much of Wessex? I settled for *The Rattle Bag* and a translation of *Eugene Onegin*.

> But lo! from out the morning valley
> The rosy-dawn brings forth the sun,
> And with good cheer and merry sally
> The name-day feast is soon begun.

No rosy dawn today. Now that we were ready to go, the worst thing was waiting all over again. The weather had changed.

18 June. We began to rig her and all our bits are scattered on the grass.' 'You're not intending to fly to Ireland in that?' Simon had watched David testing her yesterday. 'Why don't you christen it Dow Jones?' But in a fit of depression I had named it the Undertaker.

A strong westerly wind develops and we abandon any thought of flying.

19 June. Rain. Dense heaped-up cumulus swollen with water, extending up into the sky like giant cauliflowers are causing the problem.

'Muck,' Graham says. This is what pilots call the glories of nature that get in the way of flying microlights – water-filled cloud-cover lowering down at us. I begin to wonder if low pressure induces high blood pressure. I have dressed like a knight before a tourney, donning my new 'Ozoo' flying suit and white helmet. A waste of time – it rains all day.

20 June. All around are silvery grey clouds of a different texture which I have difficulty telling apart. I hardly care if they are cirrus, cumulus, cumulo-nimbus, cirro-cumulus, strato-cumulus. A wind is forecast that will blow them away, and sure enough by one o'clock the sky is clear and I dress up again. We begin to rig. Damn. Just as it seems we can take off black clouds reappear. Rain. We de-rig hastily.

21 June. I hardly dare look outside. A clear sky and leaves stirring gently. No muck. No muck whatsoever. The day is promising. Downstairs in the kitchen Simon is trying on his ancient evening suit in preparation for a night out at Glyndebourne. The cat has left her place on the Aga and is gazing out of the door at singing birds.

'It really doesn't look too bad,' Simon says, adjusting his braces. I rush upstairs to put on my quilted Ozoo once more.

When Graham appeared it took only a few moments to push the

trike out from the barn and fasten on the wings. By now the procedures had become reflexes. The Undertaker looked spruce and ready for its inaugural flight. The tank was full of petrol, the gear oil had been changed, and Graham had managed to tie on the spare can with a web of ropes. The baggage space was crammed with our effects and a place had been found under Graham's legs for another small bag. At the last moment I rejected the blue zip cover in favour of something less heavy.

The Pegasus XL might be a more advanced machine, but it was no more comfortable than the Eagle in which I had flown in Ireland. Once again I sat in the dominant mating position, with Graham's helmet stuck in my chest. There was just room for our two bodies squeezed tightly together to fit in, my legs curled round Graham's bottom and finding some room ahead at the front end of the fibreglass pod. I was holding up the control bar which fastened on to the wings which the manufacturers had painted gold, together with all the rest of the tubular metalwork. The effect was less smart than vulgar. Graham had fitted two sleeves of rubber over the bar making it easier to hold.

The engine started on first pull with the roar that had frightened the sheep and I pulled down my visor. David rushed up to take a photograph for Solar Wings' files. To left and right I could see the familiar faces of the current set of microlight enthusiasts. Eric, John, the middle-aged doctor, Jim, a fellow Irishman who owned a pub in Sligo and had come all the way from the west to learn to fly, Keith who had crashed his single-seater a number of times, and the usual group of adoring girls.

It was a day of warm sunshine above some unmenacing clouds, a day of escape from the torment of delay. For weeks past I had seen those faces and the ones before them contorted in despair as they peered out of the caravan that Solar Wings felt obliged to supply for their frustrated flying clientele and realized that they faced another period of disappointment. Now we could get away, soaring into the blue, looking down on Clench Common and Marlborough with a sense of purpose.

With a full creaking load of two bulky men and their baggage, the Undertaker just managed to hop off the ground and over the trees. At last we were leaving the familiar red brick farmhouse, fields, woods, thatched cottages, wandering country lanes, little Pewsey, the long fingers of the Downs and the dark reflections of the Avon Canal, the landscape which I loved and hated.

For this inaugural flight we aimed to cross the Severn and land near Tintern Abbey. I had had plenty of time to plan a route around England and it seemed to be as wayward as a butterfly's flight. (The microlight usually invited comparisons with insects rather than with graceful birds – I might have learnt more watching bumble-bees than seagulls. That Frenchman had chosen the perfect name for a vehicle such as this one with his *Pou de Ciel*.) In general we would avoid urban areas and all their difficulties and there was much more of England which was out of bounds because of aviation restrictions. I wanted to see as much as possible as fast as possible before crossing the Irish Sea. And now at last we were on our way.

This was flying as children imagine it. 'Poop poop! Faster, faster!' Mr Toad had roared in his shiny new car. How he would have loved a microlight! Hooray for Amelia Ann Stiggins on the back of a motor bike, Wendy and her brothers flying with Peter, all passengers on magic carpets or on the brass bed in *Bedknobs and Broomsticks*! This was the flying of dreams, flying in a toy. We were moving in a bubble of air down over Millshill towards Devizes, then making a giant loop towards the distant Welsh hills.

In a microlight you fly visually, rarely losing touch with the ground and for this reason going through cloud is always best avoided – hence the fuss about muck. Our height was about 1,200 feet, mandatory in England, and our speed was forty-five miles an hour, although a headwind slowed down our progress. Since I was not the pilot, I had infinite time to inspect the scene passing so slowly below, without wasting a moment of sympathy on those earthlings cursing a semi-permanent nuisance overhead. I had plenty of time to notice the ground plan of a manor house, whose chimneys looked so strange from this height, the contours of a hill, a distant church spire, a dog right below stirred to frenzy at our passing shadow, a man urinating behind a hedge. Flying at this height and speed in an open cockpit without protection against the elements, gave a sense of unity with the surrounding air and nature down there which was totally lacking in conventional aircraft, where the cabin was closed in, keeping out the wind and sun and the flickering movements of air currents or thermals rising from the ground.

We reached two very distinctive landmarks, the White Horse of

Calne and above it an obelisk on a hill. I knew this was the Lansdowne obelisk put up in 1845 to the memory of William Petty, the seventeenth-century physician, cartographer, ship designer and organizer of the Down survey (where measurements were put *down* on maps), Ireland's answer to the Domesday Book, source book for plantation and exile.

As we flew across the centre of Calne, once home of the pig and bacon industry, I looked down on the handsome Lansdowne Strand Hotel with its coat of arms and a weathercock pointing to the word 'change'. Weathercocks lose their visual impact when seen from above. The hotel was smarter and sprucer altogether than the dear old Lansdowne Arms in Kenmare, also named for Petty's descendants, which I had known so well in my childhood.

Petty came to Ireland in 1652 as Physician General of the Puritan army and later acquired a lot of wild land along the southern shores of Kenmare River. He had loved the views of the Kerry mountains. 'For a great man that would retire' (he meant himself) 'this place would be the most absolute and the most interesting place in the world for both improvement and pleasure and healthfulness.' His descendants retained his Irish property, gained notoriety as landlords and made some amends by planting one of the world's most beautiful gardens (some day, I thought, I'll fly over it), but kept their headquarters here in Wiltshire. Below us were the formal 5,000 acres of Bowood, principal seat of the Lansdowne family. I could see the dark circle of trees and walls, a set of gates with a church close by, a mansion, a lake and an adventure playground. The adventure playground has become as much an adjunct of a stately home as its trees and follies and Capability Brown landscape.

Circling above the little figures moving from the wooden galleon to the swings and slides and clustering around the ice-cream stall was like looking down on Brueghel's *Children's Games*. Should we land and join them, run in like the girl from the helicopter in *Treasure Hunt*? I hardly wanted to interrupt the flight at this stage. Besides, I had visited Bowood a few weeks previously on a rainy day, as rainy as any in Kenmare. I had seen the exhibition commemorating the tercentenary of Petty's birth, which showed plenty of evidence of his restless genius, and early maps of Ireland, the ground chain for measuring distances and an engraving of his famous double-keel boat, an early catamaran. His investigations had included 'Concerning ye

Plagues of London'; 'A Computation of the Late Loss per the Fire' (the Fire of London); a 'Dictionary of Sensible Words' and 'Concerning the Sweetening of Seawater'. He did not appear to be interested in flight.

'The man will not be contented to be excellent,' Charles II said of Petty, 'but is still aiming at impossible things.'

Among his contemporaries he was most famous for reviving Ann Green. John Evelyn wrote of it:

> his recovering of a poore wench that had been hanged for felonie, the body being beged (as costome is) for the Anatomie lecture, he let bloud, put to bed to a warme woman, and with spirits and other meanes recovered her to life; the Young Scholars joyn'd and made her a little portion, married her to a Man who had severall children by her, living 15 years after, as I have ben assured.

I had examined the lengthy genealogical tree showing how Petty's daughter had married Lord Kerry, whose family later became Lords Shelburne, then Lansdowne. Back in England the family acquired Bowood and took a prominent part in English country life. Its members included a viceroy, proof of whose achievements was upstairs in a glass case, baubles of empire, including some garish presentation caskets in filigree silver which the viceroy had considered 'putting into the melting pot when I get home'.

In Ireland the Dereen estate was developed by various Lords Lansdowne, who planted thousands of giant conifers imported from America, some of which are over 140 feet high today. These kept away some of the bleakness of Kerry and sheltered a garden where the almost constant drizzle has encouraged azaleas, drinys and acres of rhododendrons. Its most famous feature is a forest of New Zealand tree ferns surrounding a damp walk named King's Oozy where you feel that if you lay down for more than half an hour you would be covered with moss. The magnificent shelter of the garden cannot wholly shut away the stormy Atlantic and the smell of seaweed in a land where eighty inches of rain fall annually and small farmers have made a hard living and talk of old evictions.

How classical, neat and prosperous Bowood seemed by comparison, its tourism well organized. As we flew above the little temple and the terraces leading down to the lake, I recalled how Thomas Moore, enchanted by Bowood and its noble owner, took up residence on the edge of the park and dedicated his first volume of *Popular National Airs* to Lord Lansdowne. And earlier Maria Edgeworth had been painfully conscious of the difference between Bowood and Edgeworthstown. 'Never were people more kindly, more cordially received. Could we forget the contrast between everything around us and everything at home, we might enjoy all the comforts and luxuries and smiling and politeness of which we are surrounded.'

Bowood's green parkland with its pulsating nucleus of houses and tourists moving round the signposted routes slipped behind us. Now we came upon the M4 strapped across a piece of Wessex, very unlike the ancient road which Hardy described where 'the wheels of the dairyman's spring cart as he sped home from market licked up the pulverized surface of the highway, and were followed by white ribands of dust as if they had set a thin powder-train on fire'. We skipped over a lot of cars on the wide grey metallic ribbon stretching from Bristol, free to go exactly where we wanted. But almost immediately we were in cloud.

In Ireland the only limiting factors about landing had been the pilot's skill and the size of a field. The chances were that the farmer and his family would be watching you and very likely, when you were safely down, if you had avoided hitting any of his precious livestock, he would bring you in for tea or whiskey. Around here things were less informal with a special rules zone stretched out from Bristol to help us avoid hitting planes like Concorde, an air traffic zone around RAF Lyneham, and plenty of other restrictions. (There are so many aircraft aloft that it is hard to believe the statistic that in England two out of three people still have not flown.)

But it is seldom hard to find a place for a microlight to land. It may lack the precision of a helicopter, but its requirements for landing are still very modest. Graham kept a map strapped to a board on his knee to help him pick out landmarks below, a road, a village, or a small airport, and soon we found one on the Badminton estate, a grass strip and a hangar, amenities for affluent owners of horses coming to the trials. Here was the second great estate we had come across at random in a day of not very fast travel pace. Thirty per cent of England is still in the hands of big landowners.

As we taxied up a girl appeared at the small control centre. 'That will be a pound.' A modest sum for the pleasant exercise of flying

over the Beaufort chimneys and landing beside them. As we lay on
the grass I had a fantasy of maids coming out carrying silver trays
loaded with thin slices of bread and butter and Madeira cake. We
didn't have a Kit-Kat between us. We looked up and contemplated
the enemy.

'The clouds accumulate in very large masses, and from their
loftiness seem to move but slowly ... small clouds passing rapidly
before them ... floating much nearer the earth may perhaps fall in
with a stronger current of wind, which as well as their comparative
lightness causes them to move with greater rapidity; hence they are
called by windmillers and sailors *messengers* and always portend bad
weather.' John Constable's obsession with clouds began with the
problems of his family's windmills. Skyscapes was what he called his
studies of clouds and aerial perspectives.

We lay longing for a patch of blue. Who doesn't? A few. Hudson
wrote of how in convents and harems the windows were so arranged
that people could only look up, 'because there is no male form, no
shadow nor reflection of one in the void above, and those who have
been fenced in from harm in this fashion must have hated the blue
sky'.

'A cumulus-nimbus can reach up to 30,000 feet and produce winds
of 200 miles an hour.' That was a very long speech from Graham. He
had been more articulate in letters. 'I hope and believe that the project
will be a very enjoyable one for both of us.' So far our communication
had consisted of curt exchanges about our common interest, which
had been a sufficient talking point. Watching the sky I recalled
unsatisfactory pairings of travellers. Eric Newby and Hugh Carless,
Peter Fleming and Ella Maillart. The independent traveller prefers
solitude. Did Graham feel like Sinbad with the Old Man of the
Sea?

After an hour the clouds dispersed and it seemed that we were not
going to be sucked into a vacuum or struck by lightning. We put on
our helmets, strapped ourselves in and took off over the broad stretch
of runway grass which instantly gave way to an oblique view of
fields, trees and cornfields.

The Severn appeared as a muddy brown inland sea empty of boats.
On the far side I could see wooded hills and a wave of mountains
behind, while below us the towers of the bridge had a Babylonian
solidity, a sense of power and purpose associated with great architec-

ture. It was well not to see the queues of people in the service
restaurant waiting to be fed, the children playing Road Blasters and
Hang-on Raiders in the amusement arcade, or the man whose car had
broken down on the M4 and who sat in it waiting to be towed away.
I looked down at the silver gleam of a sandbank and the arcs of the
bridge stringed like giant lutes and wondered idly if Graham would
like to fly under it. I declined to bring up the idea over the intercom,
although, given the scale of the structure, the feat did not look all that
difficult. The preceding bridge with close-set arches hadn't deterred
Richard Hillary, when, during his training as a pilot in 1939, a friend
beat him to the dare.

> From then on the bridge fascinated and frightened me. I had to fly
> under it. I said as much to Peter Pease . . . 'Richard,' he said, 'from
> now on a lot of people are going to fly under that bridge. From a
> flying point of view it proves nothing . . . it's extremely stupid.
> From a personal point of view it can only be of value if you don't
> tell anybody about it.'

The Undertaker crossed the Severn very slowly at about the speed
of a bicycle, taking ten minutes, flying over sandbanks, tidal rivulets
of mud and brown water. Downstream the estuary opened up and a
factory spouted black smoke. We were beating into the wind like a
small boat, while little by little the Welsh hills got closer. Suddenly
we were among them; at one moment we had been over water, now
they were all around us.

Shafts of light illuminated the narrow valley where the Wye wriggled
and turned on its way to the estuary. The sides were deeply grooved
with rocks on which perched patches of trees, out of reach of the axe.
Above them appeared a pattern of agriculture which had been largely
dispensed with in the England we had left on the other side of the
Severn. Here was a reduction in scale, little cornfields turning golden
brown, protected by hedges, instead of being part of EEC prairies.
Modest-sized farms with blazing white farmhouses, small rectangular
yards and outbuildings were surrounded by fields and pastures
properly squared off in decent sizes on a scale suited to farming by
human beings instead of by machines.

Graham was pointing and dipping a wing as we spun in a circle
like a coloured top. In the pool of dark green light that stretched

down along the banks of the Wye, Tintern sprang up, a vast honey-coloured shell standing out grandly above the river and town and the tourist buses at its feet.

We chose a hayfield just above the gorge as two farmers watched us skim over the trees and taxi to one side.

'My God, I have never seen one of those before!'

Not only the Welsh lilt reminded us that we were already far from Wiltshire, but the realization that in this bit of Wales at least, a microlight had not become a nuisance, but was still a source of curiosity. After closely examining the machine that had given them such a start coming in on top of their heads, the Welshmen made no difficulty about its being left on their land while we went down to the abbey. They watched us remove the wing and leave it lying on the grass. There would be no need to re-rig – when we returned we would just check a couple of nuts and bolts and make a quick inspection before going on our way again.

We walked down a path through woodland smelling of crushed garlic to the river where Tintern was surrounded by buses and cars and tea-shops. A party of pensioners in funny hats were taking photographs as we joined the queue for tickets to visit this exemplar of the imaginative splendours of the romantic vision.

Since the 1780s tourists have come here to view the remains of the medieval monastery established for monks of the Cistercian order by the Norman lord of Chepstow, Walter FitzRichard. In those early days of tourists the romantically inclined were stimulated to go and commune with nature in the Wye valley by the Reverend William Gilpin, whose books and essays did much to arouse popular interest in picturesque travel and influence tastes in art, literature and landscape. In fact he did not consider Tintern quite picturesque enough and thought that the regularity of the gable ends could be adjusted – 'a mallet judiciously used (but who durst use it?) might be of service fracturing them'.

Early tourists dodged beggars, hucksters and guides to seek romantic ecstasy at a site chosen deliberately for its inaccessibility by stubborn monks seeking solitude for the contemplation of heavenly things. By the late eighteenth century Tintern had become comparatively easy to reach overland via Gloucester and Ross, or by sailing down the Wye past delicious scenery punctuated by picturesque castles at Chepstow and Goodrich. The Wordsworths took several days walking to

> Behold these steep and lofty cliffs,
> That on a wild secluded scene impress
> Thoughts of more deep seclusion.

'No poem of mine was composed under circumstances more pleasant for me to remember than this.'

Visitors made moonlit visits and looked at the high Gothic walls and arches with the aid of burning torches. They avoided 'unpicturesque cottages and pigsties built with the consecrated stones of the violated ruin'.

A traveller in 1851:

> The building bursts upon you like some gigantic stone skeleton; its huge gables standing out against the sky with a mournful air of dilapidation. There is a stain upon the walls which bespeaks a weatherbeaten antiquity; and the ivy comes creeping out of the bare sightless windows; the wild flowers and mosses cluster upon the mullions and dripstones as if they were seeking to fill up the unglazed void with nature's own colours.

When the ivy was stripped off in 1915, the ruins in the wooded valley ceased to promote the same degree of visionary delight. The romantic will always make a case for the retention of ivy on ancient buildings, however many times he is reminded that it is a slow destroyer. He will value the aura of menace and impermanence.

In Ireland I had seen the 'before and after' effect of ivy-stripping at Tintern's daughter house, standing on Bannow Bay. Founded by William le Mareschal, Earl of Pembroke, in 1200 in fulfilment of a vow taken when he was in peril of drowning from shipwreck, Wexford's Tintern fell into planters' hands after the Dissolution, when the Colclough family turned the chancel and the tower into living quarters and lived there for 400 years. The last Miss Colclough went into a nursing home where I visited her and was shown her photograph album with its views of the abbey as a comfortable Anglo-Irish dwelling-place. The drawing-room with its Edwardian clutter had been converted from the nave, a tennis party was pictured in front of the abbey steps with the squat little building behind in its thick ivy mantle. Meanwhile, well-meaning authorities were already turning it into a tidy place, and the descent from the romantic to

the prosaic after the ivy was torn off was an instantaneous transformation.

Unlike Tintern in Wexford, the great ruins of Tintern on the Wye
have the proportions to withstand the loss of nature's adornment and
still impart wonder and mystery. Since Gilpin's time their splendour
has resisted the puny vulgarities of tourism, although it is increasingly
difficult to experience what Rose Macaulay described as 'this melancholy pleasure in ruined grandeur and pathos'. In particular, midsummer was no time to try to capture thoughts of a more deep seclusion
as the buses streamed off the A441. We merged with the hundreds
making their way along the gravel paths, following the signs in
English and Welsh, past the uniformed attendants in peaked hats,
jostling with the others among the soaring ribbed arches of the
western front, examining the warming house and cloisters with the
mob. A few took the tour very seriously, tracking down details of
ancient monastic routine with the aid of guidebooks, or, like the
woman in the museum, reading out bits of Wordsworth to a bored
child. The bits about Dorothy, of course:

> Oh! yet a little while
> May I behold in thee what I was once,
> My dear, dear sister . . .

Like Gwen John, Dorothy has outstripped her brother and been
elevated to middle-class icon alongside the female Brontës. The
power of feminism has made William, Augustus and Branwell take
back-seats.

But most visitors were in light-hearted mood, and there was
nothing solemn about those who had just been viewing 'indescribable
grandeur and beauty' and now crowded into the souvenir shops to
buy little Welsh witches in tall hats, dish towels and T-shirts. 'They
went to Wales and all they brought back was this lousy T-shirt.' Why
should that arouse universal mirth? 'Heavenly father, look down on
us your humble obedient tourist servants who are doomed to travel
this earth taking photographs, mailing postcards, buying souvenirs
and walking around in drip-dry underwear.' Having selected their
hucksters' wares, they wandered outside and listened to the Mon-
mouth Brass Band playing old favourites, *Edelweiss*, *Hear My Song
Violetta*. There was little hope of capturing the scene 'with an eye

made quiet by the power of harmony, and the deep power of joy', so we went back to our own noise-maker which was being splattered with a gentle Welsh rain. Big pearly drops came down as we huddled for our protection in our flying-suits on the wet grass under the microlight's wings. We had plenty more time for cloud-watching before the sky cleared and the last menacing cumulo-nimbus in the shape of a Welsh dragon with a gaping mouth was dispersed by westerlies. At last Graham could say, 'That rubbish won't be coming our way' as we wiped down the perspex trike.

The rain hadn't affected the engine and she started first pull. This time there was no easy runway or even a good length, and we squeezed down at the edge of the field heading uphill. Full throttle, full power, bouncing over the wet grass and pushing out the bar before we were airborne. As we swung over the gorge, I could see another tourist bus arriving and another letting off a load of stick figures which began to move around the car park, while shadows crept along and closed in on them. The noise of our engine drowned out the brass sounds of *Now Is The Hour* as we rose higher and the figures dwindled into ants. The Gothic proportions of Tintern ceased to be under the spell of the Welsh Tourist Board and offered once more a view of unsullied and spellbinding magnificence.

Up and away. But first we needed to refuel, since the four-gallon tank which Graham had roped on at Clench Common had been emptied at Badminton. The spare tank was an essential which gave us assurance of always being able to take off; its contents would last on average flying conditions for a couple of hours. Graham's knots were secure, and throughout the journey the can never wobbled or threatened to break loose. But a refill was necessary and spotting a garage from the air would become a routine part of a day's flying. Some petrol attendants would look very startled at the sight of the Undertaker landing in a field adjoining their garage and taxiing as near as possible up to their forecourt. We always used five-star. The petrol-oil mixture of fifty to one had to be exact, and Graham, refusing to trust me with measurements which might later lead to problems in the sky, always insisted on filling up the can himself.

CHAPTER FIVE

Slimbridge and Avebury

Sun sparkled on the brown sedgy waters of the Severn Estuary, a funnel-shape reaching down from Gloucester to the Bristol Channel. A tiny steamer was clawing its way past the bridge upstream with the tide which could reach a speed of thirteen knots with the famous Severn Bore. From above, the most dangerous waterway in Europe looked peaceful, lines of moving wrinkles and mudbanks visible as harmless brown smudges. I could see Berkeley Castle standing out from its trees and the derricks and cranes of Sharpness. Beyond that we knew was the Dumbles, 200 acres of grassy salt-marsh lying outside the sea wall. Along the river an area of 1,000 acres of what are called the New Grounds, created by pushing out successive sea walls composed of mudbanks stretching along the Severn and a boundary to the east made by the Gloucester and Berkeley Canal, mark off the Wildfowl Trust at Slimbridge.

We could not fly anywhere near the place. Slimbridge abhors small noisy aircraft which upset ducks, shelducks, geese, steamer ducks, Brent geese, whistling ducks, flamingos, screamers, eiders, pochards, whooping swans and all the other nervous, restless, resident, migrant, or nesting wildfowl there, whether they fly in or are penned in amiable captivity. Peter Scott had written to me:

> If you are passing this way please look in, but not in your microlight. We have a 'no low flying area' over us to prevent disasters to our birds which become terribly upset if low aircraft pass over, and in the case of our flamingos it has prevented them breeding more than once in the past.

The microlight had to be left a good way off, out of the protective bubble of airspace.

Barry Stewart, one of the fifteen ground-staff employed as wardens, was feeding the birds. Most of his life Barry had been a twitcher, eyes glued to binoculars on the look-out for unusual avian species. In the days when he had been a policeman he had spent his free time watching Arctic terns near his home, or chasing rarities like the white-throated sparrow which had necessitated an overnight visit to Belfast for him to number it among his visual trophies. In due course he had thrown up his policeman's role to come and work in this place, which was paradise. His bedroom, overlooking Rushy Pen, which in winter is filled with the hooting of thousands of swans, had almost the same view that Peter Scott enjoyed from his studio looking out 'upon water and birds and the green fields of Gloucestershire. A pool with islands reflects a flush of the setting sun in the ripples made by the ducks and geese that are swimming in it.'

Work was joy for Barry, wheeling his trolley like a waiter with hors-d'oeuvres, offering sand-eels from Norfolk, grains of wheat, brown bread, chick-crunch and flamingo soup containing nutritious pellets and milled shrimp to keep feathers pink.

The birds knew exactly when he was coming. 'We don't try to influence them, particularly in summer when there is plenty of food.' But the gluttons were waiting for him. The sound of the cart made the trumpeter swans peal out and bob up and down in excitement, and the flamingos rush around in a welter of fluffy pink feathers. The geese and duck, surfeited by breadcrumbs thrown by visitors, were less interested and their rations were quickly retrieved by scavenging gulls.

One of the main aims of the Wildfowl Trust is to bring people and birds together and in this it is overwhelmingly successful. Those who remember Slimbridge in the early days regret the changes brought about by popularity.

Summer migrants are mostly wingless and come in from the M4 and the M5, from the lines of little boats along the old Gloucester and Sharpness Canal, and from the nearby caravan parks. When the gates open at 9.30 there is already a small crowd waiting and at the height of summer Slimbridge will attract 1,000 people and more during the day. The reserves run by the Wildfowl Trust around the country receive over 600,000 visitors a year, of which Slimbridge gets nearly 200,000 to view the largest and most comprehensive collection of wildfowl in the world.

A line of cars was waiting at the canal for the lock-man to rack them over the little wooden bridge by hand. Another queue had formed outside the office near the bust of Peter Scott, binoculars around his neck, looking down benignly over a bed of roses. The pathways leading down to the pens were crammed with bird-watchers viewing ducks which had lost some plumage and flamingos a little jaded in the heat. 'Is that Donald Duck?' a child asked its father as a fat mallard waddled up. Ducks and geese followed people all over the place like eastern beggars, looking for the breadcrumbs visitors were encouraged to buy in large paper bags. 'Please stop.' 'Please go very quietly, wild birds may be near.'

In the tropical house photographers were trying to record small bright creatures darting through the trees. 'There he goes.' A scarlet arrow zoomed past, and then an African jackana stepped out from dense green foliage and faced the barrage of cameras pointed in his direction. In the restaurant diners faced fillet of plaice, steak and kidney pie, strawberries and cream and jelly. In the shop visitors could buy feather brooches, nice reproductions of ducks and geese by Peter Scott and tea towels decorated with Jemima Puddle-Duck. This was the first evidence I had seen of the Beatrix Potter cult. Income from the trust's shops totals £150,000 a year. Leaflets urged the crowds to adopt a duck – £5 a year – or support a goose – £7 a year – or patronize a Bewick swan for £15. Others urged conservation, education, recreation. A portrait of the Duke of Edinburgh reminded buyers that bird-watchers are well connected. The Queen is patron, Prince Charles is president.

Sir Peter Scott is in favour of creating wildernesses that are forbidden to any sort of visitors at all, since any human presence may threaten an environment and the wildlife it supports. These places would be very far from Slimbridge, where you look at people as closely as you look at the satiated ducks, at the lady in tight pink trousers who appears to have eaten too many breadcrumbs, at the dark girl in glasses who has just bought a leaflet to help her identify different species, at the intense bearded man whose thick bottle-end spectacles are almost as bulky as his binoculars, the small boy making farting noises, the old lady who looks like the Queen Mother in her pastel blue cotton with her white hat perched to one side of her head, who has fallen asleep on a bench.

Groups of bird-watchers, wearing badges and carrying expensive

Leica binoculars that emphasized the seriousness of their enthusiasm, were making their way to the hides, grumbling because it wasn't winter. Winter, when the posh migrants fly in, the Bewick swans, pochards, tufted duck, pintail and geese that come over 2,000 miles from Siberia, is the time for serious ornithologists. In summer time the wild swans and geese have left this avian Serengeti for their breeding-grounds in Greenland or on the tundra shores of the Kara Sea. Only a few black-tailed godwits and other commoners parade up and down among the flocks of seagulls.

In the Holden hide they were viewing a kestrel.

'Do you see him?'

'I can't identify him.' They spoke in whispers. The more unusual birds had special dossiers on their colouring and bill patterns and had been given whimsical names, Lemonsplodge, Primrose, Antony and Cleopatra, Stars and Stripes.

'There's a couple of yellow wagtails in the next little curve.'

'Oh lovely!'

'I can't identify them,' someone was saying, peering through glasses from the high Acrow tower.

'Small or large tortoiseshell?' Two women were admiring butterflies on the specially planted buddleia. A couple were studying the Barnacle Goose Supporter Scheme. There were no barnacle geese here now, of course, they were away in Spitzbergen or Siberia hopefully rearing families, but at any time of year you could adopt a far-away goose with an enormous plastic ring on its leg marked with numbers which could be seen from 200 metres away.

'You get an arrival report as soon as your very own personal goose is sighted coming into Caerlaverock.'

'Suppose it never arrives?'

'You get a new goose for the year after. They try and give you your money's worth.'

At present seagulls dominated Slimbridge in flocks as thick as those I had watched on Sandymount Strand back in Dublin. Once again I mused on the links between birds and airmen, which are not always happy ones. On aeronautical maps Slimbridge is marked as a restricted area and high-flying jets, helicopters, microlights and private planes of wealthy tycoons are all warned away. The potential damage aircraft and birds can do each other is a mutual hazard. Seagulls are the most frequently struck birds and the speed of the aircraft turns a soft feathery body into a lethal missile. About 5 per cent of bird-strikes cause damage, which includes smashed windshields, blocked air-intakes, broken pitot heads and holed structures. In late summer the risk of striking birds is higher, because young birds have not yet learnt that aircraft are a hazard, while older birds are enfeebled when they are moulting their feathers and do not always get out of the way. In autumn or spring migrating birds and pilots share navigational features like rivers and shorelines which they may both be following, so that the risks of collision increase, and birds of prey have been known to attack aircraft.

I had been reading a chilling Civil Aviation Authority leaflet on bird avoidance which conveyed the effects of bird-strike in prose that might have been written for Hitchcock. 'If the windshield is broken (or cracked), slow the aircraft to reduce wind blast, follow approved procedures. Use sun-glasses or smoke-goggles to reduce the effect of wind, precipitation or debris, but remember to *fly the aircraft* – don't be too distracted by the blood, feathers, smell and wind blast.' If the pilot is near the ground he must endeavour not to do anything that will lead to a stall or spin. Gulls, pigeons, lapwings and even swifts can hole light aircraft windshields.

Perhaps it was better to muse on the more obvious link between airmen and bird – on bird as inspiration and the source of passionate envy to frustrated earth-bound mortals. Would man ever learn to fly like the birds? Among those who believed it possible were the brave tower-jumpers through the ages, using their cloaks or sad attempts at wings as they hurled themselves into space. Eilmer of Malmesbury crippled for life, Armen Firnian saved by his cloak in AD 852. John Damian, hurling himself off Stirling Castle, on his way to France, who fell into a dunghill. And the men who died, Boloni, Bernoun and Franz Reichett, whose jump from the Eiffel Tower like a plummeting bat was caught on early flickering newsreel, were considered presumptuous. They had ignored the Bible lesson.

Then the devil taketh him up into the holy city, and setteth him on a pinnacle of the temple,

And saith unto him, If thou be the Son of God, cast thyself down: for it is written, He shall give his angels charge concerning thee: and in their hands they shall bear thee up, lest at any time thou dash thy foot against a stone.

Jesus said unto him, It is written again, Thou shall not tempt the Lord thy God.

The urge to fly might be the sin of presumption, but it persisted and some people never lost their optimism. Sir George Cayley, who laid the foundations of modern aerodynamics, was convinced that 'this noble art will soon be brought to man's convenience'. (Sir George did not try to fly himself; he sent up a 'boy glider' who was about ten years old in the machine he designed; later, his coachman, ordered to go up, gave notice. 'Please Sir, I was hired to drive, not to fly.')

The frustration of not being able to fly was passionately expressed by the Frenchman Louis-Pierre Mouillard, who enviously studied buzzards in Egypt during the 1870s. 'If there be a domineering tyrant thought, it is the conception that the problem of flight may be solved by man. When once the idea has invaded the brain, it possesses it exclusively. It is then a haunting thought, a walking nightmare, impossible to cast off.' Fifty-six days before Wilbur Wright's flight of 852 feet in fifty-nine seconds, a pessimist called Simon Newcomb pronounced that human flight was impossible.

Otto Lilienthal's brother wrote about Otto's ill-fated experiments: 'He is constantly calculating and holding up to our admiration and emulation the wonderful economy of nature as applied to the flight of the larger birds.' Lilienthal particularly admired the flight of storks. Peter Scott's interest in gliders was natural. 'Perhaps the greatest appeal of gliding is the simplicity of the basic components. In a glider you are competing against gravity. When you are going up you are winning. When you are coming down, you are losing.'

Lilienthal's flying machine was a pioneer hang glider. He began to test a prototype in 1889, and he, too, leapt off towers. Then in 1892 he and his brother moved to the Rhinow Hills near Berlin where wind conditions were good and there were slopes to jump off. He made over 2,000 glides, at times soaring to 65 feet, 'over ravines and crowds of people who looked up in wonder'. One glide covered 1,000 feet. He flew for five years to gain five hours of flight.

Lilienthal believed in wing curvature (so did Daedalus, according to Ovid). The wings of his glider, which had a span of just over 20 feet, were fixed and they offered the stability of an arrow or a fixed missile. The problem, which he never overcame, arose out of sudden wind gusts which shifted his glider's wings. He allowed for this by moving his body-weight from side to side or back and forward, to alter his centre of gravity and maintain equilibrium. He could manage shallow banking and an awkward change in direction, but the way he flew was filled with danger. He was killed in August 1896 in a No. 11 model, flying too high – the glider nose-dived and he broke his neck. His last words were 'Sacrifices must be made!'

Hang gliding became a fairly reliable way of flying almost a century later. Hang gliders still have the sting of danger, but they are not programmed to kill in the same way as poor Lilienthal's models were. Their flight, which has been described as 'quiet, uncomplicated and free', is the nearest to the birds. The pilot, lying prone, has a bird's-eye view of the ground and no other flying machine will give him that. He flies noiselessly except for the whistle of wind in the rigging.

I flew in hang gliders for a time and felt the bird's freedom of flight which a little microlight buzzing through the skies can never impart. I remembered the constant excitement from the moment the kite was rigged, the waiting for take-off, the Terylene wings flapping as it struggled to get away. I started in a model called a Cloudbase, making bunny-hops in the same way as Lilienthal did, and for a long time most of my short flights ended up in briar bushes or near to walls. Later I became more ambitious, exchanging the Cloudbase for a Super Scorpion. That was long ago, a decade ago, aeons in modern flying development. Like the microlight, the hang glider has changed radically in a few years and recent models are far more acutely attuned to the laws of aerodynamics and so are nearer to the birds.

'Watch the birds,' I was constantly told.

I had flown like a bird, soaring, floating, swooping over Mount Leinster and the Sugarloaf. But one or two landings were not good. My family got tired of taking second place to a heavier-than-air, fixed-wing glider.

I thought nostalgically of hang gliders as we buzzed doggedly back across the Severn. Although with a microlight I had sacrificed ecstasy for purpose and Graham and I were masters of direction, we were still at the mercy of the weather, which was about to confront us again. Just across the river we flew from sunshine straight into grey cloud and rain, where we were instantly being bumped and battered, the microlight making little nauseous swoops. We landed quickly.

'The earth approaches very fast – that streaming past so marvellously quick that the eye sees only a rushing stream, a turbid liquid of clods and stones melted to porridge in the eye.' David Garnett's description of landing in a small plane is exact, although, in this case, vision was blurred by rain.

We sheltered under the wing until the rain reduced to a drizzle and I could hear birds singing and caught sight of a hare bounding across the wet grass. While Graham headed for the nearest village to get something to eat, I took up the usual sky-watching. Would that threatening bank of vapoury cloud continue to be a problem? How long would I have to go on sitting in a wet field with cows for company? Beyond them was an embankment, and a railway line, and a couple of InterCity trains rushed past, too fast for the passengers gazing through the windows to notice more than a blue and yellow blur of the microlight wing. If they did spot it they would probably think it was a tent. I remembered how W. H. Hudson scorned railway passengers ignorant of the 'great green country' of Wiltshire:

> They all know it 'in a way'; they have seen Salisbury Cathedral and Stonehenge, which everybody must go to look at once in his life; and they have also viewed the country from the windows of a railroad carriage as they passed through on their flight to Bath and to Wales with its mountains, and to the west country . . . For there is nothing striking in Wiltshire.

After Graham returned with a can of lemonade, chocolate and crisps, we left at the first opportunity, when the clouds folded back a little more firmly and a weak sun emerged. Soon we were flying over Wiltshire woods and fields, another seething motorway, and now and again an ideal English view, a church spire, a thatched cottage with coloured pinpricks of flowers, a miniature farm surrounded by the ugliness necessary to modern farming, shining tin sheds, the gleam of rain on concrete, a flurry of white plastic feeding-sacks. A village cricket game gave pleasure, the little figures in white standing out from the baize of the pitch. Someone was coming up and bowling and I could see his arm swinging over, but before the batsman replied, I was looking down on a Palladian doll's house. A curving avenue, the trees foreshortened, led to a handsome miniature brick building

with projecting wings, a maze of roofs and a cupola. A car drove up
and I could see two dogs rushing towards it, as a man and a woman
got out.

The wind was increasing, and the microlight began to tremble and
dip its wings in the frothy air. Graham was struggling with the bar to
keep some balance, but just as things seemed about to smooth out,
another gust would hit us and put us off course. Flying in turbulent
weather feels like sailing on invisible waves. A boat buckets around
the sea, but at least you can see each wave as it threatens you. When
you are flying, you are dealing with unseen forces, where, even in a
cloudless sky, thermals can tear you apart.

I should be getting used to this, bad weather again, visibility
reduced and the country smudged over in greying light. Soon another
squall was trickling across the perspex of my helmet, as the clouds
forced us down to a few hundred feet and the microlight pitched and
rocked. I worried about my teeth. Could the expensive dental bridge
so recently and painfully installed fly out and fall to the chalk below?
I kept my mouth firmly shut.

The view over Wiltshire was restricted, a few murky rooftops, a
grey shadow which could have been a wood, and then straight in
front of us a headland decorated by a white horse profiled in turf. It
stood inanely, its huge head slightly lowered as if waiting to be petted
or fed.

The sight of this apparition made Graham change course and he
landed quickly almost on the head, missing by a few feet the top of a
high chimney that was part of a cement factory down the hill.

'Is this Pewsey?' he shouted at a man in the car park as we taxied
up.

'No, Westbury.'

'How do we get to Pewsey?'

He pointed towards the railway line.

There was no shelter and it wasn't worthwhile heaving ourselves
out. We sat in torrents of rain while the microlight threatened to fill
up like a bath. Graham had made a rare navigational error and
chosen the wrong White Horse. Pilots of small aircraft appreciate
white horses carved out on hills, as such graffiti on a grand scale have
an invaluable function as landmarks. There are theorists who say they
were meant to be seen from the sky, a signal from neolithic man to
his gods as they sailed past in their flying saucers.

Before the gods that made the gods
Had seen their sunrise pass
The White Horse of the White Horse Vale
Was cut out of the grass.

This was a less ancient nag. There are six white horses in Wiltshire, none of them very old. Instead of the White Horse of Pewsey, we had landed on the White Horse of Westbury, dug out of the turf in 1778 by Mr Gee, a steward to Lord Abingdon. Mr Gee dug up and destroyed a really ancient white figure, as he thought the earlier one with its beak and long tail ending in a crescent moon – an Iron Age symbol of fertility – was a bad imitation of a real horse. It may have been a dragon. There is a legend that it celebrates King Alfred's victory over the Danes at the battle of Ethandun in AD 878.

Looking over the edge of the hill at its rump, I thought that Mr Gee had made a crude job of his equine quadruped. We had landed on an exceedingly windy exposed place that stood up 754 feet over Westbury and the surrounding countryside. It was a place for lovers to drive up their cars, for girls to exercise ponies, where the occasional hang glider could be seen seeking thermals on a warm summer's day. Not today.

We decided to risk a final flight. We started the engine and Graham took off quickly leaving the dismal horse behind and began to follow thick straight rails running over darkened fields. I recalled the old jeers about wartime American pilots weak in navigation concentrating on railway lines. Whyever not? In the failing light I could see the gleaming tracks leading us on, bars of silver clear and visible in an uncertain world. Here were places where I had walked during previous weeks. Draycott Hill, Golden Ball Hill, Gopher Wood, dark in the evening and in the rain. Another torrent and we were flying by our nose. Hemingway, travelling with Scott Fitzgerald in an open touring car, was halted by the rain ten times in a single day.

'Scott then asked me if I was afraid to die and I said more at some times than others.'

This was the worst yet, and flying soon progressed from the unpleasant to the dangerous. It was hard to control the microlight and difficult to see. There were no handy windscreen wipers, no protective screen under which we could crouch, and from the soaking, spewing, open cockpit, the smudged undulating shapes on the ground became very menacing. We were immersed in a force that had liquidity and strength. Ahead of me I could just see Graham making ineffectual efforts with one gloved hand to clean off the stream running down his visor. The rain increased and decreased with the rhythm of a hand on the scale of the White Horse working a pump.

We were about 800 feet up where occasionally the grey cloud shredded and for a moment we could see something clearly below. Peter Scott had been forced down over Marlborough in an attempt to get a prized gold C badge for gliding – some other giant Marlborough cloud had pushed him to the ground. We were not looking for medals, only for an arrival. Then we saw another White Horse grinning up at us. This was the right horse, the one designed for the committee which was organizing the celebrations in Pewsey for the coronation of King George VI in 1937. (There was an old one somewhere underneath.)

Graham landed skilfully almost in the dark. He had made the decisions and battled the clouds. I had merely been a seasick passenger. We got out stiffly, feeling that we never wanted to see a microlight again. Drenched through, we discussed without enthusiasm plans to press on next day in a southerly direction.

Next day I welcomed the wind and the rain. 'Full storm,' I noted in my diary. 'Two lows over Scotland, flying out of the question.' On the following day, a Sunday: 'The storm is still raging and any thought of flying nightmarish.' I wrote with something like glee, with none of the old frustrated yearning to be aloft. The farm was warm and comfortable, and I spent the day watching Diana preparing rams for a show. One dribbled, another refused to stand still, a third had some defect in holding its head and one of the judges was known to be prejudiced against this failing. Would it be worth it? Was it worth considering entering any for the Royal Show? Talk of sheep had a soothing effect. I was resigned to never leaving Clench. My bones would become fossilized microlight spars, my winding sheet would be Dacron wings and I would be buried in Simon's back-yard among rusty discarded machinery.

The Faux flock was a remnant, a reminder of the old days of shepherds with their crooks and dogs, of reddlemen and sheep fairs attended by gypsies with their lurchers, piebald ponies and fortune-tellers, held in mysterious remote places like Yarnbury Castle and Tan

Hill which could only be reached by horseback or on foot. Locations of the old fairs were often near ancient landmarks like Iron Age forts. Shepherds walked their flocks for days over the downs or followed 'shepherd's lanterns', the white stones that marked the tracks over the downs.

I had been reading Hardy. What exactly were reddlemen? Diana knew. A reddleman was a gypsyish sort of traveller who moved about in a cart containing all his worldly goods, selling reddle and lamb-black. According to Peter Gurney, author of *Shepherd Lore*, 'his four-wheeled cart, his face, his clothes and even his horse and dog were stained . . . a lurid red'. The principal use of reddle, which was made from red ocre and size, 'was at tupping time when a ram's chest and underparts were smeared with it, so that he left a mark on each ewe he served. Any infertility could thereafter be checked.'

Easier ways of discovering the virility of rams meant that the reddlemen had almost gone by the time Hudson was observing the lives of Wiltshire shepherds. The shepherds themselves survived up until the Second World War, passing long tough healthy outdoor lives looking after vast herds of Hampshire Downs, Oxford and Dorset Downs, Cheviots, Exmoor Horns, Ryelands and Kerry Hills, which made the downs resound with their clang bells, rumblers, cluckets and frog-mouth bells. During the 1930s the thin downland soil was still suitable only for sheep, which flourished in what was known as the age of the Golden Hoof. A few old men can still remember the last time that the sheep was king. Then the demands of wartime and the development of artificial fertilizers brought arable crops and the extinction of the old shepherds, who went the way of bustards.

Towards evening I noticed that behind one more storm cloud spilling its rain came patches of blue and gold and the flotillas were less threatening. Some clouds were shaped like torpedoes, others had become shoals of frightened fish, one was a dwarf's head with a long curling nose stretching out of sight. This was not a scientific assessment of next day's weather, but the signs were promising and there was a pink glow in the sky, shepherd's delight.

In the morning we started all over again, putting on our flying-suits and checking everything, wings, engine, bolts, fabric, safety harness, throttle, can of petrol. We took off over the downs across Savernake Forest and busy Marlborough enclosed by its hills. We flew over the house of Roger Upton where I had seen his six peregrine and two gyr falcons sitting in the garden on their stands dressed in little leather caps. Roger was continuing a tradition for falconry on the Wiltshire Downs, and later that day I would see an old photograph showing a happy group of people, hawks on wrists, setting off in a coach for a day's sport, around the turn of the century.

We continued to fly over familiar country following the line of the main road, a house, a farm, a curve of the downs, the little Norman church of St Nicholas at Fyfield where the vicar or someone was burning leaves. The smoke moved leisurely – today we would have no trouble with the wind. We flew on and Avebury appeared.

It is eerie that so many places seem to have been designed to be viewed from the air long before anyone had ideas of flying. From the height of the microlight about 1,500 feet up, Avebury invoked unease with the suggestion that the ancient complex was laid out as a living map, mysterious as those lines in Peru that were made for the gods. White horses, Stonehenge, Avebury – Wiltshire's landmarks disturb the imagination as perpetual enigmas. Avebury's major monuments are concentrated within a radius of about three miles of Avebury, and I saw them as we swooped in, the almost perfect cone of Silbury Hill, the East Kennett Long Barrow covered with trees, the restored West Kennett Long Barrow and the avenue of great stones leading up to the circles of Avebury composed of giant grey lozenges planted in the grass.

The stones are sarsen stones or 'grey wethers' (because they are said to look like sheep) taken from round about, the remains of the sandstone that once covered the chalk downs. The Avebury complex lies between the 500- and 600-foot contours on a wide undulating chalk shelf below the escarpment of the west side of the Marlborough Downs. The area – well wooded in ancient times – supported a large population. It may have been situated on main trade routes. Calcined bones of ancient sheep have been found deeply embedded in the chalk crust with Roman coins, flint arrowheads, flakes of pottery and all the detritus of prehistory.

Archaeologists and others have been pecking away around here for centuries. Early excavations were shamelessly informal, like those of Dr Tooke (or Toope) of Marlborough, who made a mess of the South Long Barrow looking for bones. He wrote to John Aubrey: 'I quickly perceived they were humane, and came next day and dugg for them, and stored myselfe with many bushells of which I made a noble medicine that relieved many of my distressed neighbours.' Archaeologists have been complaining for a long time about Dr Tooke's damage – he wrecked proper appraisal of the forecourt and eastern chambers. But much more destruction was caused by local farmers in succeeding centuries, quarrying for flint and chalk, breaking up sarsens for building, and cutting a wagon road through the centre of the rings. The looting was stopped only in 1883 when first Silbury Hill and then West Kennett became the first monuments to be protected under the Ancient Monuments Act.

At Windmill Hill excavations have revealed the remains of a large prehistoric village with evidence of neolithic sheep farmers, traders, cultivators of buckwheat, barley and flax grown on ground tilled with digging-sticks and antler hoes. They ate crab apples and raised sheep, goats, pigs and many cattle, as their animals' bones attest. With flint-tipped arrows and spears they slaughtered wild animals, wild cattle or aurochs, deer, horses and cats and foxes for their fur. All the people who lived here left shards of pottery, Windmill Hill ware, Peterborough ware, Mortlake and Fengate styles, late neolithic flat-bottomed Grooved ware and Beaker ware which heralded sophistication, since the Beaker people were the first to introduce metal into Britain. Occasionally a dead child was thrown in with the rubbish in the ditches around Windmill Hill.

John Evelyn wrote about 'divers mounts raisd, conceiv'd to be antient intrenchments, or places of burial after bloudy fights'. Richard Jefferies pondered on the 'grass-grown tumuli on the hills to which of old I used to walk, sit down at the foot of them and think "some warrior has been interred here in the anti-historic times"'. Excavations of West Kennett Long Barrow made more mysteries with the discovery of forty-six individuals interred there, of whom over a dozen were children. They may have been members of an ancient dynasty. The adults were arthritic and several of them suffered from spina bifida; one old man had a broken arm, an abscess on his shoulder, his big toes were deformed and he had died because of the leaf arrowhead in his throat. They were all dolichocephalic, long-headed, indicating that they were North European and not Mediterranean people.

The mystery of Silbury Hill has defeated archaeologists who have been investigating it for centuries, getting Cornish miners to help. A Duke of Northumberland, a Dean of Hereford and a railway engineer all made explorations, none of which revealed very much. Professor Atkinson tried harder for four years, beginning in 1967, and a few years ago the BBC tried again. They know how Silbury Hill was built, but not why. It is the biggest man-made monument in Europe and the volume of material moved in cubic feet is just about the same as the smallest of the three pyramids of Giza. It was built with great care in stages, and with a turf core and chalk walls that were so securely combined that it has hardly eroded over 4,000 years.

We flew directly over the symmetrical flat-topped dome of tightly packed chalk until it appeared as two concentric circles of faintly differing greens. I would also like to see Silbury from the air in winter when it is snow-covered. Although its purpose is unknown, the researchers know one thing – work began on it in late July or early August after some of the harvest was in. Through a turf core they discovered, along with weeds and grass grazed by ancient sheep, traces of flying ants winged for late summer mating flights.

No sign of any burial has been found during investigation of Silbury's inner core.

The village of Avebury has always been in conflict with the stones round about. The church is ancient, the manor house old, and for centuries those who lived among the giant megaliths were uneasy. In medieval times when plague raged, villagers followed a directive from Benedictine monks to dig pits and bury the great stones, which they did until one stone topped over killing a man. After that they retreated. When John Aubrey guided King Charles all round Avebury and up Silbury Hill, there were scarcely any houses within the circles. But later people moved back inside and made a little town, doing terrible things to the stones. While William Stukeley the antiquarian was recording and mapping the complex at the beginning of the eighteenth century, he chanced to witness the destruction by a farmer of 'the Sanctuary', stone circles at the end of the West Kennett Avenue. After that the stones continued to be destroyed by quarrying and being broken up with a steady thoroughness that suggests a continued hatred for ancient mysteries. (In Ireland destruction of prehistoric stone remains did not begin until twenty years ago, when superstition waned and the bulldozers began their work.)

A campaign supported by respectable gentlemen and churchmen was begun to save Avebury. Then came the flamboyant man from Dundee who exchanged preserving marmalade for preserving

Avebury. Archaeologists have compared the social effects of the making of Avebury to the Apollo space programme. Huge efforts by large numbers of people over centuries contributed to the mapping out of holy places for solemn religious purposes. To those chanting, heaving, toiling, vanished crowds, spurred by religious ecstasy, and perhaps the odd Druid whip, to heave boulders into sacred patterns must be added the final figure of the Marmalade Man. Alexander Keiller bought Windmill Hill in 1924 to prevent Marconi putting a radio mast on top. Over the years he bought more and more, excavated, tore down unsightly sheds and garages, exhumed and re-erected the old stones. Before he came the village of Avebury had been, in the words of Sir John Lubbock, another gentleman antiquarian who had Silbury in his possession in the 1870s, 'like some beautiful parasite, grown up at the expense and in the midst of the ancient temples'. After Keiller had bought a fair amount of houses and pulled them down, the rest of the village survives, subdued. The stones of Avebury have taken over again, to be worshipped by tourists.

You get a better class of tourist here, I was assured by the barman at the Red Lion. What about the Moon Maidens? I had walked by their caravans parked under Silbury, reading the notices in the trailer windows – WE ARE THE MAJORITY – BAN THE BOMB – and noticing in particular one young girl with long flaxen hair playing a pipe. It appeared that other Moon Maidens had been and gone, threatening a Red Alert in a countryside terrified of the army of hippies on their way to Stonehenge. The Wiltshire police would be keeping an eye on these ladies. In any case, 'Silbury isn't important'. Silbury does not attract a lot of visitors. The A4 between Marlborough and Bath runs right by it and it is a twenty-minute walk from Avebury. It is one of the most unvisited of the mighty prehistoric monuments in Europe.

People prefer Avebury, but only certain people. Avebury's ancient complications are less attractive to modern sun and moon worshippers than the compact midsummer measurements that attract the long-haired crew to Stonehenge. So I was assured. You did not get hippies or skinheads or yobbos on motor bikes breaking up everything. There were no hippy slogans as in neighbouring Stonehenge: FREE THE STONES. As yet Avebury didn't make a good day out for mums and dads with kids screaming for ice-cream and crisps. These people were essentially from the A-B group, who considered themselves decent middle class with a high enough standard of education to appreciate what Avebury meant. Here they found satisfaction in their faintly erudite enthusiasms like archaeology and folk history. Babies were strapped to them fore and aft – the middle class eschew push-chairs, preferring to take baby back to the wild like a little chimpanzee.

'It did as much excel Stonehenge as the cathedral does a parish church.' Reading suitable texts aloud in front of the object of your pilgrimage was practised by the serious tourist. No doubt the Bostonian accent delivering Aubrey's famous comment was nearer to the Old Restoration voice than that of the shrill woman standing under one of the thinner, straighter sarsens. 'Phallic! This one's male!' A party listened to a guide with more than the usual solemn earnestness. None of the casual admiration of people going round stately homes – there was awe at Avebury.

Two Hindus were dowsing stones with copper rods they had bought in the Henge Shop, referring repeatedly to another purchase, a book on spiritual dowsing.

'We are looking for energy spots.'

The directions were quite clear.

1. Relax. Don't work when there are distracting physical influences.

[This wasn't easy on a fine summer's day. The number of people here was not nearly as great as at Tintern or Slimbridge, but there were still too many for concentration].

2. Clearly define and visualize the object of energy being looked for.

3. Go in search, concentrating on the question, but keeping the mind still.

4. Remember you are in control.

I removed my distracting influence and walked along to the corner of Frog's Lane where I met Jim White posting a letter. I accompanied him back to his house, one of the new council houses situated in Avebury Trusloe just outside the main village, where their unsightly appearance is less prominent. A robust man of eighty-six, who walked briskly with the aid of a stick, he was interested to hear that I was Irish. The Whites came to Avebury from Ireland during famine times and stayed here – unusually for emigrants who generally sought out urban areas. Jim could remember the old times before Keiller's clean sweep. There weren't many survivors who could recall the old days – women of course. Fifty widows were left, but only three old men with memories.

'So what was it like?'

He looked out of the window across his neat garden. 'Different.' When he was growing up Avebury had been a small intimate place where the economy was based on farming. There had been a proper little town with three bakers, three shoemakers, three doctors, two blacksmiths and plenty more shops and people. He could remember some of the old names: Tommy King, the last knocker-up of the village, Fred Kempster who had been over eight feet tall and weighed twenty-seven stone, William Robinson who created a violin out of one of Winston Churchill's cigar boxes which was played by Yehudi Menuhin in a broadcast to America after the war.

Jim had been one of a family of ten, six brothers and four sisters. As children they would sit on Silbury Hill looking out for clouds of dust which would mean something was coming. Traffic had been scarce, but you got the odd visitor. Sixty years ago they came from places like Swindon in horse-drawn wagonettes. Everything was horse-drawn of course. And then in the 1920s you got the charabancs and early buses, but even they hardly disturbed the peace. You could sit in the main street for hours and nothing would go over you.

Jim had worked as a carrier with three horses and a wagon taking loads to Calne and Marlborough. He had been part of farming life. The old farm labourer had vanished and most of the surrounding land had changed hands. And then Mr Keiller had come along and changed everything. And then there were the tourists. The big number of visitors began after the war.

Over the years Jim and his surviving contemporaries had experienced a double shake-up. First there had been the Keiller clearances, and then more recently most of the old houses he remembered had changed hands in the current rural revolution. They had been bought by outsiders at prices that local people had progressively considered bordered on fantasy. Fifteen or twenty years ago they had marvelled when a cottage went for £15,000 or £20,000, but now no one was surprised any more. The fate of country people ending up in council houses was universal, but here in Avebury they had an initial sense of exile when they had to take second place to stones.

Among those who still clung to their picturesque cottages facing each other across the main street were the two daughters of James Peake Garland who had once owned the neighbouring Manor Farm on which many of the important sites, including the Great Kennett Avenue, were situated. In the 1930s when farming had been difficult, their grandfather, over a glass of whisky, had allowed the newly arrived millionaire from Scotland, land of clearances, to replace many of the fallen stones. In those days the circles which the tourists circle so reverently today had been largely toothless. Early photographs of the Great Kennett Avenue show plenty of the sarsens deeply buried in the grass. They were resurrected, trees were felled, ditches cleared to make the rings and avenues stand out, and the odd house that stood in the way was knocked down. And now it was all tourists and interference from English Heritage and the National Trust which had killed the village they remembered. You had to put up with tourists, stones and sheep. At least sheep farming had always been a part of life, and everyone knew the old joke about the special breed that grazed on Silbury with two long legs and two short ones.

There is plenty left of the village nestling in the sanctuary of the circles and the pretty houses contribute to Avebury's attraction. People who live here say there is a high-water mark bisecting it and below the Henge Shop things are a good deal quieter. The little museum was crammed with people craning their necks to view the famous scissors of the barber surgeon whose skeleton was found by Keiller crushed under a stone. Cameras were at work – to Peter Tate, who ran the museum, one of the most irritating things about tourism was what he called 'clickology'.

'They go in for arty photography. You can see them stalking stones as if they were on safari.'

Peter disagreed with the critical comments I had heard about the state of Avebury and believed that the village had been lucky to have a discerning patron like Keiller with unlimited enthusiasm and money to back up his extensive plans. Villagers had prospered because of him.

'Look at them sitting down in the sun enjoying themselves. What's wrong with that?'

The great barn, restored by the Wiltshire Folk Society, offered a blacksmith's forge, cider and cheese presses and a programme aimed at country folk – learn to make corn dollies, a Rare Breed weekend (sheep? dogs?), harness-making, traditional pipes. A lady from

Swindon, who had learned by attending night classes, sat at a spinning wheel and demonstrated how to make balls of wool. Outside folk dancers gathered in the sun, the men in blue embroidered smocks and hats decorated with cornflowers. They all carried red and white handkerchiefs. There were two groups, one from Swindon and one from New York, and they took turns dancing to a fiddle and an accordion which played old favourites like 'Ascot-Under-Wych-wood'. Before one o'clock they moved on to the Red Lion where they continued to whirl away in front of the camera-hung crowds until they broke for lunch.

The Stones Restaurant offered a mainly vegetarian menu. ' "Stone-wich", the "wich" has to be seen to be believed, freshly made to order with our own bread.' At the Red Lion a German had ordered a dish of whitebait.

'I wanted them cooked singly.'

'Sorry, sir. They've been cooked in butter in a block.'

The red beard quivered. 'Bring chicken instead.'

Outside the dancers were drinking pints of beer, sweat streaming down their faces, resting while the crowds moved round them, round Windmill Hill, walking down the West Kennett Avenue, looking for a site beside a stone to have a picnic.

At three o'clock the bell of the small United Reform Church began ringing. The church, an elegant example of nonconformist classical built in 1707, stands just outside the southern inner circle of stones where today Christianity was upheld by a congregation of three old ladies sitting in the bottle-green interior listening to the cracked organ. When Mr Brettnell, the lay preacher, got up to speak, a passing Hercules drowned his voice.

Outside the flow increased as the afternoon wore on. The car park was full up, so was the larger one for buses just outside the village. Groups gathered outside the post office to read notices in the window. 'Wanted active person, three hours a day for bottling up and general duties.' 'Lost small tortoiseshell cat named Moppet.' 'Stay in old cottage with person born in the village and enjoy home-made marmalade and jam.' A lot of jam for sale – was that Mr Keiller's influence? Someone was talking real estate. 'They want a million.' That was the old manor house which had a resident ghost, not Mr Keiller's, whose headquarters it had once been. Soon it would be sold, and the purchaser would plan a theme park for Avebury.

In the antique shop at the top of the village they were inspecting Mr Perry's paintings. Mr Perry, an old man known locally as Mr Avebury, painted naively on anything he could find. Sarsen stones, an interior of the old manor, Silbury's cone, more stones, were recorded on board, pieces of paper, hardboard and plywood. The bells of St James were ringing out as the last customer abandoned his search through the bits and pieces of scrap that the proprietor had found round about and kept in a small plastic bag. The rich days of trophy-hunting were long over and there was nothing more than bits of brass, some shoe-buckles and a piece of metal from an old car. In the old days you could pick up arrowheads and sharpeners in the chalk all around here, but such things have become very scarce. Generations of shepherds and farm workers kept heads bent and eyes open for treasure and dug into barrows and earthworks like Hudson's Dan'l Burdon going out in his spare time with pick and shovel.

'Maybe, Caleb, you've heared tell about what the Bible says of burnt sacrifice. Well now, I be of opinion that it was here. They people the Bible says about, they come up here to sacrifice on White Bustard Down, and these be the places where they made their fires.'

The builders of the first Saxon church of St James were much more wary than the later United Reformists and, when they chose their site, conspicuously avoided the pagan ring. The lady deacon considered that the carving on the stone font of a winged serpent biting the tunic of a figure which in turn strikes it with a staff must be Anglo-Saxon. Others believe it to be a Norman carving on a Saxon font. The head, which may have supported a mitre or a halo, was damaged in the nineteenth century when a metal staple was driven into the rim of the font to hold a plug. He may have been Christ or St George subduing evil. There is a theory, which archaeologists detest, that the dragon is linked to the Druidical practices that so fascinated William Stukeley that he took holy orders to help him reconcile the Druids' 'patriarchal religion' with Christianity. He saw in the serpentine plan of Avebury 'a snake proceeding from a circle! the eternal procession of the sun from the first cause!' Stukeley's solar serpent and sun disc have been linked with ancient Egyptian beliefs and mystery-seekers, and ley-line worshippers believe that here on the font is depicted the triumph of Christianity over serpent worship. (The serpent has even been identified in the dear old Green Dragon in Marlborough.)

The church underwent the usual Russian doll changes over the centuries, enlarging from Saxon to Norman to development by the Benedictines whose priory was somewhere near (no trace of it has been found and no one knows where it was, another victory for the stones). Restoration in the fifteenth century had got run down by the nineteenth, when the Victorians smartened up a lot of things.

The most recent development has been the appointment of the lady deacon – she can marry and bury, but ancient conservative forces forbid her to hold communion. Avebury seemed a suitable place to reflect on the current primitive controversy over the ordination of women. Here at St James women were in charge of ceremony, five of them standing in the belfry pulling at the tasselled ropes. In a country where only 13 per cent of the population attends church regularly, there is still respect for the outward and visible signs and the bells had recently been repaired. Money had been raised in 1981 to recast them in the Whitechapel foundry; now the new lot, together with one relatively old fellow cast in 1719, were calling the faithful.

But in a pagan place few took notice. Among the last of the tourists, a few paused to listen to the peals ringing out over Avebury's rooftops across the topiary gardens of the manor where someone was still photographing the peacocks and the stones that had been implanted thousands of years before the coming of Christianity. By the time the deacon, standing under the Norman arch, began to intone the Magnificat, supported by a sparse group of Christians, another two or three gathered together in God's name, everyone else had gone. I had gone too, back to the microlight, to make a final triangular circuit of Avebury's stones and Silbury Hill in the silken evening air.

CHAPTER SIX

From Salisbury Plain
to Brighton

There was a royal story in the Sunday papers about the Prince of Wales asking an American painter how to paint clouds. 'Oh that's the easiest thing in the world. You just soak a Kleenex in paint and daub it all over your sky.' Constable didn't paint clouds like that. Prince Charles had been aghast. 'But that's cheating!' This morning the clouds we were avoiding looked very much as if they had been smeared on the sky. Kleenex clouds was another term to add to the list that obsessed us, high cirrus, towering cumulus, the aerial cauliflower, cirro-stratus, nimbo-stratus and the cumulo-nimbus capillatus, a pompous term for a storm cloud. Storm clouds can go through two development phases, bald (calvus) and then hairy (capillatus), terms to describe their initial state and final conformation.

We drifted over ripening corn, beginning to turn from green to yellow. The plough has been at work for centuries on Salisbury Plain, not just since the Common Market made farmers greedy. Sixty years ago, when pasture was increasingly falling victim to newer sharper ploughshares, observers like Hudson regretted the changes. 'There is a certain pleasure to the eye in the wide fields of golden corn, especially of wheat, in July and August; but a ploughed down is a down made ugly, and it strikes one as a mistake, even from the purely economic point of view, that this old rich turf. the slow product of centuries, should be ruined for ever as sheep-pasture.'

Here was green turf below me, where I could see a wide furrow on which tanks were playing war games. Red flags as bright as poppies flew over various ranges on a mini-battlefield farmed under a complicated system where a farmer fool enough to plant a crop would find to his cost that a few weeks before harvesting summer manoeuvres would require his field.

The army has been here for a long time. Someone complained in

1910: 'To the lover of Salisbury Plain as it was, the sight of military camps, with white tents or zinc houses, and of bodies of men in khaki marching and drilling, and the sound of guns, now informs him that he is in a district which has lost its attraction, where nature has been dispossessed.'

Nearly eighty years later, cruising at 1,000 feet up, I could see the army as benevolent preserver. All those stretches of grassland kept for war rehearsals were old and unchanged from the sheep days, apart from the odd neat barracks with names like Delhi, Agra and Jallalabad.

We were covering the expanding view that stretched from the needle of Salisbury Cathedral to Stonehenge, a tiny spiky crown attended by lines and lines of cars. Here was England in swarming time. I could see how in summer a population of 60 million rises up and moves around, settling on any enticing spot – stately home, holiday camp, butterfly farm, wildlife sanctuary, leisure centre, amusement park, cathedral, or ancient monument. Below were hundreds and hundreds of people gathered to contemplate like John Evelyn 'a stupendious Monument, how so many, and huge pillars of stone should have been brought together, erected some, other Transverse on the tops of them, in a Circular area as rudely representing a Cloyster, or heathen and more natural Temple'.

When Constable paid his visit in 1836 Stonehenge was remote. He trudged on foot over the plain and carried away his pencil sketches to be transformed into a comparison of permanence and transience in his great melancholy water-colour of the enigmatic monument which was also an expression of grief for his wife. His background to Stonehenge is a study of cumulo-nimbus set with a double rainbow, a favourite theme, one of nature's most transient effects, which, for all God's promises to Noah, can be interpreted as a fleeting symbol of hope. The shadow of the shepherd on a stone which waits to be blotted out as the cloud moves over the sun echoes the impermanence of man's place on earth. A hare bounds away to the left as swiftly as the rainbow will vanish. In the distance is empty space, no fence or ticket office, merely a long windy walk to sketch the bluestones carried from the Marlborough Downs and distant Pembrokeshire.

Constable wrote on the mount of his picture: 'The mysterious monument of Stonehenge, standing remote on a bare and boundless heath, as much unconnected with the events of past ages as it is with the uses of the present, carries you back beyond all historical records into the obscurity of a totally unknown period.' For over 2,000 years Stonehenge was in use as ancient calendar, ancestral ossuary, temple of the gods and place of human and animal sacrifice. Now it is a car park. I watched the corralled cars, and more coming down the road to join them, reflecting metal which flashed in the warm sunshine. A bumper crop.

We flew on. Our destination was Great Durnford, a beautiful village with a medieval church and a handful of ancient houses bordering the Avon river. The old manor house was almost completely shrouded in trees, beyond was the green square of a cricket pitch and the burnished thatch of cottages. Up in the sky was bedlam, no place for a bumbling microlight, whose noise was low-keyed compared with the roars and screams in the heavens. This part of the Wiltshire sky was reserved for those who roared out of the high-wire security fence of Boscombe Down. There seemed to be scarcely a daytime moment when the air wasn't shattered by helicopters or sonic booms inflicted by test pilots undergoing noisy training.

Inevitably the last part of our journey was by more prosaic means on the ground. At Kingfisher Mill, Aylmer Tryon was feeding the trout, an easy enough task, since the river ran under his house. He lifted a wooden board in the floor, and there, gazing up, were pop eyes of silvery brown fish waiting to swallow the crumbs dropped to them. When Boscombe Down permitted, his surroundings were peaceful with the perpetual gurgle of water, and the green woodpecker, emerging from the trees and preening itself on the lawn of the magical garden, did not seem too fussed by passing aircraft. Inside the house Aylmer's friends had painted an avian tribute to his interests all over the walls and up the stairway. Each bird had been painted by a different hand, and there were very many, so that walking upstairs produced an effect of being accompanied by flashing feathers.

At present Aylmer's primary interest is the Great Bustard Trust. This is a registered charity (like 160,000 others, including Eton). It was founded in 1980 with one aim – to bring back the bustard.

Great bustards are stately birds about the size of turkeys with pale lavender-coloured heads and necks. Their feathers are warm brown with bars of black on their backs, white below and white on wings and tip of tail. The wings are also decorated with black flight feathers. During springtime the males, which are much larger than the females, grow long white whiskers and indulge in intricate courting.

To quote the exuberant literature of the GBT:

It is a sight few ornithologists have been privileged to see. The performance is purely visual; the male stands still, cocks his tail up and forward so that it lies flat along his back, inflates a large sac down the front of his neck and twists his wings (with the primaries still folded in place) back and over, thereby exposing a cascade of brilliant white feathers while the normal shape of the bird is transformed into what one German naturalist called 'a heap of snow on legs'. The pose may be held for many minutes. Scattered across a plain or hillside the males send out their signals to the females in one of the most exhilarating spectacles in nature.

By such heroic efforts of selective breeding the males have evolved to become very large – around forty pounds in weight, which qualifies them as the heaviest flying birds in the world. They are not graceful flyers, more of the bumble-bee type, and are better runners over plains and steppe particularly in Spain and Portugal, on the Hungarian puszta and the Russian steppes. In the middle of the eighteenth century there were plagues of great bustards in Russia. Shoots were organized, and children taken out of school to collect bustard eggs. But since then the numbers of bustards have declined. They are shy birds which need plenty of room and the generous prairie habitat they favour has dwindled everywhere. In many parts of Europe they have become extinct or there is only a remnant population, and they are considered an endangered species. There are 25,000 of them left world-wide, which seems quite a large number to me, but the trust is worried.

England's bustards became extinct in the mid-nineteenth century. Before that they were found in numerous open habitats and in parts of Scotland. Gilbert White wrote of 'bustards on the wide downs near Brighthelmstone', the old name for Brighton, observing elsewhere that they would not let a human approach within three or four furlongs. But they have been particularly associated with Wiltshire, where large flocks used to be seen on Salisbury Plain. A great bustard is included in the Wiltshire coat of arms, and traditionally a bird was served up roasted at the lord mayor's inaugural banquet in Salisbury. This would have been a male bird whose flesh was considered coarse, 'but the hens and young are excellent for the table'. They were hunted ruthlessly. Hudson, writing at the beginning of this century, met a shepherd who told him:

> Once I shot an eagle, but that was the only eagle I ever saw. Since the hills have become broken with the plough, such birds have been seldom seen. There haven't been any wild turkeys for many a year. I have heard my father say that he killed two or three no great while before I was born. They used to call them bustards.

In his book *The Birds of Wiltshire*, published in 1887, the Reverend Alfred Smith, a Wiltshire ornithologist, described how a boy captured one of the last of these great birds on 3 January 1856. In 1987 Christie's auctioned a painting illustrating this incident. There are White Bustard Downs and, somewhere, a Bustard Inn. There are three stuffed bustards in the hallway of the Salisbury Museum.

After they became extinct, there was little encouragement for them to return. For instance, on 26 April 1909, a stray bustard blown in from Europe was seen by a Mr Deakin of Waden Hill near Avebury.

> I was going round the sheep and heard a very peculiar noise over my head. On looking up, I could see it was a rare bird. I turned my horse around and fetched my gun, and happened to meet the keeper, J. Buckingham, who looked after the game on the farm. The bird being very wild, I asked him to take the gun and rode around the brow of the hill and attracted its attention while the keeper crept up the hill and shot it at 62 yards off.

You might imagine that with all the motorways, suburban estates and tracts of land under the dominance of the army, this area would be unsuitable for timid and vulnerable birds. But the army, anxious to promote its conservationist role, had come to the rescue. The Ministry of Defence works hard at public relations, aware of widespread resentment that it controls 92,000 acres of the plain. It counters criticism of the presence of 70,000 men who annually rush about playing noisy war games with tanks, artillery and aircraft, by pointing out all the plants and butterflies it helps to maintain, and the pre-Roman farm settlement and other archaeological sites it protects. Soldiers are not allowed to cut their own camouflage, but must obtain it in advance from foresters employed by the army.

The Ministry of Defence had provided the precious bustards with a large guarded enclosure on Portland Down. To reach them we had to make our way through high-security areas, past a Bikini Battle Zone, a Limit of Battle Zone and other intimidating places heralded by warning notices and marked with a complicated system of markers to avoid protected sites. Driving past some heavily armed, black-faced figures in camouflage jackets with twigs sticking out of their helmets, we reached the storm centre of army command, a quiet area of old downland. Here was a piece of traditional Wiltshire with rolling hills and sheep. Aylmer could remember plenty of places like this before the plough moved in. Now he stopped his car and took out his binoculars to watch a stone curlew vanish into some juniper bushes and I was reminded of the enthusiasts at Slimbridge. Stone curlews, which were sometimes known as 'thick knee', Aylmer said, were almost as hard to preserve as bustards. I missed this one, but learned that it had long wings, yellow eyes, knobbly knees and a wild cry 'to gladden the souls of those who hear it'.

Further on we reached a grove of pines. Near here the Great Bustard Trust had put up a large wire cage where it was hoped that eight assorted birds would breed and then eventually be released to colonize the surrounding land. The area was strictly off-limits for soldiers.

Sadly the reintroduction of the great bustard has not been easy. In 1970 a batch of birds was imported from Portugal to join a wild female from East Germany that had been found exhausted on Fair Isle. After the birds were turned loose in this fox-proof pen, they settled down happily, but they refused to breed. A new lot of birds was obtained from Hungary, but they too were unable to produce any chicks. Today there is little hope of obtaining more Hungarian birds, since they too have become a protected species in Hungary. It does seem possible that their reluctance to breed may have something to do with soldiers, or the noises of distant tanks, aeroplanes, or jets, and these distractions may interfere with their elaborate courtship rituals.

They are not very bright birds and become easily confused. At least one handsome bustard felt aggressive towards Aylmer, believing him to be another rival bustard. Aylmer got down from his car and climbed into the little wooden tower from where he could look down into the pen, where it was hard to see anything since the birds had reverted to their wild condition and were hidden in the long grass of the enclosure. Looking out, Aylmer caught sight of Ketto's familiar grey head, and then he appeared, a very fine-looking bird, his neck pale grey, his back and wings speckled black and russet, and his wonderful pale mandarin moustaches that signalled his masculinity sweeping back from his beak like shimmering banners. As he bounded up in stately fashion like a dressage horse, he made curious loud sighing noises declaring his anger, which a passing jet drowned out.

We were flying over Salisbury Plain again, a westerly wind behind us which meant that our speed increased so that instead of chasing cars and lorries along the motorway below, we were actually passing them. True, they had to slow down. I could see them trickling into a narrow pathway constrained by dots that must be cones and I realized that beneath me was an example of the dreaded contraflow.

There were clouds above the plain which brought Constable to mind and his obsession with the clouds and the sky, 'the chief organ of sentiment'. My favourite Constable cloud is in the Municipal Art Gallery in Dublin, a pleasant gift from Edward VII during one of his difficult visits to his Hibernian dominion. It shows thin fleecy clouds being chased away by the wind and warm golden light shines through them. The air pressure has increased and good weather is expected. One of his loveliest 'spots of time'.

It took him years to get his clouds right. 'I have done a good deal of skying . . . The sky is the *"source of light"* in nature – and governs every thing . . . My skies have not been neglected, though they have often failed in execution, no doubt from an over-anxiety about them, which will alone destroy that appearance which nature always has in her movements.'

He once wrote a note to himself: 'Whatever you do, Constable, get thee rid of anxiety. It hurts the stomach more than arsenic.'

He painted another rainbow behind Salisbury Cathedral. The spire and the hoop in the sky, another expression of the eternal contrasted with the ephemeral, was the result of the challenge of a subject 'only a madman would undertake'.

Today around Salisbury there were clouds he would have liked to have painted. Clouds above and crowds beneath, their presence betrayed as usual by their cars. Weeks ago, during the bad weather, I had joined them on a blustery day, sauntering with the queues, observing the hordes of cameramen tilting their cameras in the struggle to get all the cathedral body and spire into their lenses. The building is on chalk, and for ages has lived with the threat that a drastic change in the water-level could dry out its foundations and undermine it. During dry summers (not this one) its trustees keep anxious check on water gauges.

People wandered comfortably in the cathedral close, viewing its old houses and ancient city walls, the cloister and the chapter house and the famous view from the water meadows looking back. In the chapter house a party of French schoolboys gazed at Magna Carta, one of only four copies which date from 1215; the others are in Lincoln Cathedral and the British Museum. A woman laughed when someone leaned over the glass case and read out how 'no widow shall be compelled to marry so long as she prefers to live without a husband'. In the museum a party of German schoolboys were enjoying the mummified black rat which had died after gnawing its way into William Longspee's skull.

That was the first occasion that I had seen mass tourism in England at close quarters. The effect of the crowd in and around the cathedral has been compared in a good Wiltshire analogy to 'a flock of sheep on a burning day in summer, grouped about a great tree growing in the pasture-land'. It was difficult to analyse why those viewing what John Evelyn called 'the compleatest piece of Gothic-Worke in Europe, taken in all its uniformitie' did not evoke the same unease and sense of disproportion as similar flocks carrying cameras and babies around the stones of Avebury. No doubt the contrast was subjective and superstitious, but I found the presence of so many shuffling in under the Norman nave and soaring spire was uplifting. The cathedral absorbs them, although it makes them pay a pound. You can hear them mutter 'Voluntary donations be damned' as they trickle in. Is the man in khaki shorts huffily handing over his money a tourist or a pilgrim? It does not seem to matter.

I paid my money and wandered around reading the warning notices about falling masonry, noticing the little office for the Spire Appeal. Inside the door the great organ played as I was distracted and intrigued by the marble figure of Thomas, Baron Wyndham of Finglyss of the Kingdom of Ireland gazing at the trippers. The baron had chosen Finglyss for a title as a perk for being Lord High Chancellor of Ireland. He died in 1745; his statue was imposing, but no one else took notice of it – they were busy examining the effigies, Sir John Montacote, who fought at Agincourt, Walter, first Lord Hungerford, who fought at Crecy, Willian Longspee, founder of this marvellous place. Then prayers boomed through the loudspeakers and everyone stood still in their tracks as if they, too, had been turned into stone.

Today we flew on towards Winchester, and beyond. The ground passed underneath in every variety and shade of green, dark green stripes of woodlands, lighter green for crops, varied now and again by a savage patch of yellow which was a field of rape. A castle appeared, encircled by fading rhododendrons, a fortress which even from 1,000 feet up looked phoney, a country club or hotel, or somewhere for old people. I could make out stirring among a line of chairs on a terrace, and glimpsed slow moving figures. We passed over villages, each one bloated by housing estates, council estates and tentacles of housing developments. Our flights over Wiltshire had shown a succession of more or less preserved rural landscapes where new housing was kept within bounds. But under us now were successive reminders that England has the reputation for being the most heavily urbanized country in the world. As we passed yet another long-established nucleus surrounded by an amorphous failure of planning, I wondered about Bernard Levin's warning that sooner of later, if someone had their way, the whole of England would look like the centre of Birmingham. Here was a farm, which must be an old farm, and beside it a flourishing motorway, and then a new spiral-shaped development with fuzzy lines from tendrils of roads and bungalows reaching into fields looking like superfluous hair. Here was a village where clusters of houses were linked to some housing estate. From the air they presented clear immediate evidence of wild or greedy speculative planning, with little houses clustered together and then suddenly a thin tentacle and another cluster reaching out over a tract of country like dry rot.

The sprawl vanished and beneath us was parkland planted with fat ancient trees. There was not a bungalow in sight now, only an undulating expanse of rolling woodlands and fields. Many of these magnificent trees at the full height and glory of summer would perish in the hurricane in a few months' time. There were enough summer and autumn days left for a certain number of people to fly over Midhurst's forests, mostly in helicopters, and perhaps a few would take a last look before the October destruction. We were above the Cowdray estate covering 17,000 acres, over the largest privately owned woods in England. The storm would destroy about 750 acres of trees.

In a jewelled setting in a great park we were looking down on a game of polo.

Mr Gaunt, who managed the Cowdray estates and looked after the polo lawns, had to be tracked down in his office, where the telephone beside him was ringing all the time. I learnt how the first Lord Cowdray, whose bust adorns the little museum in the ancient castle built by the Fitzwilliam family, was a Victorian contracting tycoon from Yorkshire who acquired the Cowdray estate and took its name for his title. The Pearson empire which he founded had expanded enormously; among other enterprises that it owned was my publisher. I learned that for all Pearson's numerous multi-national concerns, Lord Cowdray was most famous by far because of his association with polo. We had flown into the heart of Mr Polo's possessions.

In Midhurst, which I was told repeatedly was the loveliest corner of the loveliest county in England, it was hard to get away from polo. Banners advertising matches decorated the mains street and the *Midhurst and Petworth Observer* gave details of games and chukkas. 'The sporting tides turned in the Prince of Wales's favour at Midhurst on Sunday when his Windsor Park polo team scooped the Cowdray Park Challenge Cup.' It was big news for a select group of people. More players arrived in their helicopters; the various machines were recognized as they landed and their identity broadcast over loud-speakers.

'Here comes Lord W—' Did someone add 'Whoopee!'? Only the elite could sort out the good and the great players and recognize Julian and Neil and Robin and Charles and Eddie and Galen and Henrik and Howard and the rest. A notice beside the airfield: 'Neither the owners or organizers will accept any liability for damage to persons or property caused by the use of aircraft on this field.' The Undertaker was parked far away.

At the River Lawn, perhaps the most prestigious of the half dozen or so lawns set out around the park, the spectacle seemed to confirm the prejudices of the uninitiated about expensive yuppie sports. Here were neat shining little horses with their legs in bandages. Here were their owners in their tight white trousers, leather boots, Lock hats, sweaty T-shirts with tiny distinguished logos over the breast, carrying a selection from a quiverful of sticks resting on the back of the Land-Rover or in the chopper.

I quote John Board: 'Polo is supreme, even if the polo itself is not transcendently wonderful. The speed, the rush, the "hurl and the crash", the instantly changing scene as one side or the other seizes the fleeting chance, the sight of gallant, well-bred horses, the thunder of their little hooves on the turf, giving their utmost of grace, speed, courage and obedience, all impress a wonderful experience.' It is considered a game for the brave as well as the wealthy, compared to playing hockey from helicopters.

For days before a match the two groundsmen, under Mr Gaunt's supervision, had rolled and smoothed the grass to baize. At Cowdray it was a proud boast that no game had been cancelled because of bad weather and players could remember an early season game taking place in falling snow. One of the lawns might become too wet after a heavy downpour, but then the game could be transferred to higher, dryer ground near Amersham. Opposite the River Lawn was a marquee the size of a circus tent which had sheltered the members during the unseasonable weather that had kept me grounded in Wiltshire.

Behind the River Lawn, a stretch of green sheeting by the river was the ruin of Cowdray Castle, cursed and destroyed by fire in 1793. Midhurst was tucked away in a corner which H. G. Wells, who went to school here, remembered 'with its odd turnings and abrupt corners and in the pleasant park that crowds up one side of the street'. Because of bad weather this was only the third time this season that the River Lawn had been in use. Last week you would have needed a boat. Management and control of lawns meant well-established caressing methods of looking after them. The groundsmen pricked and rolled, the grass was never cut too short, and it was trodden in by locally recruited treaders: pensioners, schoolboys and ladies in silk scarves.

At the entrance to the marquee the Polish groundsman, who had fought in the battle of Monte Cassino, watched the big cars continue to arrive and arranged them in lines as their owners stepped out. Two women wore gold and silver polo brooches laced in diamonds, carrying their club colours which cost £1,500.

'How are you, Benjie?'

'Looks like a good game.'

The bell clanged for the second chukka as one of the two referees galloped up and threw in the ball to reactivate the square dance of horses, white-topped riders and whirling sticks. The click of the ball was not much louder than the click of the white ball at the end of a billiard cue as the polo ponies, sweaty in a moment from all the commands and skills of their riders, ran and zigzagged down towards the yellow scoring posts at the far end.

'Great shot from Bethell!' The commentator's voice on the loud-speakers was gentle and unagitated with none of the urgency of horse-race commentary.

John Board:

There is no grander or more exciting game to watch, and it has the advantage of extreme simplicity, so that it is easy to understand more or less. In the first place there can hardly be an Englishman with soul so dead who does not thrill to the sound of high-bred horseflesh generally giving its utmost of gallantry and furious en-deavour.

'Never do that again! You can damage a person like that!' An angry shout was directed at someone who had made a foul hook.

The loudspeaker calmly told us what we were watching. 'It's a good-looking ball, just wide.'

Some spectators watched with their dogs on leads; one of the few nuisances from this crowd, the equivalent of hooligan behaviour on a football pitch, came from those who ignored the warning to keep their dogs under control. Here was further evidence of the Labrador cult. What particular advantage does this amiable creature who runs to fat have over other breeds? Most of those skirting the River Lawn were trim, kept away from the pâté, and looked ready to go off at any moment with Purdy-bearing owners in pursuit of game birds. There were faint cries of 'Well played' from the groups round the lawn standing or sitting in front of their Range-Rovers and such like. There was little cheering, just squeaks of joy.

A well-dressed pair were unpacking the hamper they had brought out of their BMW decorated with a sticker saying 'Cowdray Park Polo Club' and a silver-mounted polo player screwed to the bonnet. A group of Americans wore flared leather breeches and fringed

Texan hats. In general, clothes lacked Ascot flamboyance and had more an air of expensive utility. There were numerous quilted waistcoats and chocolate-brown jackets with felt collars. Some were in garden party outfits like the woman who was talking about the Argentines. 'Do you know how much they used to get for coming here? £10,000.' Did she mean £10,000 a season or a match? That was before Mrs Thatcher had dealt a crippling blow to the game in 1982. Had it been an effort for some of these spectators to vote for her subsequently? The Argentines who used to dominate the game have not been back, even though they have been involved in other British sports since the Falklands War. In polo, however, their reacceptance has been delayed because of the Guards Polo Club, some of whose members belong to regiments who suffered badly in the South Atlantic. The Prince of Wales is colonel-in-chief of the Welsh Guards.

The bell rang for the end of the chukka. The sweating ponies provided a jarring note to the peaceful scene, some of them looking as if they had brought the good news from Ghent to Aix. A mounted umpire in a striped shirt acquired a large ice-cream.

'Could you please tread in?' asked the loudspeaker, chuckling. 'The exercise will do you good.'

City people, merchant bankers, landowners and the rest, put down their wineglasses, got up from their picnics and began treading on hoof-marks with their good shoes to smooth down faint scars on the green turf. Some may have had colonial backgrounds, like the old man with the hooded eyes who must have remembered back before the war when throughout much of the British Empire polo had been a caste pastime with its own social mores. Even war did not put a stop to it. And now, with the new wealth, it had revived and was flourishing. The polo clubs belonging to the Hurlingham Polo Association have more than 700 players, although a lot of them, alas, play with a very low handicap. Playing polo is proof that you are smart and rich, even if you don't play very well. The top polo occasions draw up to 15,000 spectators.

My programme, listing Lord Cowdray's thirty-one ponies and carrying advertisements for Cartier, Heidsieck and merchant banking services, also informed me that polo was described many centuries ago by the Persian poet Firdausi. It continued to flourish in the Himalayas. I had last watched the game in its cradle, five years ago at a mountain pass in northern Pakistan where teams from Gilgit and

Chitral had gathered to play a championship. Ponies had walked in glaring heat to a wild dusty spot from places twenty and thirty miles away. Tribesmen had camped for days near the roughly marked-out pitch, swarthy pipers had played bagpipes through fierce chukkas contested among the mountains which are traditionally the home of the game.

The first club, the Silchar Polo Club in Cachar, was founded in 1859 by soldiers and tea planters. By 1862 the Calcutta Polo Club was established, and the game spread like wildfire in a land of cheap ponies which could carry around fairly old horsemen, provided they kept reasonably fit. Polo continues, nurtured by the wealthy, regarded with a reverence that has survived the past.

Before the war Roald Dahl shocked a major by mentioning games played with hockey sticks and bicycles. 'He glared at me with such contempt and horror and his face went so crimson, I thought he might be going to have a seizure. I had been found guilty of a great and unforgivable. crime. I had jeered . . . at the game of polo, the sacred sport of Anglo-Indians and royalty. Only a bounder would do that.' In fact bicycle polo, reputed to have started in Ireland, is now regarded as a respectable branch of the game, offering good training for the transfer to horseflesh. I had watched small boys playing it in Gilgit.

More than a century has passed since the game was seized from Asia and turned into a holy pastime. Its survival has been put down to 'the indestructible resilience of the English and is one of the most reassuring phenomena of this atomic age'. Forget about the Argies, and the pampered Americans too, who have produced some of the game's most aggressive players. For the price of maintaining a string of polo ponies you could send the same number of boys to public school.

Not everyone found it an ideal spectator sport. Parked among the cars and Range-Rovers was an ambulance belonging to St John's Ambulance Brigade, inside which two attendants were listening to a cricket match on their radio. Coming to Midhurst was one of their duties, although they seldom had much to do. They treated a few cuts and bruises, but the worst they could expect was a broken collar bone. They never watched a game.

'What happens to the horses when they get older or turn out to be no good?'

'Belgian hamburgers,' said the older man in the fancy black uniform.

The bell rang again, and, beyond the yellow goal posts, lines of ponies looked after by girls waited to take over from the latest batch of exhausted animals. Above their polished leather boots the white breeches of the riders were stained green and their T-shirts soaked with sweat by the time the final chukka was over and the red-faced winning team stood in a line outside the marquee to receive the prize from a lady in a gorgeous hat.

The suave team captain kissed her on both cheeks to a few polite hurrays and a patter of clapping. When a magnum of champagne was opened there was no indecorous waving and fizzing about in the manner of vulgar racing drivers.

We were flying over Midhurst where it was high noon in every respect. The storms of October were still far away. The stock market crash would not have much effect on the Pearson group which was ultimately responsible for the cosseting of the beautiful landscape below. Its interests in banking, engineering and oil would continue to flourish; further publishing companies would be gobbled up, the *Financial Times* would celebrate its century and would further appeal to Americans to whom it had been introduced the year before. But all the money in the world could not save Lord Cowdray's trees.

The parkland with game coverts passing slowly under our wing was an unsullied landscape that would have you believe that the sceptred isle was an unchanging rural paradise. Above all, it seemed reassuringly permanent. But this was the last summer that most of these oaks and beeches would shine in their summer green and bronze. Trees are mortal. A decade ago elms would have been woven into the tapestry below.

In a few months' time the forest would be devastated. The tempest would come in October when the trees still carried their foliage and the autumn leaves clinging to their branches could give them more bulk and resistance. Instead of giving way and bending, they would stand up and perish.

The Cowdray estate included over 6,000 acres of forestry, the largest privately owned woodlands in the south of England. In the park where the first Queen Elizabeth had picnicked under the oaks, casualties would be catastrophic; in the pleasure grounds exotic trees like mulberry and cypress would be floored, while elsewhere oaks, beech and chestnut would perish. The Gold Medal Plantation, 800 Corsican pines planted sixty-five years ago, which had reached heights of 100 feet and had won attention from the Royal Forestry Society, would be slaughtered – all but four of the 800 trees would be brought down. There had been nothing like it in the south of England since the great gale of 1703 which destroyed the old spire of the twelfth-century tower of Eastbourne Priory opposite the present estate office, toppled the first Eddystone Lighthouse and brought misery to John Evelyn.

> The dismall Effects of the Hurecan and Tempest of Wind, raine and lightning thro all the nation, especial London, many houses demolished, many people killed: 27 and as to my owne losse, the subversion of Woods and Timber both left for Ornament and Valuable materiall thro my whole Estate ... the damage ... is most Tragicall: not to be paralleled with anything hapning in our Age in any history almost, I am not able to describe, but submit to the Almight pleasure of God, with accknowledgement of his Justice for our National sinns, and my owne, who yet have not suffred as I deserved to: Every moment like Jobs Messengers, bring the sad Tidings of this universal Judgement.

Green trees and lush meadows stretched from Midhurst to Petworth, where the proximity of two great neighbouring estates preserved the land in its ancient beauty. The houses and motorways and the outer reaches of southern suburbia were kept out of this oasis of low, rolling, wooded country reaching towards the ridge of the South Downs. We flew over a field full of ponies and riders, a miniature of Cowdray Park, a pony club meeting with tents and horseboxes. Presumably most of the riders were girls, given that the ratio of girls to boys in a pony club is something like nine to one. Although pony club polo is increasingly popular, with 300 players, not a lot will aspire to rise to the heights of Claire Tomlinson, the highest handicapped female player in the world. Of ninety-five members of the Cowdray Park Polo Club in 1987, three were women.

A village clung to estate walls enclosing another stretch of parkland where columns of trees and a man-made lake had been laid out by Capability Brown. These were the grounds of Petworth where the foremost English master of garden design had swept through a Frenchified garden, in the style of Le Nôtre, rejecting a rigid pattern of flower-beds imposed on nature in favour of the sort of scenery that he persuaded his noble clients they wanted.

From the time he began chatting up the quality when he was chief gardener at Stowe, Lancelot Brown demonstrated his powers of persuasion. He was an architect as well as a gardener, who gave the English landowner a natural view from his mansion – no carved stones or statues to be seen, but soft acres of turf, artfully arranged clumps or belts of special trees with here and there one planted singly to become a park giant.

The October destruction would change for ever this cherished landscape which we were seeing at the height of its maturity, and the great house behind would enter a new phase of its history. Scores of trees, including many of the famous immense sweet chestnuts, would fall. Few people would see again, as we were seeing from the air, the panorama with shining water, meadow turf and grassland and the distant view of the South Downs, stitched together by carefully placed trees. The lakes appeared like black holes fringed with water-lilies.

We flew past the house in a pearly white sky. The long pale west front in local sandstone with its double lines of casement windows edged with shining Portland stone – forty-two on each floor – described by Horace Walpole as being 'in the style of the Tuileries', was built by Charles Seymour, sixth Earl of Somerset, around 1688. In France Louis XIV was carrying out grand plans, and here in Sussex the Proud Duke created his château in imitation. The architect is unknown. The landscaping of the park came later, after 1750, when Brown worked under the patronage of the second Earl of Egremont whose house and park were blended into a combination of magnificence that had reached its apogee as we saw it. It will not look the same for a long time. 'The park looks like the aftermath of the Somme,' Lord Egremont wrote to me at the end of October 1987.

Photographs of big houses taken from above are nothing unusual and they do not convey the pleasure of the extra dimension of seeing in real life an architect's massive plans from the air. This bird's-eye view of Petworth echoed the fashion in the late seventeenth century for painting 'Prospects', when the artist used his imagination to lift himself to where we were and integrate house and grounds for his client's delight.

Prospects became popular after 1660 when the Restoration encouraged a renewed interest in architecture as a domestic demonstration of wealth. Portraits of houses and grounds were records of possession to stand beside people's portraits of themselves. They did not aspire to high art, but were more or less aerial maps. They were the only kind of landscape painting under the Stuarts and the idea of depicting the territory beyond the estate walls did not seep back into paintings until interest in nature was resumed and Brown appeared on the scene.

Peace had come to England and the great houses represented social concord and enlightened patronage. Not only were they recorded in paintings, but there was a spate of poems about them, listing in glorious real-estate language all their attributes: walled gardens, parklands, farms, streams, and the people who worked in them, fishermen, huntsmen and farm labourers. Herrick, Carew and Ben Jonson wrote flatteringly long poems about their patrons' possessions. So did Andrew Marvell, describing Appleton House, an ex-Cistercian abbey in Yorkshire, listing its sheep, bullocks, kine, purpled pheasant and so on. After the weary struggles of war he wrote of Appleton's trees:

> But I retiring from the flood,
> Take sanctuary in the wood;
> *And, while it lasts,* myself embark
> In this yet green, yet growing ark;
> Where the first carpenter might best
> Fit timber for his keel have pressed.
> And where all creatures might have shares
> Although in armies, not in pairs.

Constable came to Petworth, but of course the house is more particularly associated with Turner. When Thomas Hardy observed the skies Turner recorded in vaporous water-colours, he wrote that 'what he paints chiefly is light as modified objects' and wanted to use writing in the same way to intensify his themes. I had a modest familiarity with Turner from the selection of water-colours in our National Gallery in Dublin where I remembered a little crayon and wash drawing of 'Sunrise at Petworth', which the artist had dabbed in 1826, an orange blaze of morning sun rising from behind dark blue hills. It seemed ironic that this tragic vision of life, so many storms and shipwrecks displaying the violence of nature and the helplessness of man in the face of natural catastrophe, should have mellowed in the congenial atmosphere of this great house and freed his vision into recording a succession of peaceful light-infused park landscapes. 'October Gale' would have been a stupendous subject.

Seen from the air, cricket seemed an even duller game than I had thought. Perhaps I had been watching too much polo. Just inside the high stone walls that surrounded the park, the figures in white dotted round a field seemed immobile and we were moving fairly slowly above them. There was plenty of time for us to go off and land quite far away and return through the narrow curving streets of the village that seemed like superfluous limbs of the big house, past the antique shops, parasites of beautiful places. Half the cars in southern England were parked hard by Petworth. Inside nobody on the cricket pitch appeared to have moved. The home team was playing a team from Emsworth near Brighton. I talked to an old man watching the match, who had worked in Petworth as a gamekeeper before the war, one of twenty-five. During the war he served in the navy and a year or so afterwards he ran into his Lordship.

'I know your face'.

'Yes, my Lord, I worked for you.'

'You were one of the bloody gamekeepers!'

Around that time, 1947, his Lordship, that was Lord Leconfield, a nice old-fashioned country gentleman who could always be relied on to put a pound into the box for a local charity, gave the whole place to the National Trust and it hadn't ever been the same since the public had been let in. The old gamekeeper looked past the batsmen and the little pavilion into the park where he could see some deer and a woman stalking them with a camera. When he worked here, the paths would have been kept clean of weeds and the grass cut properly – not left to the deer to chew. That was the sort of thing that happened when these people took over.

Still, the deer, presumably descendants of the ones Turner painted, were handsome to look at. These were fallow deer, which unlike sika and red deer, which tame easily and then become a nuisance, make good park beasts because of their timidity. Fallow deer are not native to England, but were probably introduced by the Normans. Around thirty-five deer parks were listed in the Domesday Book and these grew to around 2,000 in the Middle Ages. In Tudor times there were about 700 but many were destroyed during the Civil War and they dwindled after that to around 400 in 1900 and 143 in 1949.

Now deer parks are popular once more as places for the summer swarm to visit. According to the British Deer Society, there are 240 in Britain and sika and fallow deer are more in demand as ornaments than they are as venison. A fallow deer carcass is worth around £50, while a live buck can be worth £750. As Richard Jefferies said, 'a park without deer is like a wall without pictures'.

Deer in a park which admits visitors are useful as scavengers, since they will digest almost anything apart from plastic bags.

Down beside one of Capability Brown's lakes a man sat under a large green umbrella beside his fishing-rod, half asleep, while another threw crumbs from a paper bag into the water.

'You stupid bloody thing!' he complained to a duck trying to nibble his bait, 'I haven't come all the bloody way here just to catch you.'

He was one of twenty policemen belonging to the Sussex Police who had come here on a specially arranged outing. The days when rod-fishing was considered a solitary sport offering time for philosophic contemplation to rich men who caught fish by themselves, or perhaps with their ghillies, appear to be numbered. Now it flourishes as a group activity, preferably competitive. Lakes dug out in the eighteenth century for the discerning eye of a landowner are put to a new use by the National Trust, offering sport to groups like these policemen, who choose somewhere new to fish every year. This was their first time at Petworth, and, I gathered, probably their last, since for all the metal boxes full of hooks and flies, the rods wrapped in long canvas cases and the tins full of maggots, no one had caught anything larger than the tiddlers that had to be thrown back.

Tourists were still waiting to buy tickets, even though in half an hour the doors would be closed for the day. For many visitors the size and splendour of the rooms can be intimidating in a house designed for show rather than for ordinary living. The crowds had a faintly crestfallen air as, up until the last moment, they moved around the Marble Hall, the Beauty Room, the Square Dining-Room, the Carved Room, encrusted with Grinling Gibbons, and the Turner Room with long rectangular views of the park shaped in Cinemascope to fit the narrow spaces designed for them.

The twenty-two oil paintings by Turner at Petworth, the biggest collection outside the national collections, are a reflection of the discrimination of the endearing third Earl of Egremont and the congenial atmosphere of the big house during his time which mellowed Turner's vision. Neither Turner nor Constable was in the least intimidated by the overstretched grandeur of the Proud Duke's design while they enjoyed the hospitality of the grand old man, the third earl, who, according to his descendant, was 'humane, cultured, observant, sprightly, accurate, shrewd, eccentric, benevolent, well grounded in the classics . . . a winner of five Derbys and five Oaks'. The melancholy grandeur of Petworth is softened by his memory, and perhaps Benjamin Robert Haydon's well-known account of him should be read over loudspeakers to visitors as they are processed through the great barracks. Although Haydon shared the contemporary frightful deference for noble Lords, you cannot help sharing his affection for Lord Egremont.

The very flies at Petworth seem to know there is room for their existence – that the windows are theirs. Dogs, horses, cows, deer and pigs, peasantry and servants, guests and family, children and parents all share alike his bounty and opulence and luxuries. At breakfast after all the guests have breakfasted, in walks Lord Egremont, first comes a grandchild whom he sends away happy. Outside the windows moan a dozen black spaniels who are let in and then he distributes cakes and comforts, giving all equal shares . . . The merest insect at Petworth feels a ray of his Lordship's fire in the justice of its distribution.

I remembered the charming glimpse of Constable at Petworth enjoying relaxed hospitality observed by his biographer, C. R. Leslie, who was staying in the house at the same time in October 1884:

It was on this occasion only that I had the opportunity of witnessing his habits. He rose early, and had often made some beautiful sketch in the park before breakfast. On going into his room one morning . . . I found him setting some of these sketches with isinglass. His dressing-table was covered with flowers, feathers of birds, and pieces of bark with lichens and mosses adhering to them, which he had brought home for the sake of their beautiful tints.

The late afternoon sun threw out spokes of light that fell on the lines of doomed chestnuts outside the casement windows, while a guide pointed out Turner's paintings of the view, noting the location of the trees and how little most things had changed in a century and a half. Next summer's visitors would have a different, sadder commentary. In the café the last scones, cake slices and little tubs of strawberry jam were being served up. In the Carved Room Henry VIII looked disapprovingly at a woman wearing tight purple shorts.

Another part of Petworth is not on the general guided tour, but open on special occasions to people who manage to qualify as 'connoisseurs'. Among these hallowed rooms, in the study at the southern end of the house, overlooking another wonderful view, the present Lord Egremont was reading a poetry book. A fluffy dog was chasing a ball on the polished floor, while his wife and children were elsewhere in a kitchen. Here was an apartment as grand as those on show to the public, showing all of Petworth's intimidating splendour which had been tamed into a family room.

It is a common ungracious lament that the National Trust not only preserves the past, it mummifies it. Heaven knows, Ireland has suffered because there is no equivalent saviour, and plenty of its heritage has succumbed to neglect, destitution, decay, fire, rot and the Four Horseman of Profit, Prejudice, Progress and Vandalism. Big houses in Ireland on show to the public can expect to earn a fraction of the income of those in England, since there is never anything like the show of numbers. The number touring Petworth this one afternoon would be the equivalent of a wet summer's attendances at Bantry House. But small admission figures have not prevented the National Trust from doing fine restoration in houses on show in the North of Ireland, sometimes, thanklessly – soon the Germolene Controversy would erupt when Lord Belmore jeered at the trust's taste in decor in Castlecoole. Although so much of its effort is rightly a source of pride, the problem of atmosphere has never been overcome. The careful settings, the matching of contemporary wallpapers and the restored bed-curtains admirably evoke a house's history, but you have to do without the dust, teacup rings and hair combings that give a place the breath of life. Perhaps carefully supervised eccentrics could live among the visitors, preferably mad and old in carpet slippers with dogs or a string of children.

At Petworth the ideal has been achieved without the need for eccentricity. In the southern suite, which is almost as formidably formal as the places where the public are permitted to wander, there is more overwhelming carving by Grinling Gibbons and among the paintings kept out of the public eye is the loveliest Turner, of the Park embellished by mythical ships sailing on Capability Brown's lake. And here is something like domesticity.

It might seem easy enough for the current Lord Egremont to work out a life-style that offered enjoyment of the best possible things in the best possible world. In addition to 20,000 acres in Sussex, the Wyndhams once owned property all over the British Isles. The family had strong Irish connections through O'Briens, Beresfords and Irish Wyndhams and before 1903 had owned 43,000 acres in Ireland. The Irish properties were forfeited by Wyndham's Land Act, the work of a brilliant cousin, George Wyndham, great-grand-son of Lord Edward Fitzgerald and publisher of Ronsard and a special edition of Shakespeare. As Chief Secretary of Ireland he had been foremost in implementing Balfour's policy of killing Home Rule by kindness. Back in England the family suffered the usual landowning problems, and property in Lancashire, Dumfries and Yorkshire was sacrificed to death duties, although a swathe of Cumberland, now called Cumbria, managed to escape the taxmen.

Then there was Petworth. In his elegant autobiography, *Wyndham and Children First*, John Wyndham, the previous Lord Egremont, described the house as 'surely one of the most beautiful white elephants in Europe'. At the end of the Second World War the vast edifice, unrelieved by servants, was more of a burden than ever until he managed to persuade his uncle Charles, Lord Leconfield, to hand over house and contents to the National Trust. 'It was certainly one of the bravest things that I've ever done. He could have struck me out of his will. Happily he didn't.' He was rewarded by enjoying a wonderful compromise, keeping the glacier of the trust to run the public rooms beyond the doors on the sunny side of the house – all this and a breathtaking Turner as well. 'History has always echoed to the sound of clogs going upstairs and the tinkle of tiaras coming downstairs. My family, despite a good many setbacks, have managed so far to stay on the landing.'

Today, the present Lord Egremont was walking up the private back-stairs to examine some rare books in Turner's old studio, now used as a book-store. It is north-facing, situated at the very far end of the house above the medieval chapel with its smiling wooden cherubs. We went up another staircase and passageway right beyond the tourist orbit, and opened the door to the north-east bedroom which Turner used to keep locked. He had painted there happily in seclusion, only his lordship being allowed in.

Up in this dim, quiet place a very special atmosphere lingered on. Here in the bedroom with a high curved window which had been converted into a studio you felt very strongly the presence, not only of the artist, but also of the old earl. Haydon 'never saw such a character – live and let live seemed to be his motto'. His hospitality was on an Irish scale, putting you in mind of the Martins of Bally-nahinch or the Eyres of Eyrecourt who kept a basket of coins outside their front door for passers-by to help themselves and carved over the lintel: 'Welcome to the house of liberty.' Haydon again:

> At 70 he still shoots daily, comes home wet through and is as active and looks as well as many men of fifty. Under him Petworth was like a big inn with visitors coming and going as they pleased. They were welcome without notice. There was no leave-taking either; you didn't say goodbye, you just left.

The last tourists were going as the National Trust locked up for another day, and their footsteps echoed down the passageways, across the Marble Hall, and past the rooms hung with pictures by Van Dyck, Reynolds, Kneller, Lely and the rest. We flew off in the waning light across the park and trees and headed towards the South Downs as the sun began to sink behind Petworth and its park. I looked back at the creeping shadows and saw a tinge of the red glow of sunset that Turner had painted.

CHAPTER SEVEN

Brighton – Rochester – East Bergholt – Ickworth

We flew to Brighton where Graham had a girlfriend and a flat. We followed the long wave of the South Downs beyond which I could make out a murky expanse of sea and the lights of some boats. Then we went above a couple of little hills and reached a suburb where the girlfriend lived. We buzzed her house in slow meaningful circles which may have annoyed her neighbours. She didn't come out. She may have been watching television or making a cup of tea, or perhaps she didn't like microlights. Perhaps her relationship with Graham was another glum pilot's union. Better be a grass widow, a golfing widow, or a fisherman's widow than to be in love with a microlight pilot.

By the time we reached the small landing-field in Graham's home territory it was very nearly pitch dark. Graham put the microlight into a spinning turn; one moment we were trailing across a sky where there was just a touch of lemon light, and the next the black ground was near. More speed, straighten the wings and we were coming to land between black cloud shapes which were the lines of trees. I wondered about turbulence, wind shear and sink, as we dropped a hundred feet, fifty feet, watch out for any crosswind, and suddenly we were brushing the grass. Landing is always a bit of a miracle, but more so when you can't see.

The hangar belonged to a farmer with an interest in flying, particularly hang gliders. A few hundred yards up a hill was a small factory where they were manufacturing purer, freer flying machines, which used only the wind and didn't require a shrill engine.

Denis heard us buzzing overhead in the dark and drove down to investigate. I asked him what he thought of the Undertaker which he picked out in torchlight.

'Microlights are boring.' Echoing Diana at Clench Common, Denis

was like an old sailor who would always prefer the silent power of
sail to any alternative power that would chug a vessel along.

Graham might be a fine pilot, but he was not communicative. A
lot of pilots are like that. Perhaps it is the effect of being buffeted by
the wind, the constant exposure to varying moods of weather and the
continuing anxiety of keeping little aircraft in the air that drains away
speech.

'No trouble?' I asked.

'No.'

'I thought she sounded a bit rough?'

'I'll look at the setting.'

We took off the wing and carried wing and trike into the hangar
where there was just room to squeeze them between two light planes,
in comparison with which the microlight looked smaller than ever.

Denis drove us in his Morris Minor to Graham's flat which he had
lent to friends.

'We just dropped in.'

In the morning I looked out of the window over the rooftops to a
meeting of sea and sky, the sky marked with a couple of thin bands of
cloud. Later Graham took me to a workmen's cafe, and in a steamy
interior where everyone seemed to be friends we ordered massive
breakfasts.

'Coming up, two eggs, sausage, beans and toast.'

'Two teas.'

'Did you say chips, sir?'

'Double portion.'

We had devised a routine of eating in silence. Graham's morning
monosyllables were not yet adequate to discuss the day's flying. Yes,
no, perhaps and silence. Quite early in our relationship I had realized
that when we were flying the speaking tube which connected our
helmets was hardly necessary. I got into the habit of unplugging it.

The meal would last us for the day. When we went back to the flat
for our things, stuff which would fit into a woman's handbag, I had
another look at the view. The sky had changed colour and turned to
mother-of-pearl. Tolstoy makes Levin gaze at a sky like a mother-of-
pearl shell. 'And when was there time for that cloud-shell to form?
Just now I looked at the sky, and there was nothing in it – only two
white streaks. Yes, and so imperceptibly too my view of life
changed!'

Something had gone wrong in the hangar. We had forgotten to take a petrol can out of the microlight and one of the little struts that supported the engine had crumpled because of its weight. The lack of that one small spare meant that the Undertaker was no more airworthy than if it had crashed and turned into a piece of junk.

Graham said nothing, did not even swear. It looked as if I would have plenty of time to tour the sea-front and visit the Pavilion. The thought of being stuck for days in the Prince Regent's town was frightful.

Fortunately there was the factory up the road. The camaraderie among those who have an interest in flying machines meant that the people there dropped everything they were doing to give us a hand. Hang gliders have a bodywork basically similar to that of microlights and there are similar bolts, tubes, bits and pieces to be assembled, bolted on, zipped together or screwed in. A search around the premises meant that in a few minutes someone was able to come upon the correct spare part for our needs.

We put on our suits and helmets with an absurd feeling of relief and took off with all the style of Shah Key-Kavus's bed. Firdausi has described how the eccentric shah built himself an aircraft shaped like a four-poster bed which he harnessed to four eagles for flying power.

From Edburton we flew along between the flank of the South Downs and the sea over another densely patterned layer of England. We hovered over a golf course, an undulating emerald blanket with a paler patchwork of more closely cropped grass that were the greens, then we inspected a small lake with a marina full of boats, then a stucco castle and, beyond, a wedge of red brick houses pushing out across the fields. I had read that in East Sussex the housing has gone up by nearly 50 per cent in the last twenty-five years. The Department of the Environment has forecast that by the year 2000 there will be an extra 1 million houses built in south-east England.

At Lewes we headed north for Tunbridge Wells and a stiffly combed landscape with the occasional white-coned oasthouse. This was presumably another area dominated by the city farmer where farmhouses have become more expensive by far than the acres around them. Many city property owners are absentees, making money up in London, relying on agents to run their farms. The land they own is ornamental, at the same time making enough to satisfy their accountants.

Our intention had been to fly to All Hallows on the Thames estuary which was marked on our aerial map with a massive 'M' for 'intensive microlight activity'. We never got there, as the clouds closed in. Other aircraft fly over the clouds and have radar which makes them almost independent of wind and weather. The airline passenger can enjoy the sunlit blue above him and beneath him the crystal snowfield of cloud appears almost solid. But we were flying at about 1,000 feet with a cloud canopy over our head and the cloud pressed down like a coffin lid.

Graham tried the little radio transmitter, attempting to raise some sort of air traffic control. We had no headphones and the only way of making contact was to shout into the little speaker against the roar of the engine and the constant whistle of the wind. He attempted this a few times, without getting a discernible reply.

We were approaching London Basin and the Medway River, over unrelenting buildings, which was a different experience from flying across the friendly countryside with its nice easy fields. There was nowhere to land. Everywhere I looked were houses, factories, roads and a surprising number of railways and trains. Where would we go if the engine cut out?

We were in controlled airspace marked on the map in a huge blobby triangle around Heathrow, Gatwick and Stansted which is called the London Terminal Manoeuvring Area. Far above us strings of commercial aeroplanes were criss-crossing the saturated sky, obedient to the commands of air traffic controllers at the goldfish bowl at Heathrow and over beyond at West Drayton, part of the frenzied daily activity when they are guided through the air, miraculously avoiding each other.

Those passenger aircraft sweeping over our heads in the anxious task of avoiding collision and seeking a safe landing had nothing to do with us. What went on above us was none of our business. We were forbidden to join the mêlée above and had to keep rigidly below 2,500 feet near the airports and the capital. Under this height light aircraft, private jets, helicopters and microlights wandered as they wanted, avoiding each other solely by eyeball activity – in other words, they maintained a sharp look-out in their own crowded airspace. As long as they kept well down, they were unlikely to be struck by Boeing 747s and other large fast-moving aircraft. But down below was also quite dangerous, and we had to be careful. I watched a two-engined private jet pass rather too near, as the pilot with his passengers and their briefcases and Filofaxes sat back in their insulated cabin looking out of their windows at us.

Turbulence buffeted the wing with small hammer strokes as Graham applied more throttle. We began to see-saw and pitch and roll – one end of the wing would fall, then rise sharply as the nose made a sudden dip. Turbulence can happen very suddenly, because anything at ground level can create its own sharp current or thermal of rising air, and the urban landscape is full of thermal makers – a factory chimney on an industrial estate, the shining metalwork on a line of cars, a rubbish dump or quarry or small hill.

More bubbles of air hit us as we crossed the Medway and passed over the M20 and M2 near Maidstone. From a satellite in space these giant highways must show up on the earth's surface like Martian canals. As usual, the spectacle of trapped cars and lorries made me feel happier, free from exhaust fumes, police traps and traffic jams. We dropped down to 500 feet and skimmed over terraces of houses and the gardens behind where lines of washing were getting wet as the rain broke, lashing across our windshield and finding its way into our clothes. A red Post Office van was lurching down a narrow lane, a flag heralded a supermarket and its surrounding rows of trolleys and parked cars. A gash where earth was being excavated was strewn with derricks and cranes and now we were near the brown Thames Estuary. Where could we land?

Dark clouds were forcing us down. We were coming in over a roadway, over television aerials and back gardens, and some children looked up, little white faces and little black faces and little arms waving as we rattled overhead. A church, then a large area of suburban housing arranged in curves and centipede patterns, and now we were low enough to count the daisies on the lawns of gardens. Right in the middle of a wasteland estate I was surprised and pleased to see a small airport with a couple of runways and grass, some hangars and a control tower.

Airports and aircraft are anathema to the true traveller. In his *Visions of a Nomad* Wilfred Thesiger wrote:

I have always resented cars and aeroplanes, aware even as a boy that they must inevitably diminish the world and deprive it of its fascinating diversity. Having spent years where I never even heard an engine, I flinch every time I hear a low-flying aeroplane, a passing motor bicycle, or a lorry revving up. Airports represent to me the ultimate abomination, everything that I most detest in our civilization.

Today, however, the airport was a safe refuge for Graham and myself. A couple of officials came out to watch us taxi up as the rain pounded the tarmac and the microlight came to a halt, one side of the wing bent against the wind. We had landed at Rochester, a cheery place with a comfortable waiting room brightened by posters, helpful staff, and a landing fee of only four pounds.

Soon Graham was reading his aeronautical magazine for the tenth time as we waited for the weather to clear. A fat man bustled in and later took off in a streamlined little jet that was the airborne equivalent of a Porsche. Soon it would penetrate the cloud level and enjoy the sun high over the dark London sky. Some uniformed flying instructors looked like bus drivers. There was not much to eat, crisps, chocolates and biscuits from a machine. It was just as well we had eaten a good breakfast.

During a break in the downpour, our boredom was relieved when we walked rapidly to a garage to fill up the can with the mixture, Graham as usual overseeing the operation. A little after five the clouds shifted enough for some student pilots to begin to make circuits of the airport in very small planes. After six cups of coffee, three packets of crisps, some biscuits and a dozen pages of *Eugene Onegin*, I was looking for ways of escape.

'Let's go,' Graham said, and we ran on to the tarmac and squeezed ourselves into the flying pea-pod in the usual agonizing fashion.

Rule One. Don't be taken in by the weather when the real problem is with yourself.

Rule Two. Remember that what goes up has to come down with a bump, and once you are flying, you can't just sit it out for ever, especially over Greater London.

People have called clouds many silly things: the sheet music of the heavens, the architecture of the moving air, the shapes of disembodied ghosts. There was a haunting quality about the way they lay in wait. They would get us in the end.

I could see the Thames with derricks standing out along its banks and factory chimneys spouting smoke. We could, if we liked, dip a wing, turn and fly up west over all the new Dockland developments towards Tower Bridge. Aircraft are not supposed to go up beyond Tower Bridge right into Westminster and see the Houses of Parliament, but otherwise little machines like our own could travel almost anywhere under the network of commercial traffic. All that was necessary was keen vision.

A few months after we passed over the Thames, the London City Airport made its painful debut and soon after had to stop operations because it was considered that a pilot's eyesight alone was not sufficient guarantee for the safety of his passengers. Problems arose because city passenger aircraft were being forced to fly out of London through wilderness territory, i.e. the airspace through which the microlight was now roving. They were not being directed along safe and orthodox paths by air traffic controllers who had the power of path flight over aircraft coming into Heathrow and Gatwick. The hint came that such flying in uncontrolled airspace might be dangerous. But it appears as more and more aeroplanes clamour to fly and the number of reported air-misses increases, anywhere in the heavens above southern England is unsafe.

We were flying in a huge area of officially recognized anarchy in which we continued to be pressed down by cloud. We crossed the Thames at about 1,000 feet up at a moment when the river was putting on an old-fashioned display of sailpower. The constant traffic on the Thames includes police boats, coal barges, rubbish barges and, upstream, furious little *Daily Telegraph* launches, water taxis and the ever-popular ships of fools, pleasure boats full of party-goers dancing and drinking up and down the river's winding course. In addition, there is often some sort of pretty boat, a replica of something Francis Drake or Nelson sailed on, or a convict ship making its way up to the Pool of London, or perhaps a handsome brigantine full of South American naval cadets waiting to have their photographs taken in front of Tower Bridge. Today, beneath us, a three-master with its sails furled was chugging towards the city, and just behind it a Thames barge with a beige jib was making for St Katherine's Dock.

Crossing the Thames took about three minutes. North of the river we were enveloped in black vapour and heavy squalls of rain dribbling across my helmet. At the same time some turbulence shook the microlight as we came down lower through the downpour to about 500 feet. It was hard to see. I missed Rochester.

'Accidents are always the pilot's fault,' Graham had said that morning as we ate our big Brighton breakfast. I hoped they were not words that I would be able to throw back at him. The unpleasantness came not only from the rain, but from the clammy touch of the clouds. Down at this level traffic was nearer, every car lit up, the headlights making endless pairs of blurred nimbuses. A train passed below, then another the other way heading back towards London.

We skimmed over a roundabout as Graham consulted his map to go east, making for a second roundabout and picking out a motorway radiating out of it to follow. The black surface glistened, the traffic moved slowly. We were low enough to read the names on lorries and trucks. Keiller – a link with Avebury. Thomson Forks in bright blue – what could they be, garden forks, forklift trucks? At first we flew faster than the traffic, but as we moved out into the country, the jam eased, the wind in our face increased and the speeds of cars beneath and microlight above became roughly similar. Perhaps we were just a little faster. I watched us overtake one particular car. Sometimes he went ahead, but little by little we would overhaul him and he was well behind us when we picked up a new direction and began to follow a railway line.

The clouds stayed with us and much of the time we had to fly through menacing dark shapes that pressed all round. We were seasick and wet. One comfort was to see the non-stop housing gradually giving way to patches of fields and trees, and now we were out again above the endless conflict between town and country. If the clouds pushed us down lower we could find somewhere to land which was not someone's back garden.

The microlight hovered over a small village on the outskirts of which was a playing-field. Graham zoomed in quickly and taxied towards a large red brick school. The relief from fear and discomfort was exquisite.

As we burst out of the trike, two teachers came hurrying out into the rain to see what had landed on their cricket ground. There had not been much play that day. They watched us unpeel our soggy flying-suits and take off the wing.

'Can we leave our plane here?'

'Of course!' They were enchanted. They had never seen a microlight before.

We pushed it out of sight so that next morning there would be less chance of it being vandalized before school began. Then we walked to the Red Lion and refreshed ourselves with bitter and *Coronation Street*.

Graham's nifty navigation had brought us to our destination at East Bergholt in the heart of Constable country. On a good day its lush green vegetation, the blend of woods and meadows along the river Stour, lives up to its reputation as 'a kind of ultimate paradise of landscape'. On a good day the area gets lots of tourists.

The next day was a good one, following one of the bewildering changes in weather patterns that make an English summer such a feat of endurance. The tourists were everywhere with cameras and note-books, chasing Constable and the scenes he had loved, 'every style and stump and every lane in the village'. Identification was their pur-pose, just as it had been for those visiting Slimbridge where Peter Scott has made it easy with his leisurely walkways and hideaways out and about among the geese and swans. In East Bergholt John Constable has done much the same for those who come to search out the subjects he painted. As his biographer Leslie noted after his death: 'we found that the scenery of eight or ten of our late friend's most important subjects might be enclosed by a circle of a few hundred yards at Flatford, very near Bergholt. So startling was the resemblance of some of those scenes to the pictures of them which we know so well, that we could hardly believe we were for the first time standing on the ground from which they were painted.'

Today there were signs to help. Everyone was taking photographs of the places where Constable had painted *Boat Building along the Stour*, *The White Horse, Willy Lott's Cottage, Flatford Mill*.

'Did you get everything in?'

'Most of it.'

'Some of the trees weren't there in his time.'

'Pity about Willy Lott's cottage.'

There was general regret at the transformation from rustic retreat into a fine piece of real estate. Together with the eighteenth-century mill and the mill-house, it serves as a field centre run by the Field Studies Council, a charity that exists to promote environmental understanding for all. Lovers of nature, lovers of Constable and his favourite stretch of water were gathered here. They were the Avebury sort, pilgrims rather than tourists, with feelings of reverence bordering on worship. They had no second thoughts about the artist whom a peevish Ruskin had criticized as perceiving 'that the grass is wet, the meadows flat and the boughs shady; – that is to say, about as much as, I suppose, might be apprehended, between them, by an intelligent fawn and a skylark'.

Click. 'Who was Willy Lott, Dad?'

Everyone seemed to know. Everyone could find the passage in the leaflet they carried which quoted the invaluable C. R. Leslie, Constable's friend and correspondent. 'The little farmhouse which is called "Willy Lott's House" is situated on the edge of the river close to Flatford Mill. Willy Lott, its possessor, was born in it, and, it is said, has passed more than eighty years without having spent four whole days away from it.'

A number of people were sitting and painting the house by the waterside in imitation of the great English master. The washerwoman would have to be omitted, the wheeltracks on the water's edge, the ferryboat, the fisherman and Constable's other props. But there were still trees and water to depict, and the cottage wasn't all that changed, so that it was quite possible to sketch in a group of buildings resembling England's best-loved pictures. The efforts of these river-bank artists deeply distressed the art instructors from the Flatford Mill Field Centre, who kept trying to divert painters away from the water like hens with clutches of ducklings.

'I just wish they'd move a bit farther upstream.'

'You might as well paint some sunflowers and think they were by Van Gogh or visit Monet's house and have a go at his water-lilies.'

Groups of obstinate copycats sat firmly beside the Stour sketching very familiar scenes. This evening twenty or thirty homes would be embellished with new versions of old themes, a change from having *The Haywain* on jigsaw puzzles. These artists felt no sense of adventure; they liked familiarity, and perhaps they were right in ignoring the enticements of those at the field centre who were trying to lead them away from Constable to paint different subjects – birds, plants, landscapes, anything which had not become over-familiar. They would not be diverted from a desire to have their own repeat view of the Stour and Dedham Vale. John Peel has noted how we compare Constable's landscapes with the scenes as they are today 'and when some of the details tally, we feel we have won a skirmish with time'. A feeling of victory, of battle fought and won, is emphasized by sitting down and wrestling with pencils and paints to record the actual subjects favoured by the beloved artist. These artists might not succeed in the representation of colour and atmosphere which recorded a moment of light for ever; they might be unable to 'preserve God's almighty daylight which is enjoyed by all mankind'. But they were happy enough; gentle industry pervaded the sunlit scene.

The people at the centre had succeeded in capturing other visitors to take part in a bewildering range of alternative activities. They did not have to stick with Constable at all. They could come to Flatford Mill to learn calligraphy, natural history, photography, botany, biology, bird-watching, how to look at timber-framed buildings, stained glass design and many other things. A new group had just arrived on bicycles to study mosses and liverworts. At other times other visitors would attend the short course entitled 'Let's Look at Legumes' which would guide them 'through the perils and pitfalls of the pea family'. Or 'Herbs and Herbalists' or 'Concentrating on Compositae . . . a short course to help you with the intricacies of identifying the Daisy family'.

That course lasted two days. I felt a twinge of panic. (Graham had sensibly taken his magazine and gone in search of a pub.) Two whole days to study daisies! A passion for the natural world and its conservation, now acknowledged as part of the make-up of anyone with a smattering of education, is no longer the preserve of eccentrics or old men and women who have watched the countryside of their childhood melt away. The young have joined them in the desire to preserve and enjoy it before it is destroyed. But here it had to be enjoyed *en masse*, and I wanted to fly away.

Already it was too late, as the kaleidoscope had made another turn into another cloud pattern. The sun disappeared, and the artists gathered up their sketching materials as rain spattered into the Stour. Rain splashed down on the mill-pool and its giant golden carp, on the lines of fishermen, who like those at Petworth never seemed to catch anything, on the pilgrims in their bright plastic macs who walked, umbrellas raised, around Bridge Cottage seeking shelter in its little Constable Room or sitting down for tea in the restaurant provided by the National Trust. They quoted the remark on Constable's skies: 'When you saw them you wanted to take out your umbrella.' At Flatford Mill visitors were reduced to reading about vertebrates, woodland ecology and algae. Out on the school playing-field the microlight was getting sodden again.

I took refuge with a good many others in St Mary's Church, where we listened to the organ and read memorial tablets. An attorney, Edward Lambe, died in 1617: 'He helped many, yet took fees scarsse of any.' Unusual. On another wall extracts from Constable's own writings had been engraved. 'It will be difficult to name a class of landscape in which the sky is not the keynote, the standard of scale and the chief organ of contentment.' Later I sought out disgruntled natives, who, like those I had encountered in Avebury, were uneasily clinging to a beautiful place which had been lonely during their childhood. I talked to a butcher who got no benefit whatsoever from fans of Constable.

'You aren't going to drive down to Dedham Vale to buy a chop or half a pound of sausages.'

This man's father and grandfather had been butchers, and he had a wonderful display of photographs of the past, another country. In East Bergholt in 1890, the age of rustic innocence, his grandfather had worn a striped apron and sat in his dog-cart before carcasses hanging symmetrically outside his shop, split sides of beheaded oxen and sheep in mirror images. Other pictures showed the forge and blacksmith, and a girl in a long white dress and straw bonnet picking wild flowers near Flatford Mill before it was done up and tourism became a part of life.

'They come down here in their cars and do the Constable area in a few hours, and then they go off again.'

And here were the same sad cries about property prices. East Bergholt, too, was a place that carried the terrible double burden of being not only a centre for tourism, but a refuge for Londoners. While it rained outside, I listened to the muted hostility that I had heard in a different regional accent in Wiltshire, tales of city dwellers coming down with their fairy gold, buying up pigsties for six figures.

The rain fell the whole afternoon, and we had to wait until next morning before the clouds were reduced to cotton-wool patches and the sun came out. At Flatford Mill the students in the field centre were sitting down to breakfast. The evening before they had had a celebratory dinner of roast lamb and treacle tart before the art show at the end of their weekly course on landscape painting. Anyone who had overcome weather difficulties and finished a picture, preferably not of one of Constable's subjects, could attend.

'We had a couple of days of Constable's big skies. There's blue in the light.'

'The light's quite different down here.'

'Isn't it true that Constable painted nothing direct on his canvas, but did everything from sketches and notes?'

'Didn't he say light and shade never stand still?'

Constable wrote: 'The world is wide; no two days are alike, nor even two hours; neither were there ever two leaves of a tree alike since the creation of the world; and the genuine productions of art, like those of nature, are all distinct from each other.'

Outside the kitchen one of the girls who did the cooking was feeding the carp with left-overs. The next group of students, whose subject was 'Grasses, Sedges and Rushes', had begun to check in at the office. In the National Trust tea-house a woman was watering pots of geraniums, and along the river bank tourists had already arrived and were feeding the ducks.

'He almost bit my finger!'

'They must be the best-fed ducks in England!'

This was the sort of day that would have made Constable hurry to take out his brushes for a skyscape. He made a habit of noting weather in his diary. '5th September 1822. 10 o'clock, morning, looking south east, brisk wind at West. Very bright and fresh grey clouds running fast over a yellow bed, about half way in the sky.' Not only had he learned a bit of weather forecasting from being a mill-owner's son, foretelling wind strength and interpreting cloud formations, but he also studied an early meteorologist named Thomas Forster, author of *Study of Cirrus and Cumulus Cloud* and *Dark Cloud Study: Researches about Atmospheric Phaenomena*.

The schoolboys and some of the masters poured out to watch us take off, roar across their playing-pitch and lift over the trees. Although Constable's Stour Valley has been so delicately preserved, from up above you could see the abrupt encouragement of ugly things. On one side of East Bergholt the motorway connected Colchester to Norwich, while in the other distant factory chimneys faced the sea. A goods train passed, and we glimpsed a line of pylons striding the big fields. But the area directly around East Bergholt and Flatford continued to preserve its ancient symmetry, where the countryside was on a smaller scale. The river passed through small crooked fields, hedges had not been uprooted and trees and little patches of old woodland were still preserved. (But the October storm would come this way as well.)

We were following the river to Dedham, where barges once went up and down. The water has been empty for a long time now, and the light shines on it unimpeded. Silvery willows and dark green of chestnut and oak bordered its side as we came to Dedham, an Englishman's paradise, the sort of place that old empire-builders sweltering in tropical outposts dreamt about. I picked out all the red brick Georgian houses and the roses in every garden.

From Dedham it was a short flight to neighbouring Sudbury and the patch of the Stour associated with Gainsborough, whose statue holds up a palette. Sudbury is a market town which has escaped the full-scale redevelopment of county towns like Ipswich and Colchester, although in its suburbs there is plenty of new housing to proclaim its nearness to London and the prospect of more building to come. The centre was pleasant and prosperous, timber-framed buildings, Georgian and substantial Victorian houses echoing centuries of successful commerce. As we passed overhead I could see a market was going on, with lines of stalls leading down to the Corn Exchange. Was that Gainsborough's house and the mulberry tree in the walled garden? We were going too fast to be sure.

East Bergholt has Constable, Sudbury has Gainsborough, and the difference is corn and wool. The Constables were millers, while the Gainsborough family were woollen-cloth weavers. The painters were linked by the Stour and by a love for the landscape around their homes which makes a convenient combined tour for motorists. Beyond Sudbury were low hills covered with wheat and plenty of large country mansions like Osprey and Bat's Hall. And somewhere below was Haddington Hall where Gainsborough painted young and fashionable Mr and Mrs Robert Francis Andrews on their garden seat beside their cornfield. Probably it was Mr Andrews who proudly asked Gainsborough to paint him beside his farm instead of in the park. The lines of stubble, showing his progressive farming, and the fact that he was using a seed drill, were a prelude to EEC prairies. Gainsborough was painting at a time of revived interest in agriculture and its ideals. Changes in agricultural methods combined with some sense of a threat of siege arising from the French wars made rural landscapes a particular focus of attention. The hint of poignancy in the idea that England might be invaded would be echoed in the

Second World War. Painters tended to identify with the benevolent landlord improving his land and the contented peasants, unaffected by the tinge of revolution, working away in an idealized landscape. The swing from Georgian contemplation to Romanticism did not come until after the Napoleonic wars when orderly patriotism was less a preoccupation, and romantics could once again travel on the Continent and become immersed in picturesque touring and wilder vistas.

Mrs Andrews would be dead within a year of her lovely portrait, perhaps of childbirth. The present owners of Haddington Hall, besieged by people wanting to see where Mr and Mrs Andrews posed, discouraged visitors. Beneath us were dotted ancient Suffolk villages, old houses surrounding magnificent churches. The tranquil beauty was soothing as we flew over Kersey, with its river that cuts across a dip in the main street, then Long Melford and Lavenham. We picked out the high stone tower of St Peter and St Paul at Lavenham, a landmark across distant fields, and soon we were flying over the finest medieval town in England, viewing the ancient layout from the best possible vantage point, the timber-framed houses of wealthy medieval clothiers fitting into the medieval street pattern.

There was the Swan Hotel where the signatures of American airmen based in surrounding airfields are written on a panel in the bar. We looked down on the Guildhall and the people pouring out of buses and cars into tea-rooms and antique shops, thronging the streets, making their way into the sumptuous nave of St Peter and St Paul, vibrant with canned religious music. Once the towers of churches like these signalled islands of civilization in a perilous countryside, but now the big church with its stalls selling souvenirs had more than the whiff of the market-place. Perhaps it needed the Lord wielding a whip. I felt I had got sour since I had toured Salisbury Cathedral, and gave my attention to how height gave Lavenham an immunity from stale postcard prettiness. 'Madam, I never saw an ugly thing in my life, but light, shade or perspective would always make it beautiful.' Constable had been an unhappy boarder at Lavenham's old grammar school.

I pondered his words later as we flew above pylons — not all that much above them — which made a line of gaunt War-of-the-Worlds shadows across the country. Pylons are a great weapon in the armoury of those who wish to destroy the pleasant prospect of an orderly traditional countryside. They seem to be placed anywhere and their

immunity from sensible planning ensures a maximum rate of disfigure-
ment, which seems strange in a time when conservation has become
the big word. Why should electricity be king, when other com-
modities like gas and oil have to go underground and conceal their
traces? Pylons are unstable – no doubt in the October storm this ugly
line went keeling over with the force of the gale, like so many
others. The period after the storm would have been a good time for
conservation groups to raise some sort of outcry about these landmarks
which have become as indelible a part of rural England as the grass
and the fragile trees. For the present they provided another little
difficulty for low-flying aircraft like ours.

There were more shadows of clouds racing each other. (At Drum-
lanrig in Scotland, one of the Duke of Buccleuch's estates, trees have
been planted in clumps to imitate the shadows of cumulus clouds very
like these.) In among them moved our own clear outline, a condor
silhouette crossing fields and ditches, vanishing at a roadway and
caught again in the flickering sunlight.

After Sudbury and Lavenham the country changed rapidly into
the broad vistas and horizons of East Anglia where hedges have been
grubbed out to make land as featureless as the sea with nothing
distinct to navigate by. In a waste of golden brown we would greet a
distant spire or a clump of trees with relief as they appeared with
hallucinatory effect like a lighthouse floating in the hazy air. We flew
on through skies sweeping around our buzzing machine in space that
made you think England was a big empty place.

I knew that we had arrived in a part of the countryside which
more than elsewhere had succumbed to ruthless farming techniques.
This was the heart of East Anglia where the cattle and shire horses
have gone and the pigs have vanished inside. Since 1955 the total
number of farms and small holdings here has been halved, while the
acreage of large farms has almost doubled. Farm labourers have
almost gone the way of the big-footed horses and the old uneasy
working relationship between farmers and exploited agricultural labourers has given way to confrontation with the middle classes. I had
been told that this was another area of preserved villages which get
nicknames like 'God's Waiting-Room' because they attract the aged
and retired. But even villages seemed scarce. The aerial view emphasized the havoc where bulldozers, JCBs and power saws had done
their work with devastating efficiency to extend arable acreage.

Where were the hedges, ditches, farm ponds, road verges, green lanes and woods?

In a majority of East Anglian parishes more than half the landscape features recorded on nineteenth-century maps have been destroyed. Someone has observed that the landscape has reverted to its pre-Enclosures look. I knew these huge fields were under new pressures, that East Anglia is the fastest-growing region in Britain with Cambridgeshire attracting newcomers faster than anywhere else. The debates were beginning on what would happen next. Would the rich Grade One and Grade Two land be up for grabs? The spaces cleared for wheat looked invitingly ready to grow desirable residences with perhaps a certain acreage for low-income housing.

If the government put off decisions for long enough, the problem would sort itself out. The greenhouse effect caused by burning coal and oil and destroying forests is making ocean levels rise at the rate of a third of an inch a year, and soon it will bring back, first the fens, and then the sea. Unless there is another Ice Age, the rise in global temperature will mean that the whole of southern England from the Severn to the Wash will be under water within 7,000 years. If Graham and I postponed our flight for a few millennia, we would be flying, not over these prairies, but over a shallow inland sea.

It was a relief to fly towards a group of trees where Ickworth stood with its outstretched arms. Ickworth is an extraordinary-looking house erected on a giant scale with oval rotunda, pedimented portico and curving corridors making up an outside folly, a building resembling a giant spider-crab.

Up until now I had felt unfairly superior in every sense to the tourists. I felt myself detached from the 50 million, not to mention all the foreigners who were swarming around England looking for somewhere to go and see. But like those who went to Bergholt to venerate Constable, I had come to Ickworth in the spirit of pilgrimage. I was an admirer of its creator, Frederick Augustus Hervey, fourth Earl of Bristol and Bishop of Londonderry. I have always liked his outsized dottiness, genial charm and incorrigible frivolity. He was an ecclesiastic who refused to take religion seriously – some believed he was an atheist. In the eighteenth century you did not get appointed to high office in the church merely because you were a good Christian. As a result he was just about the only genuinely ecumenical ecclesiastic Ireland has ever enjoyed. (But once, while travelling in Siena, he threw a bowl of spaghetti out of a window at a passing procession of the Host because he had an aversion to bells.)

The bishop had a passion for travel and for collecting works of art. He also built a series of impractical houses in a spirit of outrageous self-indulgence. Two were in County Derry: Ballyscullion, which was burnt, and Downhill, a ruin on a north-facing windy cliff above the sea. (I wondered if I could eventually fly over Downhill and compare it to Ickworth.) Ickworth survives as a spectacular and eccentric example of rotund architecture. If I had the choice of meeting anyone in history, it wouldn't be Napoleon or Gandhi, it would be the fourth Earl of Bristol, preferably when he was young. Later in life, alas, he became rude and reactionary and it is difficult to forgive him for being offensive to Goethe. ('*Werther* is a completely immoral damnable book.') Even so, I am proud to claim a family connection with him through his nephew who was hanged.

Reduce speed, a slow turn across the south front and back again towards the park. The trees made a precise rectangular framework to the curves and ovals of the house. They were getting closer, a spread of plumed tree-tops arranged in a formal classical landscape. These trees, too, would suffer in the gale sweeping around England on roughly the same route as the gale which sank the Armada. In particular, a grove of giant cedars planted by the bishop was flattened. One of his enthusiasms was the widespread planting of trees, and he had bad luck with them. In 1780, he wrote how 'Downhill is becoming elegance itself – 300,000 trees, upon all banks and upon all the rocks'. Not one has survived the blasts from the Atlantic.

When you are landing a microlight you must choose an area free of obstruction, and then be sure that the wind is in the right direction before you come down. One of my failings as a pilot is an inability always to get this combination right. You may take off in a westerly direction, but in the course of your flight the wind is likely to change by a few degrees and this will affect the angle of your landing. In the microlight there were no instruments to tell you which way the wind was coming from, and you had to look out for clues. There are never any flags or windsocks when you need them, but today there was plenty of movement through the trees to guide us.

'The wind bloweth where it listeth, and thou hearest the sound thereof, but canst not tell whence it cometh, and whither it goeth.'

Graham picked a point in the parkland near the cricket ground and its pavilion and we floated down across the river, over the main gates where a woman was sitting and sketching Horringer Church, and landed at the big house with a few soft bumps.

After the grandiose prospect from the sky, Ickworth's rotunda and its arms repeated at ground level the impression of comfort sacrificed to splendour. A good deal of the house had been intended for show, to be a big musuem for the collection of pictures and statuary the bishop was amassing in Rome. He died before Ickworth was completed, having designated the domed and pillared rotunda where every massive room had its curving walls, for living quarters, and the wings, each the size of a substantial country house, as show-places for his collection. A letter written to his daughter at the end of his life ends 'The House – The House – The House'. He never saw it. After his death, his son, having considered demolishing his father's unfinished Xanadu, decided to go ahead and complete it with a revised design. The east wing became the family residence, while the state rooms in the rotunda housed the collection and were used for formal entertaining.

The bishop had been a big spender. He first came to Ireland in the manner that disgusted Swift, through influence and preference. (Swift wrote that bishops who were newly appointed to Irish sees – invariably Englishmen – got caught by highwaymen as they crossed Hounslow Heath on their way west; the highwaymen stole their letters patent and came over to Ireland in their place.)

The bishop first obtained the bishopric of Cloyne, and was then elevated to the lucrative see of Londonderry. Everyone knows about the curates' race on donkeys he organized in the sands below Downhill. He managed to make a lot of money out of Londonderry by changing the rules and collecting the fines chargeable on the renewal of agricultural leases. When he became the fourth Earl of Bristol, his income unexpectedly increased from the rents on 30,000 acres of family property which went up after the outbreak of war with France in 1793. He could afford to make Ickworth enormous. He liked his houses big: 'largeness' always predominated over convenience. He maintained he could only breathe properly in a room that was the size of an amphitheatre.

For all his faults and extravagance, he was popular until distractions like travelling and collecting works of art made him lose interest in Ireland and live more or less permanently in Rome. His passion for building lasted all his life. Downhill was a rectangular house, but later he took to curves, particularly after he met up with the young architect, John Soane, who designed him a circular 'dog house' or dog kennel. In Ireland Ballyscullion on the shores of Lough Beg was his first rotunda with arms – Ickworth was a more splendid version. There had been Downhill to visit as well. In a letter to Arthur Young he compared 'the foggy ferny atmosphere of Ickworth' to 'the exhilarating air, or rather ether of Downhill'. But when he inherited all this fine land in Suffolk he felt he had to improve it.

Although in eighteenth-century terms he was a millionaire many times over, there still wasn't enough money for his ambitious schemes. Perhaps his son tightened the budget when Ickworth was completed. I watched some of the delicate neo-classical frieze that adorns the rotunda being repaired.

'The money must have run out,' said a workman, chipping away in a cloud of dust. 'By rights this should have been made of stone instead of plaster. The problem here is that all the rusty ironwork inside has expanded.' Bits of frieze were falling all over the place.

Now the National Trust has most of Ickworth and in the usual way the current Lord Bristol is comfortably installed in a wing. Outside I walked by a notice. 'The cost of maintaining this historic garden is high. Please will you contribute towards it.' A man was tearing about the lawns on a sit-down mower. In the bishop's day and before him they mowed differently. Andrew Marvell described grass-cutting at Appleton House:

> For when the sun the grass hath vexed,
> The tawny mowers enter next;
> Who seem like Israelites to be,
> Walking on foot through a green sea.
> To them the grassy deeps divide,
> And crowd a lane to either side.
> With whistling scythe, and elbow strong,
> These massacre the grass along.

Capability Brown designed two sets of plans for the garden which the earl-bishop never got round to implementing. However, in due course most of his plans were incorporated to create another natural garden, at its maturity about to face devastation. Like Petworth,

Ickworth, too, had a lake designed to be ornamental but now providing the stately home with an added source of income. Groups of fishermen were seated on the bank; one of them told me that he had been there since five o'clock in the morning, and the only reason he hadn't got there earlier was because his alarm hadn't worked. I was reminded of the ancient *Punch* joke of the lunatic leaning over the wall and inviting a fisherman to come inside. This group was fishing for carp, which were inedible. If you were pushed you could salt them for a couple of days to take away the taste of mud, but at the end of all that they still don't make much of a meal. The best thing is to throw them back.

Nearby a man dozed with an electric buzzer set on his rod which would wake him with a sharp 'ping' when the bait was taken. From here looking down, the façade of Ickworth took up a lot of the view.

'Do you ever visit it?'

'No. There's nothing to see.'

He told me that the largest carp anyone had caught in the lake had weighed twenty-two pounds five ounces. That particular fish had been caught five times.

'A lot of people say it doesn't hurt them being caught. I don't know about that.'

He had known a number of fish which had died from 'fishing pressure' – from being caught too often. He thought capture put them off their food. Not all of them, since he had known one fish that had put on a massive ten pounds in just a few days between reluctant appearances above water.

'The water is very rich in nutrients, you see.'

There was a stir around the lake as if the wind was blowing through the rushes.

'Watch out! Water bailiffs!'

Two men appeared in a Land-Rover and began checking fishing licences. Illegal extra rods were quickly hidden, fishermen without proper documents melted away. Perhaps lurking down in the muddy depths was a monster fish that no one had ever caught or thrown back. A magnificent golden carp with the same stout figure and the same protruding eyes as the earl-bishop, sniffing the stem of a water-lily, reincarnated and spending eternity in his lake keeping watch on his house.

CHAPTER EIGHT

Towards Skeggy

We flew over Yew Walk, Oak Tree Walk and Lord William Hervey's Walk where Ickworth's tourists looked as if they were attending some extravagant house party. It was a landscape that Constable would have disliked, for all that he stayed happily at Petworth. 'I never had a desire to see sights, and a gentleman's park is my aversion.' We flew over the private church, the lake where thin fishermen's rods were visible at its edge like blanket-stitching, and the Fawn Summerhouse, and looked down on the obelisk put up by the grateful citizens of Derry who included the Roman Catholic bishop and the Dissenting minister.

> Hostile sects which had long entertained
> feelings of deep animosity towards each other
> were gradually softened and reconciled
> by his influence and example.

They could do with a figure like the earl-bishop in Derry now. If he was eccentric and perverse – in his own words, 'a vagabond star' – he was magnanimous, he believed in religious equality and he had a grasp of the contemporary ills of Ireland. 'Can any country flourish,' he wrote to a friend, 'where two thirds of its inhabitants are still crouching under the lash of the most severely illiberal penalties that one set of citizens ever laid on another?'

A last look at his magnificent folly. Perhaps the expanses of East Anglia invite the building of follies. After my flight was over and the Undertaker was no more, I returned to this part of the world to view two more situated on the east coast – Thorpeness and Sizewell. The model village of Thorpeness, erected early this century, was the brainchild of Glencairn Stuart Ogilvie, another rich man whose architectural preference was for quaintness rather than classical grandeur. With its arched gateways, turreted almshouse and working-men's club, Thorpeness was a pioneer venture in self-catering holidays. Mr Ogilvie could see the wandering crowds to come. He indulged in contemporary whimsy by naming the islands in the centre of his artificial lake after characters in Peter Pan. How fortunate it is that Peter Pan has gone out of fashion and only emerges at Christmas time; even Peter Rabbit is preferable.

I came to see the House in the Clouds in Thorpeness, the most remarkable of Ogilvie's whimsies, an elaborate piece of camouflage where a high steel-clad water-tank was covered in clapboarding and a house was perched on top of the tower. When I climbed up and looked out of its windows, I could see my old friends and enemies, the clouds, and a sweep of East Anglian coast. In the distance was the grey square of Sizewell. Let us hope fervently that Sizewell will never be given a name similar to Ogilvie's house. In fact, when you get to the grey fortress, you see puffs of thin white smoke emerging from a chimney above a low drumming of machinery. Harmless stuff, we are told.

'There is no evidence that any member of the public has been harmed by radiation from these power stations', a notice at the Nuclear Information Centre reassures tourists. No one seems to worry in case this is a lie; they are out to have a nice day. Is there anywhere in Britain that does not have its infestation of summer visitors? A few deep coal-mines, Dartmoor Prison, some inner cities? Sizewell is one of England's most rapidly growing tourist attractions. They drive in and play on the beach below its concrete walls. A child flies a kite and others are bathing.

'Who's the first in?'

'Me!'

I'd sooner step into a sea of fire. In Ireland we are perpetually worried by Sizewell's elder sister on the other side of England, leaky old Sellafield, another tourist attraction, the most popular in the Lake District. For many of us across the water the initials SRI (Safety Related Incidents) are almost as familiar as IRA. The Irishman's gut feeling that nothing good ever came out of England is reinforced by reports of what trickles out of Sellafield into the Irish Sea and lights up glowing plates of Dublin Bay prawns. We do not get much English acid rain, which is mostly blown towards continental Europe by clean west winds, but we get dirty stuff in the way of nuclear discharge from Cumbria.

The building at Sizewell, at present attracting tourists, the nuclear power station with gas-cooled reactor, erected in the 1960s at the cost of £60 million – a couple of billion at today's prices – is due to be superseded by a more expensive, more up-to-date tourist enticement. During the inquiry into the wisdom of building Sizewell B, Britain's first pressurized water reactor, the Central Electricity Generating Board gave reassuring evidence that it would be 'safe'. 'The CEGB is naturally considering what it can learn form the Chernobyl accident.' Pessimists worry needlessly about Murphy's Law, human frailty, bad housekeeping, someone going mad, the lab boy dropping something, terrorists breaking in, or some red-hot gadget wearing out. If a smallish nuclear accident on a scale far less than the one that smothered the Ukraine happened at Sizewell, London would be uninhabitable. Still, Sizewell is a cheerful place. On the beach I watched a fisherman winching down a boat and read the scrawl on the wall of the public urinal. 'Radiate here'. Picnicking families were worried only about the wind. If it had been coming from the west, they wouldn't have needed their striped canvas shelters, since the grey building would have protected them.

From Ickworth the Undertaker travelled over another portion of green and pleasant land where unwanted wheat was growing. All around for as far as we could see in a 360° arc of vision, the green ground reached to the horizon. At Newmarket, where we greeted with relief the transformation of wheatland into turf, we flew along the sweeps of grass which are the gallops. They are big enough for jumbo jets to land. We hovered and saw some little horses.

'The principal reason for Newmarket's importance as a centre for racing, training and breeding of horses,' wrote Richard Onslow in *The Heath and the Turf*, 'lies in its natural advantages. The Heath that stretches eastward and westward of the town might have been designed by its Creator as a training ground.' Looking down with God's eye you could see why the place has played a part in the Almighty's plans for running horse-races since the days when Boadicea's Iceni warriors ran their chariots here. We flew over Newmarket town and its commemorative clock-tower inscribed with the date 1837 – 'Jubilate Victoria', Ladbrokes, Tattersalls and the National Horse Museum with its pictures of smiling royalty looking up at thoroughbred horses and down on little jockeys.

On the ground I walked past ranks of caravans, cars, tents as big as houses, and parked mobile homes surrounded by flower-pots and gardens. Two elderly women watched an Australian soap opera, a man wearing a Union Jack in the form of a dirty singlet was washing a pair of socks. I passed a caravan which must have housed a French family on holiday, judging by the smells of cooking and coffee. Then a tent where lovers had drawn the flap tightly shut.

In the town I joined the merry circus once more and became a tourist. The guide who drove us around the National Stud had a horsy air himself, as if he was taking time off from training. The bus stopped at the statue of Mill Reef for everyone to get out and take photographs. Then on to photograph the six current stallions, the teaser, and the mares in their paddocks.

'They make take a bite out of you – don't say you haven't been warned.'

Rousillon and Blakeney were grazing away, looking down their aristocratic noses.

'These horses are so well bred that if they could speak, they wouldn't speak to us.'

There was a pause in camera-clicking as the guide offered words of comfort. 'Do you know, you all own a bit of them? Even the teaser? The National Stud belongs to the nation.'

The tour moved on to inspect another piece of its property, Jalmood, another busy, sleek, randy stallion. 'He's a grand old character – cheap at £5,000.' That wasn't the price he might fetch at a sale, merely his covering fee. Already this year he had covered fifty mares and the activity appeared to be doing him good. Next we shuffled over to the foaling unit, the stables with rubber-covered walls and floors, where a young man with red hair, striped shirt and tight corduroy trousers appeared and we were told once again that the National Stud belonged to everybody.

Back in the bus we went to see more, passing by training stables like Ashley Heath, a lot of them decorated with bronze statues of successful horses, a kind of *Good Horsekeeping* seal of approval. An unassuming house and yard: 'That's Lester's. You might think he would live in a castle. But he isn't at all like that.' Lester wasn't yet a fallen angel, and the murmurs were still of admiration and envy. There were plenty more people to envy; David and Jack and Sheikh Talmoud, worth millions. 'If you belong to the inner circle of racing, everyone is equal.'

From the back of the bus: 'What about the lads? How many of them can expect to become famous?'

The guide said, 'About one in a thousand will make it to the top. But that doesn't stop the others. Once you have got into racing, there's no way you will give it up.'

Newmarket was established as a sporting locality in the days of the Stuarts, with coursing, hawking and partridge-shooting. Racing came later. A few decades after the first race-course on the heath was established in 1622, John Evelyn saw 'sweete Turfe and doon like *Salisbery* plaine, the *Jockies* breathing their fine barbs and racers'. In the main street outside the Jockey Club – founded in 1712 – a list tells you the gallops that are open: Choke Jade, Back of the Flat, Long Hill, Summer Gallop. They cover an area of more than 2,000 acres, catering for well over 2,000 horses which are stabled at Newmarket – about 35 per cent of all horses in training in the country. Their number is increasing and the drift is understandable when you realize that Newmarket-trained horses have won six out of the last eight Derbys. The increase creates another problem with overcrowding, since, in spite of technical innovations like Equitrack, a training surface composed of rubber chippings and sand soaked in oil to prevent freezing which costs over £50,000 a furlong, there simply isn't enough grass to accommodate all the aspiring thoroughbreds. On public gallops they have to queue to canter.

They were out just after thin streaks of light turned the sky first gold, then pink. The trainers had them on the gallops by seven o'clock. Hundreds of elegant animals were scattered in silence here and there over the stretches of sweete turf, stable lads perched on their backs, an occasional puff of smoke and spark of flame lighting up the wrinkled little face of some old lad inhaling a dawn cigarette. Plenty of girls were on horseback. A quarter of stable lads are girls who must be prepared to do a man's job, dealing with nervous fast horses, cooped up in stables and allowed out for only an hour a day like men in prison, cleaning, then caring for them, brushing mud off them after morning exercise, polishing hoofs with neatsfoot oil.

There's a Stable Lads' Association which helps to ensure (just) a living wage of around £100 a week. With jackets buttoned up against the wind, crouched down like racing cyclists, their caps making blobs of colour against the trees, thin bodies, small bottoms, bowed legs, clipped on to shining barrels, 999 out of 1,000 programmed for failure. In Newmarket you see them everywhere, gnomes perched on bar stools.

We were flying again, above all those pinched weatherbeaten faces, squeezed dry from dieting, acid-tanned and leathery like men dug up out of bogs. A lot of the horses will be failures too, and the envious will assure you that, like polo ponies, they live with the threat of the dog food tin. We looked down on many horses in a series of views of training stables like toy farms with bright green paddocks and white railings enclosing animals owned by rich men.

Now we had a new problem, which was to avoid flying over Mildenhall and being speared not only by RAF aircraft, but by American planes, some of which are the most spectacular on this globe. The crazy privilege of microlights being allowed to share the sky with war planes and spy planes was taking us into another war zone, where the constant supersonic bangs and charging roar of low-flying jets have replaced bird-song for decades. The tolerance of the people below to the noise-makers in the sky ranging from microlights to Phantom jets is extraordinary. Microlight pilots are forever conscious that they are hated because their role up above is frivolous and the sound they make is horrible. But all aircraft noises are horrible and yet, in any protest or discussion about pollution, noise pollution has a low priority. War planes and passenger planes are accepted with resignation There may even be people who like listening to them. 'The English', wrote a German visitor in 1598, 'are vastly fond of great noises that fill the ear, such a the firing of cannon, drums and the ringing of bells, so that it is common for a number of them, that have got a glass in their heads, to go up into some belfry and ring the bells for hours together for the sake of exercise.'

Military airfields were scattered around us and navigating through them by sight was difficult because there were so few landmarks on the cornfields below. We could only do our best, keeping an eye out as we cruised at around fifty miles an hour. I told myself it was very unlikely that we would collide with oncoming traffic.

As Graham made a safe turn, I could see the enormous runway of Mildenhall to the east, a name now known not so much for its silver treasure but more for giant planes painted white with swept-back wings. Even from a great distance they looked intimidating. At the base, Little America housed servicemen and their families. A plump officer smoking a cigar, his name tag reading HENDERSON US AIRFORCE, parked his car outside the Four Seasons' Shopette, careful to pick the right place among the special parking spots for senior officers, GENERAL OFFICER, WING COMMANDER, COLONEL . . . Down the road more servicemen in battle fatigues sat down to fast food in the cafeteria. It was not these people, ready to help blow up the world at a moment's notice, casually accepting family life in rural East Anglia, who were the strangest to see. It was the group of plane-spotters, carrying books and binoculars to identify and make a note of some of the most awesome aircraft ever to have been assembled. Were they Eastern bloc sympathizers spying out secrets from the new public viewing gallery which had opened only this year? This group of tourists and pilgrims had a schoolboy look in common. In countries like Greece they would be put in prison.

A bird-control van swept down the runway as a curtain raiser. Soon the jets took off one by one. First a big four-engined plane taxied up, then behind it a KC10 fuel tanker. In the viewing area viewers noted down the US Airforce Registration. Two Five Three Six One. They consulted Jane's *Aircraft Recognition Handbook* with its end-on and side-view silhouettes and hints on recognition. They spotted a girl in a bright red dress waving out of the high cockpit window.

'I wonder who she is?'

'Perhaps she's the pilot's moll, and he's giving her a joy-ride.'

'Lucky girl.' But they were not interested in her. They listened to the jets of the KC10 whine and watched the wheels rumble as it lumbered into the blue sky. Next came a giant Galaxy and, in addition to Jane's, they looked up their essential *United States Aircraft* series.

'That's the biggest plane in the world!' The microlight would rattle around in its nose cone. The Galaxy was indeed a monster but it did not generate the pitch of excitement that greeted the next aircraft. There was joy at the appearance of the Blackbird spy plane, which was what everyone had been waiting for.

'Brilliant!'

'She'll do Mach Three!'

'When she takes off, it's like an earthquake.'

'Gosh! Perhaps she's going to Russia or Libya!'

The earth shook, the engines bellowed and the thin elongated shape leaped like a black dart into the sky to go off and photograph other men's secrets. Meanwhile, not far away, two grown men, tightly curled up one behind the other, were jogging along in a microlight.

The sun was shining and we moved through the big blue dome disturbing the peace in our small way. Beneath us was more of the nightmare harvest silting up Europe. Scribbled wheelmarks of giant machines, straight lines and curves, stretched and looped through yet another tree-less, bird-less, hedge-less stretch of EEC grain.

Richard Jefferies described a long-gone handsome harvest: 'the golden wheat, glorious under the summer sun. Bright poppies flower in the depths and convolvulus climbs the stalks. Butterflies float slowly over the yellow surface as they might over a lake in colour.' In the nineteenth century, East Anglian farms produced about sixteen hundredweight of wheat per acre; in 1985 the fertilized yield was over sixty hundredweight per acre.

Over the Broads the canals appeared to us like thin lines of dark glass. They were flowing with boats, luxurious motor cruisers, sailing boats, the odd old-style wherry, whose rusty brown sails cut the skies, and tourist boats pulling away from little piers. Skippers in yachting caps with gold braid were telling jokes to women in summer dresses.

Those who were brought up reading Arthur Ransome will remember his account of an early alliance of local Norfolk boys and middle-class children against the vulgar world of the new motor cruisers. The awful noisy *Margoletta* sitting on a coot's nest seemed to proclaim a new age and heralded the ghetto blaster. 'All the Hullabaloos were down below in the two cabins, and in one cabin there was a wireless set and a loudspeaker, and in the other they were working a gramophone.'

But the summer invasion began long before the 1930s when Arthur Ransome wrote *Coot Club*. A tourist handbook of 1890 noted how 'a large trade has arisen in the letting of yachts, boats and pleasure wherries for cruising purposes; but the inn accommodation has made little advance and is still too meagre and insufficient for the demand'.

At the turn of the century, it was considered that the locals were a surly lot who misbehaved, while the newcomers added distinction to the scene. When the trains began to bring in urban visitors, the tourists were thought of as being 'educated people with a due sense of law and order', while the 'home product' was guilty of numerous petty crimes, being 'coot potters, swans' eggs robbers and grebe destroyers; the persons who use one's boathouse as luncheon rooms or dustbins'.

As more and more holiday-makers poured into the Broads, hand-books and guidebooks were suggesting unofficial rules for good behaviour.

Do not, in the neighbourhood of other yachts and houses, indulge in songs and revelry after eleven pm at regatta times . . . Young men who lounge in a nude state in boats while ladies are passing (and I have known Norfolk youths to do this) may be saluted with dust shot or the end of a quent . . . do not throw straw or papers overboard to leeward and become offensive; but burn or take care to sink all rubbish . . . remember that sound travels a long way on the water, and do not criticize the people you may encounter with too loud a voice . . . don't go on a friend's yacht with nailed shoes . . . ladies, please don't gather armfuls of flowers, don't play the piano in season and don't turn out before eight o'clock in the morning, when other yachts are near.

The list presumed middle-class pastimes, the well-to-do in search of leisure.

The wind rustled the flags and bunting, twisted the leaves, made the water ripple and blew on the nose of the trike, keeping us almost stationary. The Undertaker's sharp buzz was a new coot-scarer. We were brand new Hullabaloos, poisoning the air around a silver grove of willow, an ancient windmill. We noted successive triangular sails of moving yachts with names like *Wild Wind* or *Concordia*, and a group of little people sitting and lying on a bank. When I looked closely I made out their tiny matchbox-sized picnic hamper, minute thermos and button plates. Another picnic party, a third, a fourth, a fifth . . .

Here are the Broads in the summer of 1903:

A scene of utter loneliness . . . a scene wild enough to enchain the imagination of man . . . The footpaths along the river walks are nearly hidden by tall drooping grasses. Many of the dykes are choked with hemlocks, frogbits and marshwort – from the marshes the shrill sound of scythes whetting and the metallic murmur of mowing machines are heard from early morn till dusk, and a fresh fragrance – the sweet scent of new mown hay . . . is in the air.

I continued to feel a new wave of guilt about polluting the sky, which I would try to modify by thinking about all the other aircraft and, further out, all the satellites that have accumulated around our atmosphere. The only airborne vehicles that have lessened in numbers during the past decades are flying saucers and UFOs, whose incidence has sharply decreased since the introduction of satellites, in the same way as ghosts became less common after electric light came in. Twenty years ago flying saucers were hardly ever out of the news. They seem to have begun as a prolonged scare in June 1947, when an American businessman spotted a chain of unfamiliar saucer shapes swerving in and out of mountain peaks, flat as pie pans, and shiny, reflecting the sun like a mirror. After that, flying saucers were reported all over the place. Many made noises, a deep organ-like note, a phenomenon noted by Steven Spielberg. In 1952 a fleet of them flew over Washington and was recorded on radar. The US Airforce was requested not to shoot at what might be a friendly intelligence from Space and a radio station gave them a warm greeting and directed them to land on a special airfield. Over the years thousands of UFOs were reported, many attributed to fireballs, meteors, temperature inversions, hoaxes, balloons, sun haloes and the Northern Lights. Even now a steady trickle rides the sky among the satellites to trouble us.

I met a sculptor in the United States who designed mobiles which he intended to plant in Space. His plan was to send them up by rocket and spawn them among the stars so that we could see them spinning from down here. Fortunately, he has not got around to it yet.

Down here, above the Broads, in spite of guilt, there was delight in flight. Oliver St John Gogarty, who flew a neat little private plane during the 1920s, recommended flying for its health-giving effect. 'Even though the danger of flying is becoming more and more illusionary every day, I would prescribe it for many kinds of nervous cases, or rather, cases of nerves. I am glad to see that women are rushing to learn.'

Graham had been in Norfolk before, but I still admired his navigational skills, as somewhere among the network of the Broads and the acres of arable land he picked out a small airfield. Sutton Meadows was used by the Cambridge Microlight Club, and a few of their machines were parked outside a small hut. They were the first microlights I had seen since leaving Wiltshire; in our semicircular tour of southern and eastern England we had not encountered one other. Perhaps they are rare: there may be hope for England yet.

Here at Sutton Meadows the menace was recognized by a notice pinned to the door of the hut which warned: 'Important. Because of complaints about lack of privacy and noise, please avoid villages, towns and swimming-pools by as large a margin as possible.' Why swimming-pools in particular? Were the echoes worse, or did pilots tend to swoop down for a closer look at girls in bikinis?

We had coffee and refuelled, although perhaps 'refuelling' is too grand a term for pouring a few teacupfuls of the sacred mix into our engine. The microlight fraternity is small and has the close relationship of other specialist sports. Graham knew the man who ran the club, who was also an instructor, and, like all instructors, had some glamour attached to his persona. I tried not to find his conversation tedious, the chat about speed, sailplanes, Section S Certification work, cruising speeds, fuel capacities, Chasers, Pegasus, Medway Microlights, Hornet Ravens, CFM Shadows, High Noise Attentuation Headsets, Sky-trikes, Hiway Demons, trikes, trikes. There were leading flyers and their endless exploits to be discussed. The latest batch of records was gone over in detail. Flying around England and Ireland was humdrum. There were all the changes and developments in micro-light technology to be gone though. I was an outsider, Graham's passenger.

At last the Undertaker was airborne again and we flew from the Broads towards the Wash, light and colours changing and merging into a milky sky as the bright sunshine we had enjoyed an hour ago was replaced by misty reflections. Another Turner where sky, sea and earth met with the dissolving imprecisions that he loved. 'You should tell him that indistinctness is my forte,' he said of a complaining customer seeking precise lines.

During the Second World War, this route across the Wash was a flight path for thousands of pilots making for Germany. Among them 617 Squadron came this way to go east and bomb the Moehne and Eder dams. Paul Brickhill described their flight in *The Dam Busters*:

> Gibson slid over the Wash at a hundred feet . . . The sun astern of the quarter threw long shadows on fields, peaceful and fresh with spring crops; dead ahead the moon was swimming out of the ground haze like a bull's-eye . . . The haze of Norfolk passed a few

miles to port. In the nose Spafford said, 'There's the sea,' and a minute later they were low over Southwold, the shingle was beneath them, and then they were over the water, flat and grey in the evening light. England faded behind.

The operation was a close-run thing. The bouncing mines, still warm to the touch because they had been filled only that day, were delivered at midnight on 13 May 1943. At 3 pm on 15 May the airmen learned of their target; they set off in the twilight at 9.10 pm on Sunday 16 May on Operation Chastise, when the Moehne and Eder dams were breached and water spread for miles through the Ruhr engulfing railway lines, a power station and factories. Of nineteen Lancasters involved in the raid, eight were lost and two more badly damaged, and 53 men died out of a total of 133 who set off in the Lincolnshire dusk. Ghosts are part of the crowded sky.

Below were the golden beaches of Holme, and eastward along the coast Snettisham and its mudflats stretching out into the bay, looking mysterious and sinister, perhaps because they were spared caravans and chalets. The moving speckled patterns of flocks of birds' wings catching the light in unison and changing colour as they changed direction, crossed and recrossed dark brown furrows of mud and shining banks of shingle. Trees made a background to massed oyster-catchers, curlews, common gulls, dunlin and others.

The fluted medieval lantern tower of Boston Stump rose up. From the air 'stump' seemed a fair description and it may have been the same for sailors and travellers taking their bearings from a distance across the marshes and flat land around Boston. Over the centuries, complaints have been constant as to why such a lovely building should be given such an ugly name.

William Stukeley's notebook of 1707 gives an account of the origin of the Stump:

Records tell us, Anno 1309, in the 3rd year of Edward 2nd. On the Munday after Palm Sunday the Miners began to digg the foundations of Boston Steeple at Midsummer following they were gott 9 foot below the Havens bottom, where they found a bed of stone, upon one of sand which lay upon a bed of clay whose thickness could not be found. The Munday following St John Baptists day was laid the first stone by Dame Margery Tilney.

Perhaps the name goes back to the seventy-year period during which the steeple was in the process of construction. The height of the tower to the top of its weathervanes is 272 feet, while the total area of St Botolph's church of which the Stump is the tower is more than 20,000 square feet, making it the largest parish church in England. Over the years Bostonians in America have kept their eye on the old church; and contributed money for its upkeep and improvement. The connection goes back to the Pilgrim Fathers. In 1630, ten years after the sailing of the *Mayflower*, a group of Boston citizens who had missed out on the initial voyage because they had been thrown into prison for their religious beliefs, sailed over to New England and founded a separate colony which they called after their home town.

We flew past the tower with its peal of bells dedicated in 1932 and recast with American money, over the market square with its statue of Herbert Ingram, founder of the *Illustrated London News*. A wedding group was being photographed – a flurry of pastel colours and movement. Everyone down there was going to get wet.

These were wet damp clouds that smelt of ocean waves although before they crossed the sea they had come out of Europe. A ridge of high pressure, formed in Poland or perhaps the distant Ukraine, had disintegrated as it crossed the Alps. The only way to escape these soft clouds was to descend very low below cloud level to view Lincolnshire at close quarters, flat as a board, without the slight undulations that marked the flatness of East Anglia. We would have to land. 'When the skies are filled with black vapours, when fog and sand and sea are confounded in a brew in which they become indistinguishable – the pilot purges of these phantoms in a single stroke.' Skimming over hedges and fields and over roadways whistling with traffic we found a farmer's field with Friesian cattle at one end and a two-storey building and yard.

Before that we had almost smelt fish and chips in the air. We had caught sight of Skegness and saw the sea and the sand and the line of gravestones that seemed to make a melancholy highway leading to that cheerful town. They were the tops of caravans and trailers – hundreds upon hundreds parked side by side in one long, nearly endless line facing the sullen North Sea, a great cemetery stretching in an arc from Skegness along the Lincolnshire coast and around the Wash. It skipped Gibraltar Point and its nature reserves. Conservationists hate caravans but you had to admire the hardiness of the people who came and stayed in them for their holidays.

Nothing prepared me for Skeggy, not even the caravans. The flat lands of Lincolnshire were not the setting where I imagined seaside holidays flourished in a traditional English combination of sea, sand and a vile climate.

'Wind SE Force Five.
Cloud amount 8.9.
Humidity 93.'

Every evening someone chalked up the weather in a shop window, a depressing daily ritual. Skegness is a durable gutsy resort where sunshine comes as a surprise. A few weeks ago there had been a couple of days which had been blazing hot (where had I been then?) and the *Skegness News* had celebrated with banner headlines and bouncing copy:

Phew! Suddenly it was the Costa del Skeggy as summer came blazing in on Sunday. In fact super Skegness was one of the globe's hotspots, warmer than Lisbon (75 degrees) Casablanca (77 degrees) and even Las Palmas (76 degrees)!

Since then weather reports had assumed their usual sad quality. People in deck-chairs maintained a touching faith in sun tan lotion which you could smell along with the chips.

This part of the coast caters for people coming from the Midlands and South Yorkshire, among whom is a relatively new category of holiday-maker, blacks and browns taking a break from inner city life. Skeggy's survival, which borders on prosperity, is an unexpected triumph. Bernard Levin has observed incorrectly that 'when the Midlands car workers found that the sun shone through all the summer on the Costa Brava and they could get a drink there whenever they wanted one, the seaside landlady was doomed.' Not so. The majority may be deserting the English seaside for the sun but there are still those who manage to enjoy English boarding-houses.

Today, in the chill of midsummer, holiday-makers shuffled along slowly in a daze, bewitched by the lines of Bingo parlours beckoning them with twinkling lights, and amusement arcades crammed with video games and gaming machines that greeted them every few yards along the front. There is no pier at Skegness any more; the great pier, 1,843 feet long, which had contributed to Skeggy's fame, was destroyed by gales in 1978. Around its stump they have built a Lunar Park which is full of movement every summer's day, wet or fine. And there were donkey rides on the beach, hotels called Grand, Savoy and Chatsworth, while the boarding-house windows proclaimed NO VACANCIES as the normal winter population of about 5,000 was swollen to 15,000. And thousands of others poured in for the day.

Good old fish and chips. Smells of batter and frying mixed with the maritime ozone of high summer were trapped below the cloud cover and a new haze, smoke from chip pans, spread over the rooftops. All the angels were singing while people dipped into their greasy bags for cod and chips, haddock and chips, plaice and chips. Those who wanted to vary their diet could chew Skeggy Rock or munch freshly made doughnuts or have as an appetizer a delicious plateful of local cockles and oysters.

I sent vulgar postcards to my loved ones, finding one in particular with a verse that summed up the spirit of summer in Skegness:

> No food to cook, no washing up,
> No daily chores to do!
> Enjoying yourself? I'll say I am –
> I ask you – wouldn't you?

Majorca and Costa del Sol, eat your heart out!

Three miles south at the northern edge of the Wash, Gibraltar Point appeared from the air as a corner of patchwork, sand dunes, marsh and trees, bounded by a golf course and a stretch of humpy sand that was strange to the eye which had become accustomed to the endless open-zip line of caravans winding unceasingly around the edges of Lincolnshire.

Gibraltar Point National Nature Reserve is a reflection of the impotence of conservationists. A tiny square of 1,000 acres, the area of one good-sized farm, saved from the caravans, is heralded as a triumph of salvation.

The wedge of flat salt-marsh and sand blending almost imperceptibly into the darker edges of sea is all that remains of a vast stretch of a hundred miles of tidal swamps and meres. A century ago this part of the shifting Lincolnshire coastline, best known for Jean Ingelow's glum ballad ('And yet he moaned beneath his breath, "O come in life, or come in death! O lost! my love, Elizabeth"') boasted the largest area of wildlife in England, which shrank to one small corner containing a tumbledown inn known as Gibraltar House, Sykes Farm, whose name has a nice sinister touch, and a coastguard station which ceased to be efficient when the sand piled up between it and the sea.

In the 1930s Gibraltar Point had an air of desolation, romance and dereliction which had to be tidied up. At first pressures of population and opportunities for development threatened to transform the dunes into a new seaside town to rival Skegness. One suggestion was for a 'Wash Speedway' linking Gibraltar Point to Boston twenty miles away. It was a triumph of the good that the point was saved for larks, whitethroats, linnets, redstarts, goldcrest, coots, moorhen and dabchick – nothing very unusual, just ordinary birds.

In Ireland we have been spoilt for wild coastline. Never anxious to learn, we are joyfully scattering bungalows along the sea-shore, preferably in the most beautiful places. However, there is still space beside the sea to qualify for that loaded adjective 'unspoilt', and there is not yet a sense of a wild sea-coast being rationed. Here in Lincolnshire I felt surprise and sadness that such enormous efforts are necessary to save so little – that every piece of coastal wildness has to be fought for, or bought, or acquired by the National Trust, or reserved for the army, or owned by the Prince of Wales.

In Skegness they were pulling one-armed bandits and flocking into the Bingo parlours while only three miles away a different crowd entirely was ringing the lesser whitethroat or sitting on some (fairly) lonely dune with notebook and binoculars, engaged in what was called a sea watch – naming and identifying little birds. In autumn at peak migration times when there were more unusual species, serious ornithologists would flock in to monitor the numbers and movements of migrants, trap them in the funnels of their Heligoland traps and ring them with very light alloy rings. It takes nearly as long to become an experienced ringer and learn not to break yellow stick-legs, as to become a microlight pilot.

A field station, a visitors' centre and the Wash Viewpoint with a ramp for wheelchairs invite individual naturalists, organized groups from schools, colleges and universities, natural history societies and ordinary visitors, including a few from Skegness. A lot of people come here and expect a sort of safari park or mini-Gibraltar. They associate the name with apes. Some visitors end up disappointed. The birds are so ordinary, the plants so commonplace.

Gibraltar Point lack the pzazz of Slimbridge and the inspired publicity. Here things are low key and most visitors are earnest and informed. They go in search of different species, looking among the stones on the beach for lamp-shells, devil's toenails and belemnites, the fossilized internal skeletons of squid. They walk among the ragwort, rose-bay willow-herb, hound's tongue, viper's bugloss, hawthorn and sea buckthorn. They go from the Spit to the foreshore to the west dunes to the new salt-marsh to the car park.

The Rattle Bag had a poem, there attributed to Hugh MacDiarmid:

> I found a pigeon's skull on the machair,
> All the bones pure white and dry, and chalky,
> But perfect,
> Without a crack or a flaw anywhere.
>
> At the back, rising out of the bleak,
> Were domes like bubbles of thin bone,
> Almost transparent, where the brain had been
> That fixed the tilt of the wings.

Gibraltar Point is a jewel, a breathing-hole, a beautiful oasis. But so small.

The east wind had become sharper and, back on the beach at Skegness, a preacher from the United Christians stood on a box and gave a quick harangue.

'If we build our lives on sand it will trickle away. Right now is the opportunity to change all that.'

He was watched by brave souls wrapped in coats and a girl wearing a hat saying SEX APPEAL – GIVE GENEROUSLY. Behind him the Swinging Pirate Ship swung and queues for the Dodgems, the Jungle Ride and the Zylon lengthened. He shivered as the wind scurried across the sand, the adam's apple in his raw neck resembling the red sac of a frigate bird. In the comfort of the County Hotel, the mayor of a Spanish seaside town, together with his wife, was being officially entertained by civic dignitaries. They were just setting out to visit the Skegness Rock Factory, no doubt to get ideas for the Costa del Sol.

We were flying, out over flat stretches of Lincolnshire. There are over 12,000 square miles of fens where once ancient shifting waters rolled southward as far as Cambridge and westward as far as Bedford. Silt accumulated over hundreds of thousands of years and gave fertility. Drainage and the help of a few Dutchmen decided the age-old quarrel between the oozing waters and the wet lands which were finally defeated and made ready for harvest.

The open fields contain some of the best agricultural land in England, where spuds and winter wheat are the principal crops, and vegetables flourish. Lincolnshire farms grow cauliflowers that compete with French cauliflowers, produce acre after acre of sprouts, cabbages and courgettes, wait on the whim of supermarkets, and employ gangs of labourers from Sheffield at £10 a day to come down and pick, cut, strip pea vines and prepare vegetables laid out on giant trays for freezers. They grow daffodil bulbs and tulip bulbs for garden centres and they are as colourful as anything coming from Holland. But the people who own the land on the coast have the best crop. Around some caravan parks lines of national flags waved in the same wind that tormented the United Christians' preacher and was striving to blow us inland.

At Sutton on Sea and Mablethorpe only the bravest were playing Crazy Golf or walking around the public garden where the plastic pink bunnies would terrify the intemperate. For a space the caravans changed to lines of beach huts along the front looking like carriages of a toy train. Cold weather and empty beaches mocked all summer plans and here was none of the spirit of Skegness.

Young Alfred Tennyson used to come here with his parents to enjoy the invigorating sea air. Infused with a wayward romantic spirit, he wrote in a spirit of nostalgia about Mablethorpe B.C. (Before Caravans):

> Here often, when a child, I lay reclined,
> I took delight in this fair strand and free;
> Here stood the infant Ilion of the mind,
> And here the Grecian ships did seem to be.
> And here again I come, and only find
> The drain-cut levels of the marshy lea, –
> Grey sandbanks, and pale sunsets – dreary wind,
> Dim shores, dense rains, and heavy-clouded sea.

Young Tennyson used to stand on a sand ridge near Mablethorpe 'and think that it was the spine bone of the world. On the other side of the land at low tide there was an immeasurable waste of sand and clay.' Holiday-makers were already coming; Tennyson's son recorded the reaction of a local fisherman to visitors to Mablethorpe:

> Nottingham and Lincoln foak mosstly coom ere . . . a vast sight of 'em soon taimine [time] they saays it is might dool plaace with a deal of sand ecod tare isn't now band nor pier like; but howsoever the wind blows the poor things a bit, and they washes their bodies i' the waiives.

No one was swimming today. A small plane skidded past us and the pilot waggled his wings. How warm and snug he must have been in his enclosed cabin, as he moved upwards and vanished into a grey shadowy bank of clouds. Microlights, keeping below cloud cover because of the danger that their fragile structures will be destroyed in billowing cloud movements, miss one of the great experiences of flying.

Flying through clouds and above clouds has always exhilarated pilots: David Garnett described the sensation as a soulless disembodied dream. Richard Hillary found a fairy city: 'I dived along a grand canyon; the sun threw the reddish shadow of the plane on the cotton-wool walls of a white cliff that towered up on every side. It was intoxicating.' Pilots still feel a special delight at breaking through the clouds. An RAF pilot was quoted in the *Daily Telegraph* in February 1988: 'I've been flying for twenty-two years now but I still get the same thrill as when I first started. On a terrible rainy day you get airborne and break out after 2,000 feet into the sunshine above the cloud, and you can't help thinking how much luckier you are than the 57 million others on the ground.'

> Oh! I have slipped the surly bonds of earth
> And danced the skies on laughter-silvered wings;
> Sunward I've climbed, and joined the tumbling mirth
> Of sun-split clouds – and done a hundred things
> You have not dreamed of – wheeled and soared and swung
> High in the sunlit silence. Hov'ring there,

I've chased the shouting wind along and flung
My eager craft through footless halls of air.
> (From *Wings of War*, ed. by Laddie Lucas)

John Gillespie Magee, a young American flying with the Canadian Air Force, wrote about flying through the clouds shortly before he was killed somewhere near here in a flying accident at the age of nineteen in 1941. Ronald Reagan quoted 'surly bonds of earth' in his speech after Challenger blew up. (In the same poem Magee wrote of 'the high untrespassed sanctity of space', not a phrase that would find rapport with air traffic control half a century later.) The experience of breaking through cloud cover is commonplace now and how few air passengers glancing out of windows feel rapture at the great white views of clouds shining under the sun. Progress has degraded a magical experience.

The wind had changed and become a strong tailwind, increasing our speed as we flew towards Grimsby and the Humber. We had to fly very low because of poor visibility; if there had been hedges, this would have been hedge-hopping. The occasional villages, farms, barns, a country house, flashed past under our belly like the images of motor bikes and cars I had watched children guide on video games in Skeggy. They put their money in and grabbed a wheel or handle, and a road on the screen would uncurl with rapidity. Here are motor bikes coming towards you. Crash! A star lights up, you have hit one, and you lose some points. Height not only gives a margin of safety if things go wrong, but allows the observer to distinguish landmarks on the countryside as aids to navigation. This is visual reckoning. Flying low confuses the senses and makes identifiable features pass in a meaningless blur. It is a basic part of training air force jets to evade radar.

Rain began to fall, so that flying low was not only dangerous but uncomfortable. Over Grimsby and its empty docks we flew in bitter smoke spuming up and hitting the cloud. Since we did not fancy the idea of being ducked in the Humber, or asphyxiated, or bumping into a factory chimney, it was time to come down out of the grey northern Lowry skyscape.

We began what had become a routine of looking out for a school playground and, among Grimsby's sprawling suburbs, we found our football field and came in low over terraces of houses and people on shining pavements looking up from under umbrellas. The Undertaker's long tapering yellow and blue wing cut across the grey sky as we landed on the grass, turned at right angles to the goal posts and taxied through the rain up to the red brick buildings of the school. We prised ourselves out of our seats and sought shelter. All the doors were shut and there was nothing to do except go back and stand under the dripping wing.

Some children rode up on bicycles and watched us as the rain poured down.

'Does it really take two?'

'How much does it cost?'

'Did you crash?'

'Where are you going?'

'Ireland.' We might as well have said the South Pole. 'DON'T TOUCH THE WING.'

They stood in a dripping group, reluctant to leave us. A man in an ankle-length raincoat, carrying an umbrella, came over leading a shaggy black dog on a lead, which got sadder and wetter as he talked. Why was it so irritating that he insisted on discussing the weather?

'You're going to be there quite a while. Terrible forecast. Nothing good for tomorrow either. The satellite picture had England blotted out. Only place to be is in the Hebrides, the cloud missed that. I don't know when it's going to take up. Every day there's rain and, if you are unlucky, thunder and lightning. We had a terrible storm the other day. Terrible. Terrible summer it's been. You're going to be there quite a while . . .'

We assented as the rain came down. From a tall chimney nearby came a flow of pale yellow smoke. The children rode away, the man and the dog moved off. We stood there for two hours without talking.

> When clouds appear like rocks and towers
> The earth's refreshed by frequent showers.

When the rain stopped and we were possessed with the urge to escape, we ignored the rising bags of cirro-cumulus. It was after five o'clock. Buckle in, petrol on, choke half open, a sharp pull and the engine starts. Face into the wind towards the terrace of Victorian cottages at the end of the games field and, before you have more doubts, let her rip. How quickly she gathered speed over the sodden grass, making playful hops that merged into bigger kangaroo leaps. Graham pushed out the control bar and, with one bound, the Undertaker broke free. She slid upwards cleanly over the rooftops and TV aerials, and the little football field, where we had spent the last two hours, was behind us.

I smelt smoke as we flew through polluting clouds that rose up from the industrial estate along the Humber. Our idea was to fly down to the Humber Bridge and cross into Yorkshire. The clouds had come down again, the far shore had vanished in a haze and a thin ghostly mist covered the ground we were flying over. Once again Graham's navigation was miraculous, as an instinct for preservation made him fly blindly, seeking out a long-deserted wartime airfield marked on our map. Then we found it, a few scrappy dark lines that made up the runway, the black shape of a long-disused hangar and an abandoned control tower looming out of the ground. As we came down to land I could see how in some places the main runway had vanished under corn and elsewhere was pockmarked with black marks that were little craters. We avoided some high-tension cables, lined up on a stretch that didn't look too bad and came in. I wondered if anyone had landed here since the end of the war.

CHAPTER NINE

Yorkshire

Nobody was about, and the place was silent except for the wind. The rusty reminders were there, the control tower with its metal windows still swinging open, the skeleton of a water-tower, some old Nissen huts, hangars and runways leading hither and thither. This was Goxhill, once a base of the 52nd Fighter Group of the US Eighth Air Force.

Barry Penrose has observed: 'Have you ever stood in the centre of a deserted runway? If you have, you know that the most striking thing about it is that it is so quiet. Airports have come to be synonymous for noise and activity but even the runways of an international airport are frozen in silence – the runway is quiet as a cathedral is quiet.' If there is such a thing as ghosts, they will be in places like these, reflecting past tensions, action, fear and boredom of waiting to go out to fight or bomb. Here, as elsewhere in eastern England, echoes of recent history reverberated in the emptiness. Like battlefields, these ruinous airbases retain ripples of violence and death. Their fate has varied but even when they have been dug up and destroyed they leave their traces in the earth like Roman roads or neolithic field systems and, no doubt, archae-ologists of the future will be able to trace the runways of the 1940s.

American airmen were housed at numerous airfields in eastern England – Bovingdon, Polebrook, Atcham, Westhampnett, Milden-hall, Molesworth and dozens of others. Seventy-nine thousand lost their lives in the European war. Later in the year I went back to eastern England to a village in Suffolk where I had stayed for many months when I was eighteen. I talked to a farmer whose memories of Metfield were older than mine. 'Sometimes, I go out in the middle of the field near the old runway and I can still see the planes coming in after a raid over Germany. Liberators. Superforts. The roar of their engines used to make the houses shake.'

All the time I had flown over Suffolk I had never given a thought to Metfield, even though the microlight had flown within a few miles of the place. Now, landing here at Goxhill and seeing the huts and hangars, I was suddenly reminded of months of misery.

After a boyhood spent in neutral Ireland, I joined the RAF in 1946. My first attempt to learn to fly came to nothing since this was not a period when pilots were needed. In an age of austerity, flying was cut down and the time I spent at Metfield during the icy winter of 1946 was my first experience of being grounded. The departing American airmen had left their pin-ups on the curving walls of the Nissen huts. In the pitted runway at Goxhill I recalled the boredom, the square-bashing and the cold of those mindless postwar months, the feeling of futility and lost opportunity. The action was over and I had missed it. The cold had to be endured – there was never anything as cold as that winter in the windy wastes of Suffolk.

When I returned to Metfield I found that most of it had disappeared after the runways were taken up in 1966 and sold for hard core. The frightful Nissen huts, the messes and wooden buildings which had housed much distress, the gates, fences and barbed wire left little trace, while ripened corn covered the places where the runways had been. You would need a summer of drought in order to see once again the changes in the disturbed ground which would leave their faint traces for centuries, perhaps for ever.

Metfield has an ancient history with a parish church dating back to the thirteenth century and it is appropriate that the aerodrome was a passing moment in its long life. The name Metfield means 'the mowed clearing'. All that remained were memories, not only my own dour recollections but more colourful moments of half a century ago that people still talked about. The bomb dump that went up in 1944 and threw up a column of smoke like the atom bomb. The Thunderbolt fighter that had come down near the village, slicing a horse in two – the pilot had injured only his nose. The Liberator, Lucky Penny, which was ill named – it had feathered one of its propellers and crashed, killing the crew. At Metfield they remember the names of those lumbering old bomb-carriers, Papa's Persuader, Pink Lady, Secret Delight, Sweet Liquidator. And the Yanks who had all the money and got all the girls.

'We used to collect their garbage and you could live on the amount of food they threw out and wasted.'

Occasionally groups of old American airmen came back to Suffolk and wandered among the places where the runways used to be, looking for traces of the past, some rusted gate, a solitary Nissen hut covered in ivy, a blistered hangar, standing out among the cornfields. At Goxhill much more has been preserved and returning Americans could easily evoke wartime memories. The runway might be pot-holed but it is there and we had been able to land on it. We moved round, peering into hangars, looking for somewhere to park. Our tiny machine hobbling along the broken tarmac was a mocking echo of past heroics. And again, ghosts were evoked, young faces in a window gazing out in disbelief, rosters of pilots in their leather jackets waiting to be called to escort bombers causing havoc in German cities.

The hangars were filled with agricultural machinery. We pushed our way through them looking for space among the tractors, combine harvesters, grass cutters, ploughs, sprayers, forklifts and trucks that were accommodated there. We managed to squeeze the trike behind a rusty harrow and thrust the wing under the empty control tower.

Now we had the problem of finding a bed for the night. We left the dismembered microlight and began walking down the runway and out on to a country road. A mile down we came across a pub and a small railway station.

'Any chance of a bed?'

'There's naught in the village,' said the girl behind the bar, peering without curiosity at the intrepid birdmen. A northern phrase – we were well above the line that crosses England from the Severn to the Wash. In Skeggy I had seen the gritty determination of northerners to enjoy themselves come what may but they were there temporarily on holiday. Here real life had begun. We still had to find somewhere to sleep. The little station produced a train that took us to Barton upon Humber where we had the usual monosyllabic meal in a small Italian restaurant. Graham and I had not exchanged more than thirty words in a week. Now he did speak.

'You should get yourself a pair of glasses,' he ventured, watching me struggle to decipher the microscopic print of the menu in the flickering candle-light. 'I don't know how you dare to fly.'

We found a hotel. Next morning the weather forecast was doubtful. There were ominous lows hanging over much of northern England as the summer went through its predictable course. The Gujerati in the paper shop near the Humber Bridge told me he had been woken by thunder and lightning during the night. What did he think of living in England so far from the sun?

'It's not a bad place, but the people are very dirty.' He pointed in disgust to bits of paper flying around the street.

Outside the railway station an old tramp lay on a patch of grass clasping a bottle. We left the stately profile of the Humber Bridge, took a train back to Goxhill and checked that the microlight was still hidden away at the airfield. The rain had stopped and overhead the sky was black and soggy.

'What do you think?'

Graham didn't reply.

By eleven o'clock a few bright specks appeared in the general gloom. Should we risk it? Count ten, go for a pee, walk up and down reciting poetry. The decision hung in the air, as usual balanced by two urgent motives – the need to escape and the reluctance to kill ourselves. The sky was overcast again.

We hung around dressing and undressing in flying-suits and helmets. At one time there was a bustle of activity when a man driving a tractor and a few workmen came over to inspect us as we were putting on our helmets. But the wind blew steadily, a stiff north-easter originating in Russia.

An hour later we took off, pushed perhaps by boredom.

There was danger even on the ground. On these runways, fallen into disuse, a constant hazard was the loose stones and jagged pieces of soft broken tarmac lying on the ground waiting to be thrown up. The body of the microlight was shoulder high and it would take only a small stone or black fragment to leap up and break, say, the tip of the wooden propeller. The propeller always seemed the most vulnerable part of the machine and I was conscious less of the idea that it could do us an injury but that to obtain a new propeller would cost more than I wanted to pay. The small triangular piece of polished wood might have been carved by Grinling Gibbons.

From Goxhill we followed the brown Humber down to the bridge which on the overcast morning had a compelling beauty. If a Martian came to inspect England he would be as struck by these majestic towers and loops of steel and wire as we would by any cathedral. As we flew by I could see sandbanks glittering like diamonds, cars filing across and factories and industrial estates spreading downriver from

Hull. On the far side a quarry had taken a raw amber slice out of a green hill. We crossed another motorway, the M62. England's roads are almost the most crowded in the world. We wouldn't be able to travel much longer, since, once again, a choked overcast sky was forcing us down. Soon we sought shelter, and Graham found another abandoned airfield with runways silted over in grass and black painted hangars emerging out of the gloom.

As we landed a rumble of thunder echoed over the runway, followed by a flash of lightning. Then another sound of thunder as a low-flying group of half a dozen RAF jets passed over our heads, leaving us to ponder what would have been the chances of a collision if we had still been airborne. We watched them loop across the sullen grey sky in a tight 'V' formation before seeking shelter in a shed filled with half-mouldy grain. There were smells of damp and mould as we sat listening to the drum of rain on the metal roof; Graham reading his magazine, myself wishing to God I had brought something else to read besides Pushkin.

> Tatanya dearly loved romancing
> Upon her balcony alone
> Just as the stars had left off dancing
> When dawn's first ray had barely shown.

Much of the next rain-filled hours were spent worrying. Today we had flown thirty or forty miles at the most. Would it ever lift? How long would we be delayed? Graham had a limited time to get me to Ireland and, as the thunder rolled and lightning lit up the sky, there seemed no reason to believe that we would ever move out of here.

Richard Bach wrote:

> The sky does not understand,
> The sky does not judge.
> The sky very simply is . . .

At five o'clock the rain ceased drumming on the tin and we emerged from our shelter to look up. The thunder had ceased and it was not raining just that minute, but the sky was filled with bullish black clouds. Graham shook his head.

The aerodrome's main group of hangars and huts. This was Spald-

ing Moor which had a busy wartime history. In *Holme Sweet Holme* it
has been described as

> a typical purpose-built Bomber Command station with the sleeping
> accommodation dispersed away from the messes, which, in turn,
> were removed from the working areas and aircraft to minimize the
> effects of the enemy. The huts in which officers and men lived
> were poorly heated by a small metal stove. Water for washing was
> more than often cold but life was lived to as full an extent as pos-
> sible.

From early days Lord Trenchard, who became the first marshal of
the Royal Air Force in 1927, concentrated on 'real estate', the
acquiring and building of airfields. In 1937, with war imminent, it
became the responsibility of Air Vice-Marshal Sir Charles (later Lord)
Portal to seek out land for aircraft in the face of furious opposition
from East Anglian landowners worrying about their pheasants and
racehorses. He received 'a barrage of letters' from Conservative peers,
eager to preserve their estates. But building airfields went ahead in the
war years and, by 1943, there were over seventy in eastern England
for bombers alone – Fighter Command was elsewhere. The Americans
had to be accommodated, and requirements essential to the air war,
such as training schools, hospitals, radio and radar establishments and
bomb dumps, all contributed to the RAF's massive budget – in mid-
war, equal to about one sixth of the total national budget.

Before the war most airfields had been just that – stretches of turf
and grass. In September 1939 only nine RAF stations had hard runways,
but as aircraft grew heavier, and night flying and operations in all
weathers became routine, runways of ballast and concrete became
essential. The standard layout for bomber stations consisted of three
runways, fifty yards in length, laid in an equilateral triangle linked at
the corners to a perimeter track fifty feet wide. As war progressed the
runways grew and, by 1944, most main runways had doubled in
length to 2,000 yards, while the two subsidiary runways increased to
1,400 yards. Each airfield worked like a military barracks, with
accommodation, stores, kitchens, canteens, recreational facilities and
sick quarters, in addition to hangars and workshops – plenty of
temporary building space to deteriorate and fall into ruin after half a
century.

At Spalding Moor the semblance of the old wartime base, although fairly crumbling and ruinous, remained intact since the typical Spartan conditions which airmen endured there had not stopped it from being used for flying for over forty years after hostilities had ceased. It was not until 1984 that Aerospace had sold off Spalding Moor for yet another store to hold surplus EEC grain.

For the second night in succession we had to abandon the microlight, find a road and walk down it looking for food and shelter. It was always odd arriving from nowhere in an unknown place without the easy familiarity of a journey over ground. From the air we had looked down on a murky sprawl which, at this level, had turned into trees, cottages and country gardens. An hour's pleasant walk brought us to the nearest village, where the afternoon had not ended, and the pub was still closed.

This was Holme, which, we were told proudly, had the distinction of being the longest village in Yorkshire. Just when we thought we were through it, another turn in the road revealed more buildings of suburban estates, of sober houses, functional and sensible, and gardens full of bedding plants where red, white and blue dominated. And roses, marmalade-coloured floribundas and bridal bouquets for giantesses trained on the end of sticks. No yuppies here.

We stayed at Ye Olde Red Lion, a new motel-style hostelry with separate chalets for the guests, all of whom were well past retirement age. We were lucky to get accommodation among the old people, who were gathered in the bar where they sat talking of foreign parts.

'We spent two years in Jinja.'

'Did you ever meet anyone who enjoyed Aden and Crater?'

'When I was in K.L. . . .'

One old warrior with an ivory-coloured handlebar moustache was a former RAF officer who talked of the days when 458 Squadron had been stationed at Spalding Moor. But no one wanted to listen to him, no was was interested in local conflicts.

'Oh, we were there, all through Mau Mau . . .'

'There are three main tribes, Hausa in the north, Yoruba and Ibo. When the civil war broke out . . .'

In the morning we walked back to Spalding Moor where I met Michael Meseller, who had also seen service in the RAF. The skies around here were full of military planes, he warned us. Look out for A10s. 'Remember, they always go in pairs.' After he retired he started a duck and goose farm right beside the aerodrome, which was just about the worst thing he could have done. When he first started he had no idea of the effect that aircraft would have on his stock. Aerospace used to test Buccaneers and the noise of jet engines overhead had proved catastrophic to the peace of mind of his Indian black runners and his fawn and white speckled mallards, which he described as being of 'the Irish type'. Worse still had been hissing balloons. And when the occasional microlight passed, the birds went mad. Their shapes hovering overhead made them appear to the geese as vast birds of prey.

Here was a new source of guilt. I already knew that we were enemies to ducks and geese from enquiries at Slimbridge but I had not brooded about it. How many innocent birds had we terrified to death as we had circled around southern England? When we departed we took good care to avoid Michael's farm.

A good night's sleep and two ample hotel meals had helped us to forget the misery of waiting. The weather had cleared somewhat and, although there had been a little more thunder in the west, the worst appeared to be drifting away. Our idea was to fly in the direction of York and then head off towards the Yorkshire Dales. Graham looked more cheerful.

From Spalding Moor we flew above the 1079 motorway, and the lorries and cars filled with drivers biting their nails, over to Pocklington, where we hovered near the church tower above lines of shiny slate roofs. It must have been market day; around the main square stalls had been set up, the coloured canvas making splashes of blue and white stripes and vibrant yellows against the grey houses in front of the church tower. A convivial group of people circled around with shopping-bags, looking for anything from stalks of rhubarb and bunches of lavender to an old gas-mask.

There were tourists in Pocklington, too, who came to the old Ritz cinema which is now called Penny Arcadia and houses Mr Gresham's collection of amusement machines. Once they were found on railway stations, piers and arcades, before the computerized games came in and they became discarded junk overnight. Mr Gresham had gathered them up, lovingly restored them and put them together. There were life-sized figures of a Belgian brass band, the first little machines with handles and tin players for games of football, strength testers, muscle developers, a Floating Lady, Dennison's Chinese Torture, and Charles

Ahrens's popular favourite of An American Execution where a poor little tin man was strapped into a tiny electric chair. There were other executions where marble-sized plaster heads were chopped off, Madame Sandra told your fortune and the Model 05 Poluphon played 'Bill Bailey Won't You Please Come Home' as we flew overhead.

I felt resignation as another gush of cloud and rain overwhelmed us, and a few miles from Pocklington we were forced down near a flock of sheep which appeared to be less nervous than Michael Meseller's ducks and geese. Swallows darted low over the wet grass. A fat man who was snagging sugar beet plants in the next field came over.

'I know all about those things. One of them crashed the other day, didn't it, and the poor sod was killed.' He stroked the shining anodized airframe tubes with their 'just polished' look. 'Heart attack. Poor bugger didn't have a chance. Must have happened high up.'

Graham went off to look for petrol while the fat farmer lingered and quizzed me about the machine's capabilities. Would it carry him? That seemed to be asking a lot, since he told me he weighed twenty stone. It would, of course – Graham and I together weighed more than that.

Some cars screeched to a stop at the sight of the blue and yellow wing and their drivers came over and joined the discussion.

'Do they use them for agriculture?'

'There were some on TV going up a river in Greenland.'

Microlights may be nothing but a curse in many parts of England but there are still some places where they are rare enough to excite curiosity.

'How much do they cost?' The commonest question. It always comes as a surprise to those who associate flying machines with transport for millionaire polo players and jockeys or the means for getting Richard Branson to conferences. The Undertaker was quite a lot cheaper than this man's Audi, that man's Jaguar.

'Great for avoiding the rush hour.'

'How much would it cost to fly over to France?'

It began to rain. Lightning lit up the sky. The fat man advised, 'Don't touch the metal. It could kill you.' The drawback to our sort of flying came falling out of the heavens.

Damn the rain. The idea of our sort of hedge-hopping was intoxicating, avoiding congested roads, congested towns and urban pressures that made the sky appear like a freeway. Running costs of this microlight were inconsiderable. Anyone could acquire a new vision of the earth. A celestial vision was not the toy of the privileged rich, and independent flight for the middle classes was a possibility. But the weather . . .

However, on this occasion, the shower and the little display of lightning were transitory shows of strength. By the time Graham returned we could take off, leaving the chatty Yorkshiremen waving up as we circled overhead.

Soon we could see the craggy twin towers of York Minster rising above the city walls and rooftops, proclaiming the faith and endurance of their medieval builders for whom it must have been like building mountains. As we flew nearer, even above the Undertaker's screech we could hear the booming tones of Great Peter striking twelve o'clock while the tourists took out their cameras and the pigeons wheeled around the towers and soaring Gothic nave.

Now we were over York with a glimpse of how the English loved and pampered their gardens, the sheen of the parallels of a well-cut lawn, the subdued tones of pampered herbaceous borders, bright annuals and lines of giant onions. Lilliputian figures were walking on the city walls among the stone towers. The city crowded round the Minster, a jumble of high walls and narrow streets, and we could make out how in places like the medieval Shambles the houses on either side of the road almost met.

We moved along, squared up over the railway yard, came down over a race-track and landed in a small park called Hob Moor which was surrounded by a housing estate. The grass was thick and wet and no one took any notice.

The heart of the city was only a short walk away. In the Minster the cleaning ladies had taken out their brushes from the cupboard below the choirstalls to dust down the medieval tombs and railings and remove bits of chewing gum stuck beneath the pews.

Say a prayer for Sir William Gee, his two wives and six children, and take note of what is written on his memorial: 'Stay, gentle passenger, and read a sentence sent thee from the dead.' As usual, almost as a reflex, I looked out for connections with Ireland – there are few ecclesiastical buildings in England without them. Sir Henry Lee, 3rd Dragoon Guards, accidentally killed by a fall from his horse in the Phoenix Park, Dublin, on 3 September 1870. Lady Mary

Hoare, daughter of the Countess of Wicklow, on her way to Scarborough for the recovery of her health, who died at York on 23 July 1798. Pity these poor souls.

A Chinese girl was finishing off a certificate for an American visitor. 'A donation of £3 will maintain York Minster for a minute.' The Reverend Kemp Welsh was bringing round another group, leading them past the crypt and the cope chests until they stood in front of the east window.

'It is as big as a tennis court. I don't play tennis myself.'

He showed them the Astronomical Clock dedicated to the air forces of the Commonwealth.

They went through air and space without fear and shining stars marked their shining deeds.

Away from the Minster I sought out the Jorvik Centre. The crowds that pack into the Viking Madame Tussaud's are infinitely greater in number than those who visit the Minster. I joined the queues, marvelling.

Once upon a time, over a thousand years ago, there were two Viking cities on these islands inhabited by tough Scandinavians of Norwegian and Danish stock. (The restless Swedes tended to go off to continental Europe as far as the Danube.) Dublin was founded in AD 841 and York was captured from Anglo Saxons in AD 861. First linked by the warrior brothers, Halfdan and Ivar the Boneless, who was described by the Annals of Ulster as 'King of all the Scandinavians of Ireland and Britain', the cities constituted a powerful unified political and economic force during the tenth century. York, convenient for a flourishing sea trade with Denmark and the Friesian coast, and benefiting from the surrounding rich farmland it had conquered, was regarded as the more important. Dublin's rulers always aspired to rule York. However, the warrior kings of Dublin, living on booty, tribute and trade, particularly in slaves, had a more lasting kingdom. York fell to English rule early in the eleventh century but Scandinavian Dublin continued until Strongbow's conquest of AD 1171.

Time passed, and succeeding generations buried Viking York and Dublin. After many centuries the remains of both cities were discovered almost simultaneously in the 1970s. In Dublin, in High Street, Fishamble Street, and Winetavern Street, and in York around Coppergate, archaeologists sifted through a wealth of Viking detritus that revealed comprehensively how these Norsemen lived. Contrary to historical tradition, they were craftsmen, fishermen and traders rather than warriors. Instead of weapons, they left evidence of their lives as cobblers, carpenters, comb-makers, leather workers and fishermen. Among the objects they discarded were chisels, awls, knives, shears, bronze pins, fish-hooks and carved antlers.

The Viking diet was closely examined and ancient wattle cesspits were searched to find remains of barley, rye, peas, leeks and fat hen – a species of weed used as a crude porridge. Vikings ate hazel nuts, wild fruits, coriander, summer savory and corn-cockle, as well as a quantity of worms. In both locations, large numbers of bones were found, beef bones, mutton bones and those of goats and pigs. In Dublin, the amount was so great that it had to be stored in scores of plastic sacks which cluttered up the digs for months before being sorted and measured by weight. Sturgeon, herring and eels were among the fish consumed.

Archaeologists traced street patterns marked by post-and-wattle walls, pathways and wattle partition fences. A few wooden houses were found but by far the most common dwelling-houses for Vikings were single-storey, chimneyless, post-and-wattle huts with rushes on their floors.

What did the city fathers of Dublin and York do about these marvellous discoveries?

In Dublin they salvaged more than 30,000 artefacts of which a selection is on display in the National Museum where needle-cases, gaming pieces, spoons, shoes, toys and jewellery give a hint of old life-styles. But long before excavations were completed, the obliteration of Viking and medieval Dublin was planned. The bull-headed Dublin Corporation, aided by the Commissioners of Public Works, was determined to build its new civic offices on the Wood Quay site. Its officials found unexpected allies in the National Museum whose hierarchy for reasons best known to itself chose to step aside and let the destruction take place. Another bizarre voice in favour of scrubbing out the old town was a Corkman, an archaeologist named Professor Michael O'Kelly, who gave evidence in a High Court hearing that 'this hole in Dublin' was worthless.

The citizens of Dublin who sought the preservation of the Viking town were led by a self-professed mendicant friar and Professor of History at University College, Dublin, Father Francis Xavier Martin. It was Father Martin who provided the impetus for protest on 23

September 1978 when 20,000 people, not all of them middle-class trendies, took part in a memorable march to save Wood Quay. Father Martin won a case in the High Court for its retention, Mr Justice Liam Hamilton declaring in vain that the site was of national importance.

In spite of a petition from over 200,000 people from all over Ireland and from abroad, protests from eighty voluntary bodies and associations, motions passed in the Council of Europe and mountains of telegrams from Scandinavia, the bully boys on the corporation had the decision overturned by the Supreme Court and got their shameful way. On the evening of 9 March 1979 the bulldozers moved in and began to rip Viking Dublin apart. Eventually Wood Quay was cemented over, huts, woven walls, gates, city walls and all. The old Norse town was once more beaten into the boulder clay. On the cemented site municipal offices of a defiant ugliness were built.

In York, first of all, naturally, they brought in a charity. The York Archaeological Trust (YAT) carried out excavations in the city for the enjoyment and education of the public. During my flight around England, I had encountered many things that benefited from charity, geese, swans, great bustards, stones, Turners, Constables, carp, fallow deer, Flatford Mill, Salisbury Cathedral, York Minster. Now it was the turn of Snarri the jeweller and Thorfast the bone carver.

At the Jorvik Viking Centre, which cost £2.5 million to build and attracts 850,000 tourists a year, the archaeological commitment is impressive. Timber and wattle remains are carefully preserved, labelled, measured, photographed, and reset where they were found. Five hundred objects are on display in the Skipper Gallery, dice, beads, coins, keys, knives and a Viking turd ten centimetres long, ten centuries old, 'rich in bran and full of intestinal parasite eggs'.

Every day the crowds wait to take part in the time experience created by modern technology and blessed by Magnus Magnusson. I queued long to find a seat in a time-car which would enable me to appreciate the most innovative breakthrough in heritage display of this century. I was carried along past polystyrene generations of ordinary York folk back in time to a plastic past where Lothin and his wood stall, Sven and his leather shop and all the marvels of Viking Disneyland awaited. Karl and Eymund gutted model fish, young Toki listened to tales of seamanship and battle exploits, and frozen figures waited to unload barrels of herrings and wine pots from the

Rhineland. Harald sat in a wickerwork latrine decorated with plastic ivy. As I sniffed the smells of tenth-century Yorvik and listened to its sounds before making my own piece of money stamped with Thor's hammer, and pushed my way to the souvenir shop to inspect mementoes of a teeming, thriving, ancient town, I began to wonder whether the Vikings of Dublin, decently reinterred, weren't better off than Snarri and Thorfast.

In 1988, millennium year, Dublin produced a pale imitation of Jorvik, also with sights and smells, re-creating Fishamble Street with actors instead of models. In York, meanwhile, the Jorvik Centre is so successful and is making so much money that the YAT is planning to excavate and develop another centre – a Roman one on the site of the Sixth Legion's fortress at Eboracum. Model Romans carrying reproduction eagles will be a further inducement to come here.

In the Minster an Afghan tourist had just bought another Minster scroll with his name, Sayed Jamel, carefully penned in large letters, and the fabric of the cathedral was maintained for another minute. The nave was still crowded and, no doubt, the Rose Window and the time-cars benefit by proximity. Then it was five o'clock, time for Evensong, and the crowds went away. The organ boomed and the choir, in red cassocks and white cuffs, assembled among richly carved stalls for a purpose that came almost as a surprise – to render praise unto the Lord. A choirboy, wearing a large gold medal attached to a loop of red ribbon, sang *Hear My Prayer*.

Next morning we took off just as the tours began inspecting the Roman tower and walls and queues were already winding around the Jorvik Centre. The microlight, squatting on the grass, yellow and blue wing outstretched, seemed a more exhilarating time experience. Small boys gathered to watch as we faced the race-track and the minster, pushed down full throttle and gaily catapulted above a train arriving at the station. The Minster was turning beneath our wing, the twin towers and ridge of the long copper roof, the Roman pillar they had discovered in the crypt, the wooden figures of English kings carved on the fifteenth-century choir screen.

We were turning into sunshine towards the York plain from where I planned to fly through the Yorkshire Dales up to the Lake District. Graham hadn't been enthusiastic.

'We could be stuck for weeks.'

Both the Dales and the Lake District were notorious for attracting rain and, without luck, we might find ourselves under a semi-permanent cloud formation massed above the lakes. If that was the case, we might as well forget about further flying.

We were above Marston Moor, where the biggest battle ever fought on British soil raged during the stormy evening of 2 July 1644. I could make out the road between Tockwith and Long Marston, on either side of which 40,000 men had faced each other a musket shot apart, standing in fields of soaking rye, the parliamentary soldiers singing psalms. Parliamentarians allied with Scots in a massed force amounting to around 23,000 men, which consisted of horse, dragoons, musketeers, 11,000 foot and, most notable, 2,500 cavalry under Cromwell's direct command.

The Royalist 'batallia' south of the road was surprised into battle at seven in the evening as the sky darkened and a storm burst on the armies. Prince Rupert had actually gone off to have dinner before the enemy advanced with all its components 'like so many thick clouds'. Fighting went on into the night under a full moon until 'the godly part' prevailed, and thousands of Royalists lay dead. The victors captured enough colours 'to make surplices for all the cathedrals in England, were they white'. Cromwell was pleased: 'It had all the evidences of an absolute victory obtained by the Lord's blessing.' As usual, the Lord was on his side as He would be at Drogheda, 'a righteous judgement of God upon these barbarous wretches'.

We were flying at the same time of year as the date of the battle, and there were still fields of ripening corn where the Royalist forces had marched to their doom. On this moody summer's day, the play of light, sunshine swiftly overtaken by cloud and rain, echoed the uncertainties of that long tragic evening. Somewhere below was the mass grave for Royalist casualties (the Parliamentarians lost only a few hundred). Prince Rupert called Cromwell 'Old Ironside' because of the impenetrability of his cavalry, advancing tight-reined at a fast trot – later the nickname passed to his soldiers. Through a squall of rain, I glimpsed the little obelisk commemorating the battle, erected jointly by the Cromwell Association and the Harrogate group of the Yorkshire Archaeological Society. In front of it someone had placed a wilting wreath.

The tailwind gave us a speed of over fifty miles an hour, which was fast for us, and we were flying low at about 500 feet, too low for the usual prospect of landscape laid out like a map. Instead everything was rushing at us and trying to suck us in, fields and hedges, a passing farmhouse sweeping by and too many trees which had all suddenly become threatening. We were too low for safety, forced by the clouds to brush the tree-tops.

It was difficult for Graham to make a judgement about landing. Most of the fields that flashed by were too small, or contained an impediment like pylons, a herd of animals, wire fences, a drainage canal, or a road was too near. Mist curled up around us. A sailor can shorten sail, reef up and ride out a storm; aircraft must land. Then a patch of light, the grey outlines of houses, and we reached Tockwith, yet another abandoned aerodrome.

Another runway pitted with holes that were pools of mud and water. As we bumped our way towards the surviving hangars and airport buildings, a lorry drove up much faster than us, screeched to a halt, and an angry face glowered out at us from the cab.

'Don't you damn well know that this place belongs to the Ministry of Defence?'

'Sorry!'

'A couple of months ago another bloody fool in a glider landed and ran into one of our trainers. Don't you realize this place isn't meant for aircraft?'

Tockwith, which had housed operational bombers during the war, had been converted into a Driver Training Centre for truck drivers. Enough old broken-down runways survived to make an interesting obstacle course for learners, who could, however, do without hazardous reminders of what the battered stretches of runway were originally intended for.

Having snarled at us, the driver then did his best to make us welcome. An empty shed was found for the Undertaker, while another driver gave us a lift to Bickerton Grange where the Lovells took in occasional guests.

Bickerton Grange was a huge house, empty now, but until recently a part of the Ockenden Venture. The Venture is small, and less well known than it should be. It was started after the last war by Joyce Pearce as an individual response to the rag-tag of suffering among the postwar refugees of Europe. Its budget is very modest in comparison with umbrella organizations like Oxfam or War on Want and its work, in co-operation with the United Nations High Commission for Refugees, is a reflection of the changing waves of the dispossessed and the helpless. For years the Lovells had brought up children from Poland and the Ukraine as members of their own family – now the Venture gives help to Afghans, Tibetans, Vietnamese and Ethiopians among others, offering accommodation to a few of the pathetically small trickle of young refugees coming to England from Asia and Africa. Here was a charity that appeared to invite a good deal more support than others I had encountered.

The Lovells had just retired and, although they were soon leaving Bickerton Grange for their own home, they found time to provide us with accommodation and drive us down to the village. Graham and I had the usual monosyllabic meal in a pub. I was reminded of how Joyce and Beckett engaged in conversation which, according to Richard Ellmann, 'consisted often of silences directed against each other'.

CHAPTER TEN

The Dales
and the Lake District

I woke to brilliant sunshine streaming in through the tall windows of
the bedroom, lighting up our rumpled heaps of clothes. Outside the
remains of a heavy dew were being dried off rapidly. If you are
uncertain about clouds and cloud formations, the presence of dew is
an infallible sign of good weather. If there is a good dew on a
summer's morning there won't be rain.

'It looks OK,' I shouted across to Graham, who stirred and went
back to sleep. The cross humours of two people flying close together
had led to a certain amount of friction. Tandem pastimes – double
bicycling, sweeping down a mountainside on your back with someone
else, invite tension. I wondered how Blyth and Ridgway got on
halfway across the Atlantic. Had their rowboat been worse than the
awful intimacy of the microlight?

By 9.30 we had taken off into blue sky – a sapphire-shot, charged,
steepèd sky as Gerald Manley Hopkins would have it.

> The glass-blue days are those
> When every colour glows,
> Each shape and shadow shows.

A tranquil blue sky and light winds offered the very best sort of
weather for flying. We were looking down on a lush sunlit tableau
stretching before us which was the same threatening country we had
blundered over the day before. 'Blue be it: this blue heaven.' The
contrast in weather conditions was more dramatic than usual, more
definite than the wobbling minute-by-minute changes in atmosphere
that affect small vulnerable aircraft. The least change in wind and
airlift causes the machine to respond, and the landscape contributes to
what goes on in the air. This patchy scenery made flying more

irregular and unpredictable than moving over the smooth sweep of the East Anglian prairies and the Lincolnshire flat lands. In the sunshine every object we passed, trees, fields, towns and lakes would link with our passage across the sky. Each would have its own particular power of absorption, affecting the air above with different degrees of temperature, creating new patterns of turbulence and changes in the atmosphere.

Before we reached the Yorkshire Dales, we flew by Ripon and then encountered new methods of farming at Lightwater Valley Farm. After the butter and beef mountains, these fibreglass cows and pigs standing beside open gates through which poured an unceasing battery of cars, heralded the shape of things to come. Here was Jorvik in the country, plastic animals for pleasure, and much more besides. As we flew over the small lake filled with paddle-boats and a complex of farm buildings, I could see the miniature railway, the Rat's Ride, the Devil's Cascade and a Moon Buggy. In the outbuilding beside the paddock, farming was explained in easy terms to those who had never seen a hen or a cow.

On the ground a notice greeted people who had already bought their general admittance tickets. 'This way to the farm . . . it'll cost thee owt.' The crowds and cars were reminders of how close we were to the industrial Midlands. The concept of Lightwater Valley Farm was brilliant, and it had been planned with the ingenuity that the Ministry of Agriculture asks for when it encourages farmers to diversify. It was so simple. Show farm animals to millions of city dwellers – and a good many country dwellers as well – who have never seen them. No need for butterfly farms or time-cars or other expensive methods of amusement devised by the leisure industry. No need for a landscape by Capability Brown or a wall covered with Van Dycks. No need for lions when hens and pigs will do.

In the mating room a hog called Randy Andy was resting. The queues moved past him to have a look at squealing piglets. Further on lines of broody hens sat on eggs and chickens were being hatched, watched by open-mouthed crowds. Each glass-fronted pen had its white-coated attendant who guarded the livestock and gently shifted people on. All the children were enjoying themselves, all the adults were bored. There was no doubt that this was the place to bring the kids, and mothers behaved with the same air of disinterested self-sacrifice as a mother hen directing her brood as to what to eat. The sight of a chicken nibbling its way out of an egg in the warmth of a large light bulb aroused little interest in fathers. Perhaps when Randy Andy was at work again.

Real country with real farms was not far off. In the microlight we turned our back on the fertile Vale of York and headed towards the most beautiful landscape we had yet encountered.

Aerial photography is another miracle deriving from flight that we have come to take for granted. First developed as an accessory of war, it was perfected with the advent of the helicopter. Television is saturated with landscape photographed from the air, obligatory for drama, documentary and nature shows. We have even become blasé about satellite photography and it is a long time since we marvelled at the blue and white marble of the earth seen halfway to the moon.

The photographic conventions that have made landscapes seen from the sky as unexciting as the helicopter preludes to *Dallas*, lack the dimension of surprise that is part of the joy of moving about in a small aircraft. Here was a delightful surprise; the division from flat land to the Yorkshire Dales seemed knife-edged. Suddenly we had left the Vale of York, pleasant enough country, and were crossing over an ancient landscape with rolling hills, deep-set valleys and stone walls dividing the little, vivid emerald green fields that you get in limestone areas. Villages consisting of neat groups of stone-built houses blended in gently. The Dales were familiar, again through television where they are associated with an ageing humorist who came here to practise as a vet half a century ago. They were beautiful. I could understand instantly that J. B. Priestley had been doing more than championing his home territory when he declared: 'In all my travels I've never seen a countryside to equal in beauty the Yorkshire Dales. The Dales have never disappointed me.'

The use of the word dale for valley is particularly associated with the north of England, although similar derivations were found else-where – Old English *dael*, Old Saxon *dal*, Old High German *tal*, Old Norwegian *dair*, Gothic *dalap*, Germanic *dalom* and *daloz*. We were flying over valleys moulded by limestone, and by rivers and glaciers cutting and shaping the earth. A profound influence on this landscape had been the activities of monasteries established here, the Cistercians at Fountains and Jervaulx, the Augustinians at Bolton and smaller foundations at Coverham, Easby, Ellerton and Marrick. The legacy of the monks still affects hill farming and a lot of stone walls beneath us could be traced back to the Middle Ages. Here were lovely ancient farms and hills where wretched modern farming techniques had not intruded, an old landscape which the JCBs had not destroyed. We followed the peaty brown River Yore, tracing the woods and meadows on its banks. Sun sparkled on the water, shone on its vaulted bridges, on limestone walls alongside, and reflected back the dale's greens and greys.

Jervaulx Abbey appeared, fallen stones in a pool of grass surrounded by flowers, meadows and trees. Before the Dissolution, the monastery, founded in AD 1156, had owned large estates in the Dales, particularly in Wensleydale. We hovered, disturbing an old lady resting in the sun on a wooden bench. There was hardly anyone else to look up at us. Unlike Tintern, Jervaulx, which is in private hands, avoids the crowds. There is no ticket office, museum, or souvenir shop; just an honesty box and a few guidebooks left near a little gate. We paused over the main walls and the cloisters, crossing and recrossing the ruins, marvelling again at the way it lacked people and cars. The old lady looked up; we were the polluters.

East Witton, with its long sloping green surrounded by grey stone houses, seemed almost on top of the abbey. It had the unmistakable air of a landlord village, an essay in improvement, the houses rebuilt in the nineteenth century. The houses and gardens were put together by the Earl of Ailesbury on precisely the same positions as previous houses had occupied on an estate map made 200 years before. Beyond East Witton we flew over Cover Bridge towards the heart of the Dales, near Leyburn with its large market square, over Colsterdale and Masham Moor, Dowdown, and endless tarns, falls and fells. Perhaps it was the day of the week. A sunny midsummer day and a beautiful empty landscape. Did the Dales National Trust frighten people off? Even the skies were empty, without vapour trails or aeroplanes. Apart from us.

A few fishermen on the old stone bridge over the River Cover looked up to watch the microlight behaving as skittishly as the swallows swooping over the water. We chugged overhead in an encircling arc towards Wensleydale, enjoying the warm summer wind. Why wasn't flying always like this? Nothing bad threatened, no rain, no evil clouds, no rocketing thermals or down-draughts, just a smooth current of air carrying us effortlessly from place to place.

We were coming into Middleham and its castle facing Leyburn, a large pink Regency house with curved wings. At one moment we were scraping the slopes of heather-covered hills, the next we were coming in at a glide on to a long green meadow enclosed by stone walls just above Middleham Castle.

A sign said BEWARE OF THE BULL, which was a little worrying. Cattle have acquired a taste for microlights, which appeal to their curiosity. Not only is the frame of the huge spindly flying creature to be investigated and nuzzled, but the Dacron wings provide a pleasant chew. The unwary pilot who leaves his machine unattended in a field of bullocks will return to find a mess. But this field had no bovines, and the farmer who owned it left his sheep and came over.

'You wouldn't get far yesterday, it be much too wet.' Like pilots, farmers are constantly aware of the weather. He assured us that there would be no trouble from rain today, nor from bulls either, and we could leave our machine for a while.

From where we landed was a short walk down to the massive tower and keep which dominated the town. The first castle, built in early Norman times, was succeeded by a sterner fortress which became the headquarters of the Nevilles of Raby. History had brought the tourists and here they were sprung out of the ground like dragon's teeth, and the empty Dales we had enjoyed that morning appeared to have been an illusion. It was as if people were invisible from up above, like figures in early photographs who disappeared with movement.

Middleham was another place where the inhabitants were trying to preserve an old way of life without being swamped. The battle seemed unequal as we watched the cameras hard at work. Why should that group of Japanese be so interested in the castle where the young Duke of Gloucester, later Richard III, spent a part of his youth? The people of Middleham suffered from the other problem as well. In the charming village many houses with names like Warwick Cottage and Neville View had been bought by outsiders, most of whom lived here for a few months, leaving them empty for the rest of the year. I talked to a lady who thought the answer to the unnecessary luxury of second homes might be to slap on higher rates for non-occupiers. It seemed a gentler response to intruders than the Welsh solution.

She had seen Middleham change from a neighbourly place where everyone knew everyone to just another stop-over for the Lake

District. It was a place that didn't need tourists, since it had its own native industry. Horses have been trained here since the days of the monks. I had seen the horse-boxes on the street and encountered Mr Foran, who came from Chapelizod and was an ex-steeplechase jockey.

'There's a power of history about this place.' The Dublin accent was still intact.

Mr Foran had had a good life, taking to racing when he was young. He had been so captivated by Fred Archer's racing colours that he had acquired similar ones and brought them over to his family in Dublin. Because of weight, he had taken up steeple-chasing; the walls of his Georgian house in Middleham were adorned with photographs taken at Thurles and Gowran Park. But Ireland was in the past and he had never regretted the move to England, nor retirement to the Dales. No place like it in the world.

While the tourists were sitting down to their hotel breakfasts, the racehorses took over in Middleham the way they did in Newmarket. By the time we were ready to fly next morning, strings of horses were clattering up the main street, past the Swine Cross in Market Place on their way to the gallops at Low Moor. There was the same mix as Newmarket, the horses and stable lads and lasses, the smells of dung, straw and cigarettes. The blacksmith was already working at his forge, the sharp tap of his hammer accompanied by the roar of the electric blower which has long replaced the old hand-bellows. Up on the gallops, trainers and owners discussed form and peered through their binoculars.

'It's hard going in this wind, George. When you ask him he just goes.'

'A big bloody horse. He won the mile and a half at Chester.'

Higher up over the village and castle walls we rigged up the microlight and waited for the sun to rise above a cushion of clouds. The clouds were black; their vacation had been brief, and they played with our plans. Would they close in or stay where they were? The forecast was reasonable but untrustworthy in a mountain region where local weather conditions tended to be capricious. Providing they didn't close in, we would continue to fly towards the Lake District. Even in this pleasant place, the urge to move was there, soon becoming a burning desire not to stay one moment longer among the tourists and horses. So we flew off. Ahead the hills formed long thin horizontal lines against the horizon, and the clouds brushed their higher tops.

What are days for?
Days are where we live.
They come, they wake us
Time and time over.
They are to be happy in:
Where can we live but days?
Ah, solving that question
Brings the priest and the doctor
In their long coats
Running over the fields.

We were circling over Middleham and I could see the long gallops and the lines of horses. We followed the green tongue of Wensleydale, dairy country once owned by the lords of Middleham and Bolton, the abbots of Jervaulx and the Metcalfes of Nappa. The light had an Alpine fierceness where the vivid green of the pasture below threw up its own kind of glare. When the sun came out, its rays bounced upwards with a particular brilliance. I blinked at slate rooftops and pools of water, and an emerald meadow squeezed between outcrops of bony limestone. The polka dots of a herd of sheep took on the sheen of stars.

When a cloud crossed the sun the change was startling, halfway to darkness, and everything was suddenly obscure and cold. In an open cockpit the temperature loss in flying always feels extreme. Choosing flying clothes in an English summer is difficult, and you can never have enough if you are in the open. In California hang glider and microlight pilots fly naked – here in Wensleydale in midsummer, dressed in an elaborately quilted flying-suit, I was being alternatively exposed to sunburn and frostbite and wondering if Biggles's leather flying-jacket had been more effective in coping with the weather.

As a cloud moved in above us and I shivered in my seat behind Graham, I unplugged our two interconnecting helmets. Up until then our conversation had been sporadic.

'What town is that?'
'Don't know.'
'Have we enough petrol?'
'Wait and see.'
'What about that aeroplane?'
No answer.

From Leyburn we followed the A684 above the southern bank of the River Ure to Hawes at the head of Wensleydale. Hawes, whose prosperity was founded on packhorse traffic around 1700, buzzed beneath us with shops, hotels, guesthouses, holiday cottages, camping and caravan sites, a Youth Hostel, a National Park Information Centre, the Hawes Ropeworks and the Wensleydale Creameries, a secret place where they make the cheese. We didn't go down. Just beyond the town the Fells closed in, guarding the entrance to the Lake District. They looked alarming, hills and Baugh Fell completely misted over in a rolling sugar-white wave. We should have landed or gone back to Hawes for a look at the Upper Dales Folk Museum. Going on was foolhardy – like the actions of monks holding out their cloaks and throwing themselves off towers expecting to fly. The history of aviation is full of references to fools.

We continued simply because we were very near the Lake District, and only a few puffs of cloud and mist separated us from our goal. We flew on and, as Saint-Exupéry once wrote, 'vomited out of a valley as from the mouth of a howitzer'. Flying is a succession of very swift episodes. One moment we were moving through half-seen misty vapour with the liverish dark shapes of mountains pressing our wings and, suddenly, the clouds were gone and I could see Sedbergh and the distant glint of water.

I tried hard to remember the last minutes in the Dales, the lonely farm with a few outhouses, a field that could have been a swamp, trails of vapour and the roar of the throbbing engine, enlarged by the claustrophobia of the clouds pressing behind our heads. We came swooping down on Kendal from the hills and made for our customary target. Graham came in with his usual style on the school playground at the edge of the town, another low approach, skimming over the houses and their back gardens and a group of children knocking a ball about. One minute we had been experiencing a heightened romantic vision of mist and hills, a very short time after we were in an urban wasteland.

When we had last been on speaking terms, Graham had warned me, 'these days the best way of seeing the Lake District is from the air.' It took only a few minutes to tidy away the wing and push the trike into an empty alley before going down into the gateway of the Lake District and encountering a crescendo of tourism. The experience of being jostled in the crowded streets of Kendal must be something like going to Mecca. Here the goal of pilgrimage is Peter Rabbit. The

power of Beatrix Potter is awesome. Mrs Heelis has crushed Wordsworth and Coleridge beneath her stout brogues.

Finding somewhere to stay was a nightmare, as we searched all
afternoon among rabbit faces, squirrel faces, duck faces, Japanese faces,
for a guesthouse with vacancies. No sooner was it found than the
impulse to hop away was more imperative than at any time during
our journey. Next morning the weather was good, very luckily since
it rains in Kendal almost as much as it does in Killarney. (How
Killarney would love these crowds – in comparison, the Americans
riding out in jaunting cars to Kate Kearney's cottage seemed a pathetic
trickle.) We were told it had been raining for weeks in Kendal but
now, for once, the sky and the waters of Windermere were equally
blue and a few little skirmishing clouds could be ignored.

The greatest lake in England was criss-crossed with boats. As we
flew over the pier at Bowness the *Queen of the Lake* was already
edging her way out of the crowded marina on her first cruise of the
day to Ambleside. All the boats in the toy pool of Bowness and the
boats out on the lake by the hundred suggested that the possibility of
collision might become as much a problem here as it is in the skies
over London. Motor cruisers speeded among the waves that flecked
Windermere, white and red sails from surfboards raced each other
towards Belle Isle, and the stripes and patchwork of spinnakers billowed
in front of yachts making white trails of foam.

We flew above Belle Isle, site for the circular house with domed
rotunda and pedimented portico built in 1775 by John Plaw, which
the earl-bishop of Bristol had seen and copied on a far grander scale at
Ickworth. We had tackled the Severn and the Humber and now, for
the third time, were over a substantial stretch of water heading out
confidently across the slaty blue expanse. The beat of the engine was
strong and reassuring and the warm breeze only tickled the outstretched wing. Graham never said a truer thing than when he
recommended seeing the Lakes from the air as we were doing, at a
perspective that changed tatty Lakeland tourism into a Dufy regatta.

Below us, having dogged the powerboats towing water-skiers, the
Queen of the Lake put into the little pier at Brockholes National Park,
a mushroom shape of preserved woodland flanking Windermere's
eastern edge. Hidden among the trees were numerous delights, heritage trails, a compass trail, a putting-green and a programme of
children's events encompassing Teddy Bears' picnics, a mini-beast

safari, tree-hugging and a Squirrel Nutkin Trail. Here Japanese visitors in particular were finding delectable things to photograph as the Beatrix Potter cult assumed terrifying proportions. Close to the tea-shop and Information Centre were amassed the same furry animals I had seen in their thousands in Kendal, but here they were life-sized, each standing in its own grotto. Some moved the way holy statues do, Samuel Whiskers spinning his rolling pin over a Tom Kitten wrapped in a drainpipe; Peter Rabbit condemned to chew an outsize carrot for ever (had he been confused, perhaps, with Bugs Bunny?); Mrs Tiggy-Winkle and a moa-sized Jemima Puddle-Duck, applauded and photographed by the Japanese party, grinned like ogresses. If you put ten pence into a machine a voice read out Holy Writ.

He lived in a little damp house amongst the buttercups at the edge of a pond. The water was all slippy-sloppy in the larder and in the back passage.

The apotheosis of Beatrix Potter has been a very serious process, a reflection of the universal preference for the lightweight. Her life and work combine ingredients that contribute to her status as one of the most popular literary figures in England. Like the Brontës, she had a dramatic and pathetic life story in her development from lonely girl with a talent for water-colour, to bereft bride, to terrifying old woman. Like Flora Thompson and Edith Holden she inspires nostalgia for a vanished idealized countryside. Her pictures have enough quality for anyone to appreciate. She herself raged when an admirer sought to place her beside Palmer and Bewick in the school of English water-colourists and to suggest that some of her landscape achieved Constable's 'Dewy Freshness'. ('Great rubbish, absolute bosh!')

Perhaps her reputation for whimsy is undeserved. In fact, her prose is simple and direct and her humour subtle. She lacks the nauseous qualities which Kingsley Amis attributed to her when, to cries of outrage, he linked her with Edward Lear. Writing about that 'apparently harmless figure' he considered that 'until Beatrix Potter came in on another flank, he did more than any other individual to foster the arch, twee, whimsical, etc. tendency that so disfigures English literature, humour, even character'.

Oh, unfair, unjust Kingsley Amis! *The Rattle Bag* had one of Lear's Animal Alphabets:

> The Dolomphious Duck,
> who caught spotted frogs for her dinner
> with a Runcible Spoon . . .
> The Melodious Meritorious Mouse
> who played a merry minuet on the
> Pianoforte . . .

Neither of these creatures could be a Beatrix Potter animal. Consider, rather, Graham Greene's opinion of the Queen of Sawrey (which did not amuse her). He observed how 'her stories contain plenty of dramatic action, but it is described from the outside by an acute and unromantic observer, who never sacrifices truth for an effective gesture.' As an example, he cites 'her masterpiece', *The Roly-Poly Pudding*, in which Samuel Whiskers, the 'old man rat', says to his wife:

> 'Anna Maria, make me a kitten dumpling roly-poly pudding for my dinner.'
> 'It requires dough and a pat of butter, and a rolling-pin,' said Anna Maria, considering Tom Kitten with her head on one side.
> 'No,' said Samuel Whiskers, 'make it properly, Anna Maria, with breadcrumbs.'

As we prepared to fly over more lakeland, to look, like the Jumblies, on the Lakes and the Torrible Zone and the hills of the Chankly Bore, the *Queen of the Lake* was pulling away from Brockholes Pier and the captain was shouting into his loudspeaker. 'A lot of the western side of Windermere was given to the National Trust by the celebrated author, Beatrix Potter.' We were drowning him out with our nasty buzzing; the passengers on the open deck looked up at the long tapering shape of our wing and a wheelbarrow-sized mode of transport almost as eccentric as the one chosen by the Jumblies.

We flew over fells, villages, narrow lanes and stone-walled pastures that the creator of Peter Rabbit first of all drew and painted, and then saved for the nation.

Once upon a time there was a young woman named Beatrix Potter. She could draw and paint and she could write stories. She sent some of her stories to children she knew. Then she had them made into little books that all children love to read.

First she wrote *The Tale of Peter Rabbit*. Then she wrote *The Tailor of Gloucester* about mice and embroidered waistcoats and 'No More Twist'. And, feeling more confident, she thought of a story about squirrels using their tails for sails. The squirrels lived in Derwentwater which is now known as Nutkin Country.

She went to the Lake District where she bought Hill Top Farm above Windermere. Six of her best-loved tales are about the village of Sawrey, while others are set in pretty places round about. They are about Tom Kitten, Mrs Tabitha Twitchit, Tommy Brock, Mr Tod, Mrs Tittlemouse and other small animals. Many find themselves in dangerous situations. One has his tail bitten off, others nearly get put in a pie, another is beaten up by a mob, and Jeremy Fisher is snapped up by a giant trout in Esthwaitewater. The stories are read by children and grown-ups all over the English-speaking world and they made Beatrix Potter lots of money.

She used her money wisely and bought up pieces of the Lake District. She bought them bit by bit, a farm here, a field there, a cottage somewhere else. Soon she owned a good deal of property.

She asked herself, 'What is the best thing I can do with all the land and farmhouses and beautiful places I have bought with the money I have made from my little books?'

And she did something that benefits us all by giving every bit of her beautiful land to the National Trust. And we can all go and see it.

But there are too many people who gain pleasure from these books and come to see the places in the pictures. If Beatrix Potter were alive today, she would not be pleased. She would not like to see us queueing up to look at her little house, twenty-five at a time. This is the house that looks just like the one where Tom Kitten was tortured by Samuel Whiskers.

We come to admire and worship Beatrix Potter but she thought of us as 'the public for which I have not cared one tuppenny button'.

Someone said 'a love for animals is the honey of the misanthrope'.

The visitors trembled with anticipation as they gathered near Sawrey, the most visited place in the Lake District. The village has become so popular that the National Trust, in a vain wish to discourage pilgrims, has removed road signs pointing to Hill Top Farm. But the readers of the 'little masterpieces' sniff out the place. They wait patiently in queues before they stoop to enter. You hear American voices, Australian voices, voices from all over the English-speaking world.

'I'm proud of her! The way she did all this for posterity!'

'A wonderful lady!'

'Simply charming . . .'

They wait to view the cottage flowers in the garden, the phlox and roses and the rhubarb patch where Jemima Puddle-Duck hid her eggs. Inside they file past the clogs which BP used to wear, and marvel at the dresser illustrated in *The Roly-Poly Pudding*. They admire the longcase clock seen in *The Tailor of Gloucester* and the doll's house food stolen by Hunca Munca. They worship a shrewd sensible countrywoman and gasp in horror at Ladybird's new desecration, the new illustrations to her stories condemned as 'the ultimate perpetrators of an unmannered assault on a beloved writer'.

Ambleside at the north-east tip of Windermere was plastered with notices: PLEASE FEED THE DUCKS FROM THE FAR BEACH — AWAY FROM THE BOATS. SORRY NO EATING OR RUCKSACKS IN THIS SHOP. A Gospel Hall said I AM THE WAY and dozens of guesthouses said NO VACANCIES on printed cards. Fish and chips were king here – just as they were in Skegness – only, in the Lake District, visitors from foreign lands, particularly the Japanese, had to be reminded that they were the Great English Meal.

The National Trust proclaimed its prohibitions. NO CAMPING. NO LITTER. NO PARKING. In the Lake District, the NT's relationship with the public, which is similar to that of an ant stroking aphids for honey, tends to break down in the face of numbers. Later in the year I read a letter in the *Sunday Times*: 'On behalf of the twelve million of us who visit the Lake District every year and love the place quite as much as that awful Wordsworth, even though we live in places like Penge and Portsmouth . . .' Twelve million? I thought of numbers in Irish terms – three times the population of the whole island of Ireland. The letter went on: 'We are made to feel like scum. Only two months ago' – that was when Graham and I were there with the Undertaker – 'you were all wittering on about how visitors fall in love with your region, buy your cottages and price your young marrieds out of your housing market. It was yours, yours, yours, wasn't it? But, last week, the National Trust launched a two million pound appeal to save the area and, suddenly, the Lake District belonged to everyone again. Priceless national asset, etcetera, etcetera. It is the visitors who have caused the trouble and it is the visitors who must pay to put it right. Well, why should we?'

Because, facing fearful odds (12 million pairs of shoes, boots, sandals and sneakers wearing away the soil), the National Trust has worked magnificently to shore up the place and to restrict the effects of poor planning and indiscriminate development. So much of the Lake District is still beautiful. Beyond Windermere we saw the dark prisms of more lakes and mournful hills and places still as Dorothy Wordsworth described them. She described skies as well.

We lay upon the sloping Turf. Earth and sky were so lovely that they melted our very hearts. The sky to the north was of a chastened yet rich yellow fading into pale blue and streaked and scattered over with steady islands of purple melting away into shades of pink. It made my heart almost feel like a vision to me. We afterwards took our cloaks and sat in the orchard. Mr and Mrs Simpson called . . .

There was tourism in the Wordsworths' time:

Monday 9th [June, 1800]. In the morning W. cut down the winter cherry tree. I sowed French Beans and weeded. A coronetted Landau went by when we were sitting upon the sodded wall. The ladies (evidently Tourists) turned an eye of interest upon our little garden and cottage.

In those days the real nuisance was the passing poor, those to whom Dorothy was perpetually generous but who annoyed her when 'they addressed me with the Beggars' cant and the whining voice of sorrow'.

The Wordsworths brought in the tourists in droves and William, more than any other single person, was responsible for spreading the fame of Wordsworthshire. 'I often wonder what will become of Rydal Mount after our day?' His favourite chair is there, his tinted glasses and the scales on which his friend, De Quincey, weighed out opium. On to Dove Cottage beside the road, near the A591, where Dorothy used to walk.

Properly, and in a spirit of prophecy, was she named *Dorothy* . . . in its Greek meaning, *gift of God*, well did this name prefigure the relation in which she stood to Wordsworth, the mission with which she was charged – to wait upon him as the tenderest and most faithful of domestics; to love him as a sister; to sympathize with him as a confidante; to counsel him as one gifted with a power of judging that stretched as far as his own for producing; to cheer him and sustain him by the natural expression of her feelings – so quick, so ardent, so unaffected – upon the probable effect of whatever thoughts, plans, images he might conceive; finally, and above all other ministrations, to ingraft, by her sexual sense of beauty, upon his masculiine austerity that delicacy and those graces which else . . . it would not have had.

De Quincey did not mention how she found time to write her journal.

After tea we rowed down to Loughrigg Fell, visited the white foxglove, gathered wild strawberries, and walked up to view Rydal. We lay a long time looking at the lake, the shores all embrowned with the scorching sun. The Ferns were turning yellow, that is here and there one was quite turned. We walked round by Benson's wood home. The lake was now most still and reflected the beautiful yellow and blue and purple and grey colours of the sky.

Dove Cottage was cold and dark. The Wordsworths had been very hard up and William had come to Grasmere in the first place in search of cheap lodgings. Guests put up with primitive conditions, except for one or two like Walter Scott who eschewed the frugal regime and made for the comforts of the Swan Hotel at Ambleside. It is interesting to compare the austerity of Dove Cottage with the cosy comfort of Hill Top Farm. A century separated the writers, and a whole concept of luxury.

Beside the museum the tourist shop sold editions of Wordsworth's poems and critical works of other Lakeland writers and poets, but even here Beatrix Potter's familiar little books took up much of the shelf space. There was some attempt to crowd her out with Woods of Windsor soap, Forget-me-not Fabric Sachets, Comfrey and Camomile Shampoo, Sweet Pea Hand Cream, Country House Old English recipes for wine and liqueurs, table mats decorated with wild flowers, Kaffe Fassett pincushions, super-soft table napkins, Wedgwood fluted jasper National Trust bud vases, and other attractive souvenirs. But Mrs Heelis is ubiquitous; her creations were stamped on soaps, table-cloths and cards.

'Who reads poetry?' said the man in the bookshop wrapping up another copy of Mrs Tiggy-Winkle. 'We have to make money.'

Knuckles of heather-covered rock were constantly reflected in giant pools of water. We were conscious of water all the time as we flew from Ambleside down to Rydal Water and then Grasmere, and from the air the two lakes gently touched each other. De Quincey described Grasmere as 'the lovely abode of the poet himself, solitary and yet sowed, as it were, with a thin diffusion of humble dwellings'. The humble dwellings have become guesthouses and second homes but, with a bird's-eye view, the 'beloved landscape' was as beautiful as ever. The caravan park outside Grasmere was nothing more than an assembly of white dots surrounded by fields, in another demonstration that caravans and trailers fade into pleasant patterns from high up in the air.

From Grasmere we followed the A591 down to the black waters of Thirlmere and above the lake Helvellyn rose above our heads, a high buttress challenging the powers of the little microlight. Above the peak were a few swirls of cloud, thankfully not as Dorothy described them: 'the shape of the mist slowly moving along, exquisitely beautiful; passing over the sheep it seemed to have more of a life than these quiet creatures. The unseen birds singing in the mist.'

De Quincey wrote a graphic description of mist in the Lake District:

> Ten or fifteen miles afford ample time for this aerial navigation; within that short interval sunlight, moonlight, starlight alike disappear; all paths are lost; vast precipices are concealed or filled up by treacherous draperies of vapour; the points of the compass are irrevocably confounded; and one vast cloud, too often the cloud of death, even to the experienced shepherd, sits like a vast pavilion upon the summits and gloomy coves of Helvellyn.

The poetically bad weather brought about 'the melancholy end of a Mr Gough who was not only a lover of the picturesque, but also a man of science'. It could still threaten the little creatures we could see wearing away the mountain with their boots until one day Helvellyn would be flat. Today they were safe and so were we – we would leave the Lake District easily. We had experienced De Quincey's wall of cloud on our entry to Baugh Fell but there were no barriers to our departure.

The black water of Thirlmere reflected the edges of forest that higher up thinned into broken screes of rock. Everything was easy for us compared to the efforts needed by the sturdy climbers beneath us. All that had to be done was to press down upon the throttle and gently push up the wings. We climbed over one edge of rock and then another, almost scraping them until another 'whoosh' of air would send us up another hundred feet. Far below was the serene green world slashed by Thirlmere and, beside the dark lake, I could see the crowded car park, then the valley leading down to Keswick and the other peaks forming a distant panorama. As the engine of the Undertaker roared its responses, we continued to bubble upwards.

This was the first mountain I had flown up and over. Down below the climbers must have started at crack of dawn and we overtook them one by one, two by two, three by three, people tramping up in their hundreds. Helvellyn would survive their boots today; he was holding up his rocky head in our direction. As we slipped over the last rocks, I thought of the patriarchal figure of Wordsworth standing there. The mountain was a favourite expedition for his family and friends and Benjamin Haydon's painting shows the poet, aged seventy, standing on the summit.

Any feelings of pleasure were instantly dissipated by terror as, just as we hovered over the peak, a roar and a blast of movement made the microlight tremble. Only recently two low-flying aircraft had collided, provoking angry correspondence in the press. 'The Ministry of Defence is quite happy to send its rowdy low-flying jets dive bombing and looping the loop around the top of, and occasionally into the side of, the silent peaks . . . A toll tax for entering Lakeland airspace seems . . . an absolute minimum here.' It had not happened yet and we had buzzed through for free.

In 1987 six pilots of low-flying aircraft died and six others escaped, using ejection seats. The Ministry of Defence claims that this represents a far better safety record than accidents for military aircraft during the 1950s.

The number of people who have had their hearts thrown up into their mouths by the roar of aircraft engaged on exercises not always easy to justify increases day by day. But although the public and the press have an undisguised loathing for jet planes coming out of an invisible sky, they tolerate them. Do they do so out of patriotism? Do they respond to the Ministry of Defence which has issued reassuring leaflets and works almost as hard as the people at Sizewell to convince us that here is another necessary and worthwhile adjunct to modern life.

Radar and missile technology has greatly increased the wartime risks to aircraft, even when operating at low level. Pilots must fly as close to the ground and as fast as possible to have a reasonable chance of penetrating enemy defences. To operate under such conditions demands extremely high levels of skill; the only way these can be mastered is by means of realistic training over land. To be realistic the training should be conducted at heights of about 100 feet above ground level and at speeds of around 600 knots (690 mph).

We had been flying at around 600 feet. At least, if you are on the ground you are frightened but safe. We were not safe at all. We were flying legitimately and frivolously for recreational purposes at something near eyeball level with these jets. So far no Jaguar or similar military plane has hit a microlight but there is always a first time.

Like those who tell us what radiation levels are safe, there are bureaucrats who decide what noise and fright levels are tolerable. It seems a cruel imposition on those on the ground, and even those who appreciate the necessity for this sort of defence training have been heard to complain. The Ministry of Defence goes out of its way to choose areas of natural beauty in Scotland, Wales and the Lake District over which to impose these fearsome defenders of England. Let lovers of tranquillity whinge about being taunted by these things, expensively trained pilots must learn to avoid somebody else's radar, somebody else's defence system.

The concept of aircraft as instruments of war, predicted in the seventeenth century by Father Franceso Lana – 'no city, ship or castle would be safe from aircraft hurling down fireworks and fireballs' – swiftly followed the solving of the mysteries of flight. One of the first actions of the Wright brothers after working out the 'flying problem' was to contact the US War Department. Then they approached military authorities in Europe. At first the English were reluctant to accept such a radical means of fighting and both the War Office and the Admiralty turned down plans for 'an aerial scouting machine of the Aeroplane type'. The Admiralty told the Wrights that 'their Lordships are of the opinion that [aeroplanes] would not be of any practical use to the Naval Service' while, in the army, the Chief of the Imperial General Staff thought that 'aviation was a useless and expensive fad, advocated by a few cranks'.

Things changed rapidly after 6 August 1914 when a German Zeppelin demonstrated how easily people could be killed from above by dispatching nine civilians of Liège with bombs. By 1917 Lloyd George was fired with the romance of warriors in the air and declaimed in a speech to the House of Commons on 29 October:

> The heavens are their battlefield; they are the cavalry of the clouds, high above the squalor and the mud, so high in the firmament that they are not visible from earth, they fight out the eternal issues of right and wrong. Their daily, yea, their nightly struggles are like the Miltonic conflict between the winged hosts of light and darkness. They fight the foe high up and they fight him low down . . . Every flight is a romance, every record is an epic. They are the knighthood of this war, without fear and without reproach.

Churchill's great tribute to fighter pilots, with echoes of Lloyd George's romantic outburst, still finds a place in our hearts. Otherwise how could we endure the torment of military aircraft without more protest?

For this microlight passenger, the sudden terror as the thing lunged by and disappeared far faster than I could see it, was mixed with envy for those masters of their fate flying their single-seater Jaguars just above the ground. A Jaguar costs about £7 million and a Jaguar pilot costs nearly £3 million to train to fly it. Each pilot is insured for £100,000 and more, and about half a dozen are killed annually. They are temperamentally equipped to face danger, driven with the endless urge to fly faster and lower. That is their job, and the feeling it inspires must be unique. The lower you fly, the faster it feels and the concentration, the training and the endless reliance on reflexes must create a unique feeling of power and achievement. They are avoiding hedges, ditches, trees and buildings, moving along at a speed just under the speed of sound. To hell with the frightened rabbits below.

CHAPTER ELEVEN

Across the Solway

One moment we were flying over long lakes and mountain farms and the next all that was left of the Lake District was a series of little peaks like tousled heads that seemed small enough to grasp hold of. Ahead the land flattened out towards the Solway Firth in a pattern of farms and fields. Beyond was the silvery glint of water and on the far horizon misty silhouettes of Scottish mountains.

The engine gave some hiccups which made it sound like an elderly gentleman clearing his throat. If you heard that noise when you were on the ground driving a car, you would turn up your radio and continue with a nagging feeling of annoyance and an idea of looking for a garage sooner or later. But in the air, two common-sense rules were instantly to be obeyed. One: if you lose confidence, land quickly. Two: never attempt to cross a stretch of water on a doubtful engine.

We landed at Kirkbride on yet another wartime airfield which was still partially used by a local flying club which kept a few machines here, while one of the buildings had been converted into a hotel. From where we came down we could smell the sea.

As we taxied up and unbuckled our helmets some pilots of proper aeroplanes came out.

'I knew a man who broke his leg in one of those things, and there was no insurance.'

'I wouldn't get into a bloody microlight if you paid me.'

One pilot was off to the Isle of Man with friends, travelling in a little Cessna, which seemed a big Cessna compared to what we were used to. A short flip to Blackpool, then on across the Irish Sea, time for a good lunch and back again.

I wondered what his scarlet aeroplane cost. They come at different prices. You can get a comfortable seven-seat, cabin class, twin-engined plane with bar, tables and toilet for around the price of a new Rolls-Royce – about ten times the price of the Undertaker. Smarter, pressurized models, with accessories like colour radar, will come to over £100,000 second-hand, and you pay over £1 million for some executive jets. I guessed this one cost under six figures.

'Are you flying to Ireland? In *that*? The *North* of Ireland? You must be mad!'

Had we never heard about security clearance? What about maps? Didn't we know about the concentration of RAF low-flying exercises around the coastline of Stranraer? About getting permission from the Chief Constable?

His friend arrived and there was no more time to pour scorn. Three stout men were obviously looking forward to a good Manx meal. Inside the Cessna's cabin they took off their jackets and, sitting in their shirt-sleeves, peered out at us with an air of bemused benevolence. They had no problems in starting and soon their red machine was a speck in the sky.

Graham decided to strip down the engine just to be sure. He managed to borrow some tools from a good-natured mechanic as I stood by and watched him take the carburettor off and clean the jets, then check the plugs and the choke. More and more small shining pieces of metal were regurgitated from the engine and put back. It wouldn't start. Graham looked grim as members of a local gun club came along and began firing at clay pigeons. A cold wind blew in from the sea and the hotel restaurant was shut.

Graham said, 'Should work.'

'Something must be wrong.'

'I've checked everything.'

'I'll give it another pull.'

How I loathed the lawn-mower way of starting the microlight by pulling a piece of cord. I didn't care to remember how many times I had been in an open boat at sea struggling with an outboard engine, pulling while the boat slipped sideways and downcurrent from the direction it was intended to go. If you were lucky, the rain let up and the *Seagull* or *Johnson* suddenly decided to make amends and avoid the dirt in its feed, too much choke, oily plugs, or whatever reason there might be for sulking. Not being a mechanical man, I used to be inclined to believe in an act of God.

'She's flooding.'

'Should you turn off the petrol?'

'Give it a few more tugs.'

Graham watched over the engine and again I tried the futile wind-up and pull. Nothing happened.

I wanted to pack it in for the time being and go into the bar for a drink. After a long flight, the Undertaker probably just needed a good rest. Engines can be temperamental even if there is nothing really wrong, but temperament is not what you need in a flying machine.

The clay pigeon buffs were firing away across the tarmac as Graham gritted his teeth, took off nuts and bolts again, puffed and blew.

'Give it one more go.'

I pulled. The microlight started.

We put on our helmets, buckled ourselves in and taxied to the runway as the shooters kindly stopped firing. A few minutes later we were heading towards the Solway Firth, dappled with frisking waves and reflected light. West of us was Carlisle, and westward, beyond the open mouth of the Firth, lay Ireland. We flew over sandbanks and shoals of shingle where flocks of seagulls were scattered like a drift of feathers.

The engine throbbed reassuringly behind my back as I reminded myself that up to now in many hundreds of miles of flying it had failed us only once. I was imbued with complete confidence in a fragile toy that had an old-fashioned air like something made out of Meccano. The pistons were running up and down the way they should, the petrol was flowing, the carburettor was doing its duty and the wooden propeller was whirling. Graham didn't seem to be worried, although it would be difficult to tell if he was. I continued to believe that the microlight was less fallible than parts of my own body.

From Kirkbride we flew south-west over Newton Arlosh and Skinburness then due west across the Firth towards Southerness Point, moving at a height of 2,000 feet, high enough for detail below to be dissolved into moving reflections of shadow and light. The scribble of the waves was interrupted by the dark shadow of wind crossing the water, while, further west, the sea was a silver pool.

As we drew nearer, a dark gritty shore and shapes of mountains behind half hidden by cloud and mist reminded me of home. Their shrouded outlines suggested a wildness and a sense of discovery that I had missed travelling across poor tamed England. And immediately there was a feeling of fewer people. Southerness, which had developed from a small fishing port to a resort, seemed amazingly empty compared to the Lake District. We flew past the ruined lighthouse, over the sparsely filled beach, the John Paul Jones Hotel and the golf course before following the intended coast, keeping close to the shoreline.

There was Castle Hill Point, Auchencairn Bay, Balcary Point, Rascarrel Bay and the whole curve around Abbey Head marking off a large patch of land designated DANGER AREA on our map. Here was the army at work again protecting the land with gunshot and explosion, just as it does on Salisbury Plain. Wherever it does its training with red flags to warn off trespassers, it creates an environmentally controlled area where the odd rabbit or rook may have its head blown off, but houses, caravans, wind-surfers, pony trekkers and chip vans are seen off. Let the army continue to do its mini-battles in rock and heather. From the air, DANGER AREA looked like Paradise.

Civilization took hold again at Kirkcudbright at the bottom of the estuary where the tide was out and a line of stranded yachts leaned on the exposed mudbanks. We flew above the small grey clean seaside town, over the walls of the ancient Maclellan stronghold, and over St Mary's Isle and Sandy Bay where a few swimmers were tackling the raw west wind and surf-boarders were dodging down to the Firth. Another caravan park, another sandy beach, rocks and sand thinly scattered with chilled people, and around the headland a lacy collar of foam.

As we rounded Borness Point, the nodule of tourism faded away and another wide estuary, Wigtown Bay, was flanked by more windy forelands where cattle stood hunched against the sky. These were colours that were shared with Ireland, peaty browns, greys and heathery pinks, and the houses were painted garishly with ice-cream tints, pinks, greens and mauves, just like houses in Kerry. Carsluith Castle, guarding the coastline, resembled the tower houses that the O'Mahoneys and O'Driscolls built to defend the shores of West Cork.

A strong westerly wind was blowing across the bay as we headed towards Wigtown. Yachts bowed over as they tacked, and their sails seemed to be touching water, although we could not see any disturbance apart from some signs of white curling waves.

The wind is blind.
And the sail traps him, and the mill
Captures him; and he cannot save
His swiftness and his desperate will
From those blind uses of the slave.

From the crowded cockpit of a yacht trailing the water like a bird with a broken wing, figures in bright yellow oilskins waved. I could see the splinter of foam around the bow, the awkward angles of deck and sail, and the bright red hull turned up in our direction so that the keel was almost visible.

Wigtown was cold and grey, dominated by the Martyrs Monument standing on a hill, enriched by a whisky distillery and a misty background of mountains. We made for another abandoned RAF airfield, where, as usual, Graham had to taxi in swerves to avoid pot-holes. There was a smell of new-mown hay and, between the broken runways, fields of barley ran down almost to the sea. The seven hours we had flown today had been our longest flight.

An elderly farmer came hurrying up. 'You don't mean that the two of you flew in that wee thing?'

Hugh Sproat, a big friendly man for whom nothing was too much trouble, owned the old airfield and the surrounding land. Sairtainly we could leave the microlight in an empty silage pit. No trouble. In fact, quite like the old times. At the beginning of the war his fields had been dug up for runways and, for five long years, he had listened to the constant roaring of planes. It was a little bit of nostalgia to have the silence broken again.

A silage pit is an excellent place to park a microlight, where no one can see it and the concrete walls act as a protection against the wind. Hugh Sproat insisted on driving us back into the town in his Land-Rover, his two sheepdogs keeping watch in the back. There was his family house, that big substantial one. Sir Walter Scott stayed there, and just beside it was the ruin of seventeenth-century Baldoon Castle. Of course, we know all about Wolf's Crag, sole possession of the wronged Master of Ravenswood, lover of the puir Bride of Lammermoor, who ended up beneath a quicksand, puir fellow? The very same. There was Bladnoch Distillery, recently taken over by the Guinness Group. A shadow had fallen on the reputation of the heavenly local product.

'The biggest disgrace in Scottish history was to let those buggers have our whisky, when all the time they were fiddling the books.'

Different places have different tourist attractions. In Wigtown visitors are invited to view places associated with the Covenanter Martyrs, victims of the Killing Times, who refused to use the Book of Common Prayer. I was shown their names on the obelisk above the town: Margaret Wilson, aged eighteen, a farmer's daughter, and Margaret McLauchan, aged sixty-three, who were both drowned by sentence of the public authorities in the waters of the Bladnoch on 11 May 1685. The enterprising townsfolk of Wigtown have marked out a Martyrs' Trail around the town and a trickle of visitors was following it down to the stakes, now reproduced in ferro-concrete, where the women were tied before the advancing tide. The elder was bound to the foremost stake, where she drowned first, the hope being that her death would persuade young Margaret Wilson to take the oath and save herself. But she would not yield, and both died, their heads thrust beneath the waves by the town's officer with his halberd. I did not expect to feel a nostalgia for Beatrix Potter.

We had arrived on Sunday when a soberly dressed procession was walking down the hill to the large Presbyterian church. Compared with sparse English Sunday congregations, this one seemed a big crowd and, again, I was reminded of Ireland. There was a friendliness about these churchgoers gossiping to each other at street corners, at the two stone crosses, one commemorating the Forty-Five, the other Waterloo, or beneath the old town hall which had functioned up until 1975 when Wigtown had lost its status as a county town.

What else about Wigtown? A local hotel had a bird garden full of love-birds, finches and cockatoos that managed to survive the raw winters. A peaty scent of warm earth mixed with ubiquitous chips hung over the town and the congregation. The fish caught round here once used to taste of whisky: an operator at the distillery turned on the wrong valve, and for years afterwards salmon and trout taken from the Bladnoch were pleasantly flavoured.

In a town famous for its beautiful whisky, our guesthouse was rigorously T.T. I have never seen a house so clean and decent. In the bathroom, towels were marked *His* and *Hers*, a little decorated cushion sat on the lavatory seat, and the nervous guest, intimidated by smells of lemon and pine, made ineffectual attempts to clean up after him. The drawing-room was a dazzle of antimacassars and framed religious texts. Our usual mealtime silence took on a holy aspect here, in quiet broken only by the scraping of cutlery on plates, until, thank God, the big red-faced man at the neighbouring table engaged us in conversation. After the usual rude preliminaries about Mrs Thatcher, which in Scotland seemed to be as customary as 'Good morning', he told us he was the skipper of a fishing-boat.

'Have ye ever met the Ruskies? They're a right lot of bastards, I can tell you. I can always tell them a mile off, they dress like penguins with stuffed shirts and black Homburg hats. Do you know why they always walk in threes? If one tries to jump ship, he gets collared by the other two. He must be mad, anyone would be raving if you ask me, what's there in Scotland?'

Next morning, looking out at the rain, I asked myself the same question.

Down in the square a group of young men were whirling round on motor bikes. On the backs of their leather jackets was the Red Hand of Ulster and the legend NO SURRENDER – UVF LIVES ON. Ireland was getting closer.

'There is scarcely any earthly object giving me more pleasure – and I don't know if I shall call it pleasure, but something exalts me – than to walk on the sheltered side of a wood or high plantation, on a cloudy windy day and hear a storm blowing among the trees and raving o'er the place.'

You had to bring Robert Burns into your thoughts here in Wigtown. He came from nearby Dumfries where he endured the humours of changing Scottish weather. It was not wind or storm that greeted us next morning, but drizzle, vanished mountains and a low overcast sky. Graham shook his head over fried egg and frizzled bacon. A maiden lady sprinkled castor sugar over her cornflakes and read a library book. It was a day of earthly humours, not one to go aloft.

Up until now, we had not discussed the problems of crossing the Irish Sea. It was so difficult to have any discussion at all with Graham. At one time he had mumbled about flares and life-jackets but, by now, he knew about my finances and, as far as I could judge, would accept that such items were outrageous luxuries.

'What about the Chief Constable?'

'I'll ring him.'

'It's essential we have security clearance.'

He didn't reply. I thought about the role of the Chief Constable and had a vision of an elderly moustached figure wearing antique highland dress slowly deliberating our fate. Drops of rain trickled down the window. How much easier to retire to a pub or tour the distillery instead of hanging around waiting for the caprices of Scottish weather to suit us.

By midday it had cleared enough to walk down to Hugh Sproat's farm and the old airfield filled with ripening barley and singing birds. The low hanging sky gave little grounds for optimism as we sat down to the familiar waiting game, which was disturbed an hour later by the sound of a car, a police Panda driven by the burly local cop who was the Chief Constable's emissary. He got out stiffly and examined the Undertaker which we had rigged for take-off.

'What do you call it?'

'A microlight.'

'What speed does it do?'

This was the first time since we had set off from Marlborough that an official presence had shown interest in our movements. Up until now we had flown around England with far more liberty than the average motorist encounters moving on the ground. But flying to Northern Ireland made authority tetchy. The other problem, that of the RAF's low-flying exercises in the Rhinns, had already been brought up by the pilot we had talked to at Kirkbride. He had thought it would be better not to fly during the day, but he did not have to contend with the awful prospect of night-flying in the Undertaker. Air force jets travelled low off the ground all over England, whether or not they were taking part in special exercises. Presumably today there were many more than usual flying over the Rhinns. Much good would that do us if luck did not go our way.

The Wigtown policeman clearly doubted that we would be able to fly to Northern Ireland at all.

'Ye'll end up in the North Channel.'

He walked around the microlight a few more times, examined our meagre baggage and produced a form.

'Sign.'

It was up to him to consider if we were a security threat. There is no reason why a microlight should not be used as a terrorist weapon; a well-equipped skilled pilot could avoid radar and helicopters, skim over rooftops and bomb targets from the air with a very small bomb. Machines as small as ours are hard to see on a radar screen. The PLO used motorized hang gliders on kamikaze missions, and the military of various countries such as Israel and Saudi Arabia have added them to their armoury.

Once again, the constable walked around us inspecting machine, pilot and passenger. We had been told he was the terror of the local lads, stopping their cars after the pubs closed. Now it became apparent that he was just curious about us, looking forward to seeing with his own eyes our little aerial vehicle take off and fly. It was another case of being willed to fly by spectators as both the constable and Hugh Sproat watched us buckle ourselves in. The sky still looked sickly. But I got in and pulled the cord, while Graham checked that the engine was ticking over before climbing in too, in front of me. He headed down the broken runway, the worst of any that we had encountered. Forty years of Scottish weather had reduced most of it to a lacy expanse of pot-holes into which our small wheels kept sinking painfully. One could make meteorological conclusions by comparing the relative wearing away of old airfields in different parts of the British Isles. I recalled some of the stretches of tarmac we had rumbled over during our flight, which now seemed as smooth as velvet compared to this.

We trundled up and down, and finally flew ungracefully into the air on our last lap of travel over mainland Britain. I was eager to be home flying the microlight myself. Although Graham wasn't the friendliest companion, I admired his expertise and was grateful to him. But I looked forward to reaching Sligo and taking charge.

Below was the spot where the two unfortunate martyrs ('So sad – both of them ladies!') had been tied to their posts. The site of their sufferings appeared as an interruption in the pattern of glossy mud-banks where a car park and signpost pointing the way to the traditional site of martyrdom attracted a certain number of visitors on this overcast day. The nearby salt-marsh would become home for thousands of geese in winter.

From Wigtown to Stranraer we flew over patches of forest and bog with the occasional flash of a jet black lake. The landscape below, the wildest we had seen, appeared and disappeared in mist, and to the usual problem of wrestling with the weather was added a nagging distrust of the engine. Halfway, it coughed a few times as I began trying to decipher a possible landing-place, while spongy wet cloud came down over us and squiggles of rain lashed our helmet shields. But troubles pass, if you are lucky – the engine ceased to misbehave, and we were through the grey tunnel and flying in bright sunshine.

Ahead was the distinctive hammer-shape of the Rhinns of Galloway and the long stretch of Loch Ryan where the sun glinted on the water and a container ship was putting out to sea from Stranraer. But first we flew above Castle Kennedy beside the Black Loch and the White Loch and looked down on a rich semi-tropical garden which was an interruption of brilliant colour in a landscape like Arctic tundra. The climatic conditions here in south-west Scotland are like those that encourage similar gardens in the west of Ireland, like Dereen created by the Lansdowne family. Those who have swum in the Gulf Stream around these islands will always be puzzled as to why its presence should encourage exotic jungle growth. In Kerry my mother grew a tropical garden where the same Gulf Stream and drizzle promoted the luxuriant growth of ferns, palms, rhododendrons and azaleas, a casual patch of brilliant forest by the sea. The plan of Castle Kennedy below us was more formal. The garden was created in the eighteenth century by an old field marshal, the second Earl of Stair, with the aid of Scotts Greys and Enniskillen Fusiliers who were stationed nearby and were supposed to be chasing Covenanters. Ignoring fashionable concepts of a natural garden, and contemptuous of the newfangled ideas of Capability Brown, the earl stuck to the inspiration of Versailles, and laid out avenues converging like the spokes of a giant wheel on a big round lily pond which we could see with its edging of bulrushes and water-lilies. Some features were named after his own campaigns, Mount Marlborough, Dettingen Avenue. More than a century after his death his successors brought in rhododendrons, camellias, embothriums, eucryphias, magnolias and monkey puzzles. Later still, the splendid *Metasequoia glyptostroboides*, first found as a fossil in 1949 in Montana, and then as a living tree in China, was introduced here; dating back to the dinosaurs, it is on the verge of extinction elsewhere, but nursed successfully in sub-tropical Scotland.

Metasequoia glyptostroboides wasn't something I could pick out, but the ramrod straight lines of the avenues and the summer massing of flowers made a fine prospect. I didn't envy the gardener riding the old grey Ferguson tractor, endlessly mowing wide acres of grass as if he was painting the Forth Bridge. This was the ideal garden to view from the air and we hovered over its seventy acres, finding the round pond, bowling-green and sunken garden, and admiring the rhododendrons, just like the visitors below.

We disturbed a flock of speckled geese on the edge of Lochinch before flying on over another patch of empty tundra. Then we were above Stranraer, ferry port and gateway to the Rhinns, situated at the southern end of Loch Ryan, a U-shaped fiord opening into the Irish Sea. As the Undertaker slowly buzzed across the rooftops, I looked northwards and caught sight of the ferry from Larne coming into sight around Corsewall Point before heading down to the terminal and the lines of waiting container lorries and cars. A train slid into the station while we were leaving Stranraer behind to cross the Rhinns in a matter of minutes to Portpatrick. We braced ourselves to fly over the North Channel of the Irish Sea.

Things seemed to be going well as we headed directly west towards the coast of Antrim with the tremendous advantage of an easterly wind behind us which was blowing the microlight along at a brisk rate. Peering ahead I made out the distant coastline more than twenty miles away, which seemed within easy reach. The east wind gave us confidence, leaving us no time for hesitations or worries about the time it had taken to cross the Severn, the Thames, the Humber and the Solway Firth. The sea ahead loomed, the horizon vanishing in light blue haze, and we set off blithely.

People have been crossing the North Channel from Scotland to Ireland for more than 7,000 years, since Larnian man went over to become the first human settler on Irish soil and leave the shells and bones of his meals on County Antrim's shore. More recently, the sea provided a challenge for Mr Tom Bower, the first to swim across in the late 1940s. (No woman has yet succeeded – Mrs Chadwick tried in 1960 and failed.) In 1985 an amphibious Volkswagen set off from Portpatrick and managed to stagger across the water. Mr J. Potts flew over in a powered hang glider in 1979. It was as well that we did not know about Mr Potts, whose achievement would have lessened our sense of enterprise and adventure. At breakfast at Wigtown in that frigid dining-room, Graham had become quite animated, suddenly infused with the ambition of most microlight pilots to break yet another record. He grunted about being the first microlight to make the flight. I had my doubts, and later discovered that laurels, if laurels are deserved, must go to Mr Potts, wherever he may be. On the other hand, knowledge of his feat might have enouraged us. If a paper dart like his powered hang glider could do the crossing, so could we.

The moment of leaving the coast and seeing the horseshoe harbour of Portpatrick pass under us was not something I experienced with pleasure. We had plenty of petrol and the engine hadn't coughed for some time, but the water which separated Scotland and Ireland was very wide. No flares, no life-jackets. I looked down wistfully on the lighthouse and the moored boats clustered inside the mole. That was the end of Scotland.

Coming the other way like Mr Bower, St Patrick had crossed the channel in a single stride. There used to be a boulder carrying his deep footprint which was later removed and used in the construction of the harbour (sounds like Presbyterians at work). On another occasion, when St Patrick was walking through nearby Glenapp, a band of savages attacked him and cut off his head. He picked it up and, putting it under his arm, walked back to Portpatrick where he plunged into the sea. Holding his head in his teeth, he swam back to Ireland. A journey by microlight should be easier.

As we headed out to sea, I looked back at the Rhinns and glimpsed the disappearing silhouettes of a pair of jets, those we had been warned about, which were doing their exercises at a far lower level than our 1,000-foot height. Today I did not envy their speed. Ours had given an element of wonder to everything we had encountered, a cloud, or field, or house projecting its own particular impression and, very often, beauty. At present, our flight was offering another novelty; although we were moving, everything seemed still. Overland every passing object contributed to the impression of speed and distance covered, but over the sea there was little to offer a hint of passage.

Except the clouds ahead. It was amazing how fast the enemy gathered, with a life of their own, ignoring the wind, assembling all together and merging into a mist that confronted us, concealing the coastline of Ireland that had been so enticing less than ten minutes ago. There was nothing more to see. We flew on uncertainly for a few minutes, hoping for a change which did not happen. Instead, more clouds were welling up over the sea. If we kept on a direct compass course, we would have reached the Irish coast without trouble, but what then? A strange countryside blanked out in soft white drizzle, rugged mountains, darkened valleys and a feeling of helplessness.

Tendrils of sea mist were curling around us and Graham turned round and shook his head in a frenzy of communication. We had nearly reached the point of no return as we curved around and flew back to Scotland. I was very happy to see the cliffs around Sandeel Bay taking shape in a long grey line, the ruin of Dunskey Castle on a rock overlooking the sea, the pincers of Portpatrick and the twinkle of lights.

Graham found a field above the town where hundreds of rabbits were skipping about on the grass beside a long white two-storey farmhouse, some fine dry stone walls and a power line that he managed to miss.

'Ireland! They'll never get it sorted out!' The farmer in whose field we landed offered his opinion when he learned of our destination. From here on a clear day you can see little white houses dotted on Irish fields and hills.

The connection has always been strong since the days of Celts and early missionaries crossing back and forth. During the reign of Elizabeth I, Portpatrick was a military transit station to Ireland. After that hundreds taking part in the plantation of Ulster had sailed across the sea from here. My own ancestor had come this way for unusual reasons. It seems eccentric now, but he fled Scotland to seek religious freedom in the north of Ireland.

The Reverend William Somerville was an Anglican clergyman who aroused the wrath of Galloway Covenanters. The fate of the Wigtown Martyrs showed the extent to which religious persecution could go in seventeenth-century Scotland. By 1690 the tables had turned and Somerville found that he had to flee for his life, together with his son-in-law and their families. His descendant, Edith Somerville, obtained the details of his escape to Ireland during seances, when the old clergyman came down from the ether and told her his story. William Somerville, 'a good and kindly man', was a High Churchman, an Episcopalian and rector at Leswalt, a parish in the Rhinns seven or eight miles from Stranraer. After the disestablishment of the Episcopalian Church, he and his son-in-law, the Reverend William Cameron, faced arrest and perhaps worse at the hands of the Covenanters. The two families fled by night. Edith Somerville described the scene vividly, telling how the ladies, 'sitting knitting by the light of home-made wax candles in tall silver candlesticks', were roused in the darkness and told to prepare to make the journey on horseback down the long peninsula to Portpatrick.

The Rev. William was a prosperous gentleman, and I am sure kept good horses. They have ever been a Somerville extravagance and, without horses in such a district as this, how could a Minister go about his parish? The plans are made at a feverish speed. The two ladies must ride pillion behind their husbands, Judith must hold her child in her arms, and young William must ride the pony and contrive somehow to hold little Tom in front of him. And while the two horses are being got ready, Mistress Agnes must drag little Tom out of bed, and must dress him and dress herself as suitably as possible for this incredible nightmare journey, while even as she dashes about the manse, she feels that it can be no more than a terrible dream.

All rousing stuff. We parked the microlight at the farm quite near to where my ancestors began hoofing it from Leswalt. Soon we were installed at the Crown Inn, sitting down to freshly caught plaice. Portpatrick is old-fashioned, a small no-nonsense seaside resort, where, if you are on holiday, you are obliged to go out fishing or sailing or taking brisk walks.

In the late eighteenth century this was the Gretna Green for Ireland, and eager couples would cross the sea from County Antrim to plight their troth in Scotland. If they were able to convince the local minister that there was no legal objection, they were married on the spot. Kirk records for the period from 1776 until 1826, when the practice was suppressed, show the hurried and secret weddings of 198 gentlemen, 15 army and navy officers and 13 noblemen.

In the days of the Plantations there was no proper pier or harbour, and travellers like Sir William Brereton, who made the crossing in 1634, had to hire a flat-bottomed boat and swim his five horses from a beach where they were lifted aboard by some sort of terrifying and ponderous tackle. A hundred years later there was a proper commercial ferry linking the two shores, but the sea voyage was far from comfortable. I own an eighteenth-century water-colour by John Nixon on which the artist has written in spidery lettering: 'Sick Passengers from Port Patrick to Donaghadee'. It shows two miserable travellers in an open sailing boat. One is resting his head on his arm, the other has wrapped himself in a shawl, and both look as if they want to die.

My ancestors fared even worse. 'It would seem that no sailing boat

was available. They were too near their parishes to risk being overtaken and, rather than stay in Scotland, they procured an open boat
and the two parsons, stouter fellows than might have been expected
of landsmen, rowed the long twenty miles of rough water across to
Ulster.'

Tomorrow, weather permitting, I would attempt once more to
follow in their wake.

CHAPTER TWELVE

Across the North Channel

We spent the night in one of the many guesthouses that the town provides for summer visitors. The days of importance for Portpatrick ceased in 1865 when the service to Larne was shifted to Stranraer. Today there is no longer a train terminus, and the lines of cars and lorries waiting for the boat are elsewhere. People have time to talk to you and pass the time of day among the lines of coloured houses rising up in tiers from the harbour.

'Would ye no like a wee bit more bacon?' called out the good lady of the house from the kitchen as I ate a massive breakfast. 'If ye intend to fly across the sea to Ireland, ye need plenty of fortification.'

Back on the slope overlooking the town we reviewed our position. There were some scattered clouds anchored by their shadows. Very little wind. The coast of Ireland was much clearer today, and I could make out a tall factory chimney that could well mark the entrance to Belfast Lough. The sight of something so solid and tangible made Ulster seem that much closer and more attainable. Anyone looking out across the sea could understand something about the dramas of Ireland's wars and colonization.

We attracted our last audience on British soil as the farmer and his family assembled to watch us rig up the Undertaker. With a full tank of petrol we took off uphill, barely skimming over a stone wall, and a moment later were circling the Rhinns. To the south-east a thick neck of land containing some of the best dairy pasture in Scotland led down to the lighthouse at the Mull of Galloway. Far to the south was the hump of the Isle of Man and scattered in front fishing-boats made black dots on the sea like fleas on a cloth. Behind us the coast of Scotland rose in waves of grand mountains.

We crossed a trim suburb where some children were kicking a ball around a field by the caravan park. As usual the caravans and tents looked neat from the air, the more so here, because they were contained by carefully tended gravel paths. As we passed the arms of the harbour I gave a thought to famous visitors of Portpatrick. Peter the Great (can it be true?) is supposed to have stayed in 1698. John Keats, returning from Ireland, called at the post office for his mail. This was a military town, and the official snapped out, 'What regiment?' Sarah Siddons arrived with her husband overnight by coach in order to catch the ferry for a theatre engagement in Belfast. Next morning they found the packet boat out in the bay ready to sail and, as they waited for a rowing-boat to take them out, the actress, charmed by her surroundings struck up a dramatic pose and proclaimed:

> Methinks I stand upon some rugged beach,
> Sighing to the winds, and to the waves complaining,
> While afar off the vessel sails away,
> On which my fortune and my hopes embarked.

While her husband gripped her by the arm, telling her, 'Egad, my dear, if we don't hurry, the vessel will be gone absolutely,' people rushed out from the houses on the shore to listen to her. No doubt hearing Sarah Siddons was more worthwhile than watching a microlight take off.

Portpatrick has been a place of transit, like Holyhead, with little time to build up a history for itself. Franz Liszt passed through from Ireland, landing from the mailboat, *St Patrick*, a sailing-boat which had to ride out a storm on the crossing. Owing to the heavy swell, she had to be run aground and pulled up on the beach by the crew with the assistance of local children. Liszt and his fellow passengers staggered ashore and, as his carriage could not be unloaded until low tide next morning, he stayed at Gordon's Inn, where he signed his name on a clean page of the visitors' book taking up most of the room: Ferencz Liszt. Next morning he set out for Stranraer where he was caught in a blizzard before being able to continue to Glasgow.

Out at sea we caught up with the ferryboat, the bulky ugly *Princess Galloway* which had left the terminal at Stranraer, made her way through Loch Ryan and curved around to begin her journey west. We would follow her route in that empty sea. Behind us Scottish mountains lingered majestically; ahead the Irish coastline took clearer shape, as low waves of hills began to stand out clearly and one glittering cornfield, picked out by the sun, beckoned us with a small dazzling square of gold.

On the sea below the Somervilles and Camerons had tossed about in their small boat, the two clergymen straining at their oars, dressed, according to Edith Somerville and the Reverend William's ghost, in full seventeenth-century fashion: 'voluminous wigs that Charles II had introduced. Their long coats were full skirted and made of fine black cloth, their long waistcoats almost reached down to their knees . . . Ladies' dress was, if possible, more unsuitable than that of the gentlemen for such an emergency.' Had they been seasick like John Nixon's passengers?

I shared with the Reverend William an intimate glimpse of the stretch of water dividing Galloway and Ulster and a link with lowland Scotland. The family crest, confined to silver spoons, showing a dragon charged with a trefoil behind and before outstanding on a wheel, had as its origin the legend of a Norman knight who had problems similar to those of St George. Later in the year, fired by William Somerville's exploit and imbued with the Anglo-Irish weakness for ancestor worship, I would return to Scotland and find the little parish of Linton on the borders where on the tympanum over the doorway of the church is embedded the Somerville stone. This shows the efforts of a certain John Somerville of Linton to spear a fearsome two-headed dragon known locally as the 'worme'. This creature, the terror of the countryside, three Scots yards long and somewhat thicker than a man's leg, had its den in an area which is still called the 'worme's hole' and had proved impervious to spear and lance. Sir John, however, the first of many engineers in the family, observing that 'when this creature looked upon a man, she always stared him in the face with open mouth', had a spear made twice the ordinary length which he planted on 'a little slender wheel of irone' which, with the aid of his servant, he thrust in the serpent's mouth. A seventeenth-century account of the incident tells how

about the sun rysing, this serpent or worme . . . appeared with her head and some part of her bodie without the den. Whereupon the servant, according to the directions, set fyre to the peat upon the wheel at the top of the lance, and instantly the resolute gentleman put spurs to his horse, advanced with a full gallop, the fyre still increasing, placed the same with the wheel and almost the third part of the lance directly in the serpent's mouth, which went doune her throat, into her belly, which he left there, the lance breaking by the rebound of his horse, giving her a deadly wound.

I felt warmly about my resourceful forebear. And about others, too, fierce border lords. The font at Linton is particularly large, intended for the total immersion of infants – but the custom was that male babies were not totally immersed in holy water. Their right arms were kept out, so remaining heathen, so that they could be used to kill as hard as they liked, without prejudicing the chance of the rest of the body of getting into Heaven.

Looking back at the Galloway mountains, I was proud to be associated with the resourceful and noble Scottish engineer, the dry-armed warriors always ready for the fight, not to mention the embattled Anglican clergyman who had rowed his family to safety just where I was flying, in the wake of the *Galloway Princess*, which had still not reached the halfway point of her journey to Larne.

Soon we overtook the ferry as we approached County Antrim; ahead was Larne Harbour and the wide arms of Belfast Lough. To the right I could see the line of the Antrim coast all the way up to Fair Head, a series of grey-edged bumps and hollows.

The little microlight was behaving perfectly. There were no warning stutters or gusty tremors of wind to shake us and frighten us. Even the radio worked, just about the first time it had functioned properly, and Graham managed to call up the local radio station. The crossing took three quarters of an hour, a leisurely passage of time sitting back and enjoying the view. We looked down the mouth of Belfast Lough, past Whitehead and Carrickfergus towards the city. The Copeland Islands, home for thousands of birds, appeared as dark smudges on the water like oil slicks. Then we headed north towards Larne where the outline we had seen from Portpatrick turned into fields and farmhouses. The scale seemed much smaller this side of the water and the first grey house with smoke pouring from its chimney was a home for dwarfs. There was the same cornfield I had seen, first from twenty, then from fifteen, then from ten miles away, the same golden lozenge shining in the sun, turned into a patch of ripening barley.

Even the dockyards and terminal at Larne seemed small, suited for

Meccano. Soon the *Princess Galloway* would be arriving and the procession of cars would begin to move off, while passengers, including the usual tough guys tattooed with Union Jacks and Red Hands, would disembark.

From Larne to Ballymena was a short hop over low sedgy green hills where the view took on a familiarity which filled me with pleasure. I was over home ground. Even the sky took on the changeable quality associated with Irish weather, sunshine one moment, a couple of breaths, then a spot of rain, and for a time the two moods blended so that we were flying through a damp rainbow of speckled light.

Graham, who had been unusually talkative over the radio, shouted back to me, 'We're probably the first.' He was still preoccupied with entering the record books. Should we have sought publicity and informed the press? I had lacked the Branson spirit, especially after my dismal attempts to obtain sponsorship. No generous manufacturer, airline or philanthropist had been interested in having a name written on the Undertaker's wing. No one had offered me petrol or anything useful. Nothing but a few kind replies: 'We wish you well in your venture.'

Graham had become jumpy. He had never been in Ireland before and, even though he had been over it for only ten minutes, he was already nervous. Resourceful and efficient in the air, he seemed to think that down there on the ground there would be a terrorist lurking under every hedge. Also, we were both worried about procedures. Would we have problems rising out of our declared aim of travelling south across the border?

We went straight to Ballymena to inform the RUC there of our arrival. We flew by Shane's Hill, Magherabone, Douglas Top and among the Slemish mountains which stretched out of sight below the misty shapes of clouds.

One sign that this was a peaceful area was the lack of any look-out helicopter over the town. Over Belfast, Derry and other Ulster trouble spots the helicopter is part of life. I was familiar with the hawklike Lynx hovering for hours over Belfast, mounted with its Marconi-Elliott surveillance camera, the Heli-Teli with colour film that can pick out faces from about 500 feet. These droning spies stay motionless above houses, capable of looking down and examining a family sitting-room or picking out a brand of cigarette a man is smoking, recognizing faces and figures, witnessing murder. In the city they are constant as the sun and moon and noisy as any microlight. But Ballymena was quiet, sprawling below us, a few factories and housing estates petering into small fields. We circled round looking for a landing-place, and found our last playing-field, a green patch surrounded by houses close to the town centre.

Because there were no brakes to the microlight, Graham always had to make sure that we would have enough room to land. The safety margin was small, and if there was any doubt it was always better to put on full throttle, go up and round and try again. Landing in a strange town was always an adventure. The glide angle had to be right and the judgement of distance correct. And now for the last time I observed how quickly life emerged from a relief map view of an urban complex, which in an instant became transformed into individual back gardens and lines of washing and TV masts sticking out of roofs. As we floated down on them, the sense of speed always became alarming and, in those last few moments before landing, vision was assailed with scores of quick impressions – a woman's startled face at a window, a milk van suddenly pulling up as our shadow cut across a street, children playing, cars, plenty of cars, one having trouble parking, an old woman burdened with shopping-bags. Then we crossed the last little terrace and the playing-field was waiting. The farm at Portpatrick seemed far away.

The Wakehurst Playing-Field in the heart of Ballymena might have been anywhere in England and I sensed that Graham was disappointed. A few people ambled over the grass to have a look, while I went off to find a local garage, where, following Scottish instructions, I rang the RUC.

'Where did you say you've come from?'

'Scotland.'

'That's a wee distance away. What do you want?'

They took their time before a group of four uniformed men drove up.

'Is she brand new?'

'I wouldn't mind one myself.'

The sun came out as we stood and watched the admiring group of flak-jacketed policemen examining the microlight. She looked splendid. I was a little surprised myself that, after such a long gruelling flight around England, the Pegasus XL had stood up so well. Nothing had happened to her apart from that one dented strut she had received in Brighton. Graham hadn't changed oil or plugs. She looked pristine.

We learned that there were very few microlights in Northern Ireland, where they were regarded as a novelty. We had the honour of being the first ever to land in Ballymena. Graham beamed at this achievement and his nervousness gave way to relief and then to gratification at all the interest. I listened as he became loquacious, pointing out the mechanics, how to start the engine, how to fly, like a salesman demonstrating a product.

'How much would she cost?'

'How long would it take me to fly to Belfast?'

They sweated in their flak jackets on this warm day. One constable had been working in his garden when he heard us overhead coming into land, a time when the noise is particularly penetrating, and it did indeed pass through his mind that we might belong to an illegal organization. Another, Sam Andrews, a young man with a bushy moustache, had always been fascinated by hang gliders. He had never seen a microlight before, and there was envy in his eyes as he examined the long tapering wing and the shiny blue cockpit.

'Oh, wouldn't I love one of those!'

Another man buckled himself in the seat and pretended he was going to take off. The others laughed.

'I wouldn't do that, Billy.'

'She's easy enough to fly – sure, there's only one pedal.'

'What about insurance?'

'What's her fastest speed?'

'My lawn mower has an engine like that!'

At last they let us go and watched us climb in and start her with the first pull before taxiing back to the far edge of the field. The throttle roared as we took off smoothly with a wave to the three RUC men. They got back into the car and drove to their barracks, a brick fortress surrounded by the usual wire enclosure, shut in by heavy iron doors, high enough to discourage mortars. As we flew in the direction of Lough Neagh, the three lunched in the cafeteria and afterwards were briefed by the superintendent about policing a local cricket match. On the outside, the barracks may look as austere as a medieval castle, but, inside, it is comfortable enough with games room and communication room whose walls are lined with maps. Above the staircase a small memorial flanked with wreaths topped by the crest of shamrocks and harp that associates the RUC with Celtic symbolism, has the names of seven local officers killed in the current troubles. 'We will remember them.' The area around Ballymena is considered quiet.

Sam Andrews, patrolling the Glens of Antrim in a police Ford Granada, whose bright orange stripe and blue overhead lights made every motorist within sight slow down instantly, gave a good deal of thought to microlights. He considered the possibilities of flying one, of perhaps eventually owning one. The patrol drove in a wide circle back to Ballymena in some of the most beautiful country in Ireland, crossing the high back of the Glens, passing numerous small farms, moving in sight of the distant flash of the sea, and then down into Cushendall on the shores of Red Bay. The Glens are peaceful, touched with the presence of St Patrick, but on occasion the Troubles intrude brutally, as they did the year before, when a young man returning to meet his girlfriend, after playing in an Orange band, was attacked and killed. The revolver in Sam's belt was a constant reminder of the possibility of violence. That afternoon, however, he continued to brood about the grand microlight that had landed on the Wakehurst Playing-Field. He wasn't to know that he had seen her off on her last few hours of flight, and he learned of her fate only many months later.

We had been told to check in at the airport at Enniskillen for customs control before crossing over the border and flying on to Sligo. But the clouds would get us before that. A wall of them blanked off an area of Donegal beyond the Sperrin Mountains, and others were massing to the west of Lough Neagh. We were approaching the silver disc of Lough Neagh with Aldergrove Airport on the far side and, to the south, the rolling summits of the Mournes on their way to the sea. The green of the fields was iridescent beside the shining lake, the largest in the British Isles, with scarcely a soul on it or around it. In midsummer I could see no surfboards, no water-skiers, just the odd boat.

At Toome Bridge we flew over the Fishermen's Co-operative where they catch and market eels. Two men were bringing in the morning supply from the trap across the river, millions of freshly caught squirming eels which would all go abroad. Local opinion has it that foreigners eat them because they are great aphrodisiacs. The office at the co-operative was in the charge of an elderly priest who may have given a thought as to why St Patrick did not expel this lot along with the snakes. They swim from the Sargasso Sea to Lough Neagh before going on to tickle French and German palates.

'Easy does it.'

A few slip out of the net as they are taken from the trap and slither on the ground. The larger ones, weighing eight or nine pounds, seem as big as pythons. In the shed across the river a group of men stand around a large wooden table carrying pincers and wearing protective gloves as eels plummet from a chute. At this late stage in their odyssey, before being packed in boxes of crushed ice marked LOUGH NEAGH EELS, they are prepared to give a painful bite.

We could see the stone bridge with the eel fishery on one side and the large walled RUC barracks on the other guarding the village of Toome Bridge. A Union Jack flew over the church tower, which, together with the octagonal spire beside it, had been erected in 1788 by the earl-bishop of Bristol, whose passion for building was not confined to grandiose curved houses – he built numerous churches all over his diocese of Londonderry.

A little fall in pressure made the microlight shiver, and the air grew darker. Lough Neagh is the largest lake in the British Isles and it has the reputation of being the most boring. The flat landscape on the sides of this inland sea is considered particularly dull. A strong westerly wind was whipping up the waters and the lough was showing its teeth. Surrounded by a bleak grey shore, the lines of frothy waves had sent the 200 licensed eel boats home and, apart from a couple of yachts and the *Lady Sara* berthed in the new marina outside Ballyronan, there wasn't a vessel in sight. A few hundred yards away a couple of prefabs and a cottage stood on the empty shore, all that remained of a tourist development blown up by the IRA.

Another Union Jack fluttered over the tower of a church in Ballinderry and, not far off, a last flash of sun picked out IRA in big black letters on a wall. Graham was pointing to the southern end of the lough, where I could see dark rain obscuring the shoreline. We changed course towards Coalisland on our way to Enniskillen, aiming to cross the border into the Republic soon after.

Flying over England I had been constantly made aware of the precious nature of green space between each urban patch, the demands of living space competing with agriculture, the destruction wrought by modern agricultural methods, the restless movement of millions of people and all the battles of the countryside. Below us now, in deceptive tranquillity, was a landscape that even more than the pleasant patch of Wales and the part of Galloway over which we had flown seemed caught in a time warp. The small family-sized farms, with their handkerchief-sized fields, whose boundaries were laid out with an exactness that suggested the use of a theodolite, suggested a way of life that retained kinship and tradition.

We were approaching Dungannon in the dwindling light of the overcast sky, and soon we were unable to look more than 200 yards ahead into dark vapour. We searched the dumpy hills and hovered above the winding roads looking for a suitable place to land, while the black clouds chased us up until the moment when Graham spotted a steep green slope above a valley.

He braced himself to find the right height and speed, the right line-up and room to manoeuvre and try again. At the second attempt he got it right with a sharp steep turn that had us almost hanging on the tip of the wing before he straightened out and swooped downwards. I was as surprised as the bullocks who watched our strange arrival in their midst.

Graham switched off the engine. 'I can't stand those stupid bloody animals.'

Heavy raindrops splattered the wings as half a dozen bovine heads came nearer. Up at the top of the fields I could see that some cars had pulled up and the drivers were peering through the shower to watch us with similar unwavering stares.

CHAPTER THIRTEEN

Clogher

When the rain stopped we took off in the direction of Dungannon, a wee distance away just over the hill, a cluster of glinting grey rooftops washed by the shower, church tower and Union Jack, walled-in barracks, sprouting radio and signal antennae and a large ugly green helicopter that had risen hurriedly and was now sidling crabwise in our direction. One moment we had been the only thing flying in the sky, the next we were charged by this clanking monster circling up on us and whirling its great rotors. I could see two small heads in giant helmets peering in our direction.

I waved my gloved hand in what I hoped was a friendly manner – like the Queen Mother. The helicopter did another circuit, making the microlight stagger, and I could see Graham was getting increasingly tense. A little closer, and the gush of wind from the whirling rotors could easily finish us.

Our sudden appearance over the town may well have been alarming, considering how rare microlights were in Northern Ireland. If RUC stations can be bombed with mortars from the backs of lorries, there is no reason, in theory, why terrorists might not vary their means of attack. Military uses of microlights are still uncertain – on occasion Graham had demonstrated their capabilities to the British Army. The IRA have not got hold of helicopters, although Rose Dugdale attempted a jail break in one over a decade ago. Since microlights are relatively cheap and, given time, not hard to learn to fly, they might easily be adapted for unfriendly purposes. We could be attempting to lob a grenade into Dungannon's defences. Did we look harmless? After my cheery wave, the thing flew away. Either the pilot recognized a pair of sporting amateurs, or he had heard from the RUC in Ballymena.

More rain came down, the low green hills became shadows beneath our wing, and a shining road pointed the way to Enniskillen. We were in Tyrone over Ballygawley, and just ahead was the Clogher Valley studded with the Three Towns, Augher, Clogher and Fivemiletown.

Augher, a pleasant village on the Blackwater, contains a castle with the rousing name of Spur Royal, built by Lord Ridgeway as a plantation stronghold in 1611. Fivemiletown is called in Irish *Baile na Lorgan*, 'Town of the Shank'. Its English name derives from the erroneous supposition that it is five miles equidistant from Clabby, Clogher and Colebrooke. Around and about they still make hand-crocheted lace. Clogher, two miles west of Augher, would be the end of our journey.

Clogher is the Regia of Ptolemy, the seat of the most ancient bishopric in Ireland, founded by St Patrick. We approached it over a dark and forbidding tangle of woods – somewhere in their midst was St Patrick's Well and Chair, the last a massive boulder, surrounded with dripping ferns.

Around it little pieces of cloth had been tied to trees, together with other votive offerings, a religious medal, a torn photo, a piece of broken comb, a nylon stocking. Perhaps if we had the opportunity to leave something . . .

The Clogher Valley, which has been described as 'the richest, fairest and best inhabited land in Ireland', was famous long before St Patrick. Neighbouring Rathmore was the ancient dwelling place of the kings of Oriel and a Bronze Age burial site is located at Knockmany. There is the usual estate and relics of a plantation family. A few miles beyond St Patrick's Chair I made out the shape of a forlorn country house with overgrown garden, long winding avenue and dripping trees. Opposite the Moutray family once owned more than 9,000 acres of a grace and favour estate here. Memories of Moutrays linger in church memorials in the small castellated estate church opposite the house. Stella Moutray, who died of a broken heart after making a misalliance with a policeman, is commemorated by a carved marble lectern in the shape of a kneeling angel. Another Miss Moutray, who played the organ, has her memorial in brass. 'Lord, who has provided such musical flowers for sinners here on earth; what must Thou have provided for Thy saints in Paradise?'

Canon O'Neill was giving his final blessing in St Mary's Portclore church to the bridal couple as we flew overhead. A wedding was a rare occasion in this small Protestant community. Old Sam Ferguson began cranking the bellows as the organist played the Wedding March and the four bridesmaids in pink dresses with white silk bows gathered behind the newly weds, the best man adjusted his red carnation and outside children waited to throw confetti.

A few hundred yards away in a cosy gate-lodge of the Moutray mansion old Mrs Clarke was making herself a cup of tea, remembering the old days when the big house was kept spick and span, and so was the garden and the walks and everything else. Now she couldn't bear to look at the place. At Augher a group of farmers was sitting down to a plateful of ham sandwiches after a busy day at the mart. The café, once the railway station, reminded them of the old days before the last train, or tram, as it was called, had run in 1941. Framed on the wall was the verse composed when the line was opened in 1887, which Amanda Ros could not have written better.

> On the 2nd of May we must now say in the present year
> Was opened up the new tramway from what we read and hear
> This lovely railway hill and dale, it cuts a glorious shine
> From Tynan to Maguire's Bridge on the Clogher Valley Line.

Outside the café cars and lorries were belting down the road a few miles to Clogher, on the next little hill a line of houses leading up to the cathedral tower topping the town. There was the old market house, a burnt-out hotel, the walled-in RUC barracks and the Bishop's Palace, now an old people's home where the matron was supervising tea. In the days of liveried servants and splendid social gatherings, the bishop and his guests had looked down the flights of stone steps that led to the little lake full of swans. Bishops of Clogher included the wealthy Robert Clayton, D.D., friend of Mrs Delany, translated from Cork, who was faintly heretical; John Garnett, D.D., translated from Ferns and Leighlin, 'pious, humble, good natured . . . a generous encourager of literature and justly esteemed, who, although he had but one eye, could discover men of merit'. There was James Spottiswood, D.D., who discovered that Beath, grandson of Noah, had landed in Northern Ireland from a second ark, together with thirty of the most beautiful women in the world, and gave his name to Slieve Beagh. According to Spottiswood, Beath is buried under a great cairn nearby, built by the same beautiful ladies, each carrying a single heavy stone.

Here at the palace where the old women sucked at their tea, Bishop John Stearne, described as 'good John', dispensed an ample table. Dean Smedley wrote of him in mildewed verse:

> Good John indeed with beef and claret
> Makes the place warm that one may bear it,
> He has a purse to keep a table,
> And eke his soul is hospitable.

This hearty and kindly friend of Dean Swift rebuilt the handsome barnlike St Macartan's Cathedral at the top of Clogher Hill before Dean Richard Bagwell remodelled it all over again in 1818.

The succession of deans and bishops whose handsome portraits hang in the porch followed on the most ancient traditions of Irish Christianity. The first Bishop of Clogher was St Macartan, St Patrick's strong man. Late in life while he was carrying St Patrick across a ford near Augher, he was heard to complain – 'I am now an old man and infirm, and my comrades have churches, but I am still on the road.' St Patrick listened to his muttering and replied: 'I will leave thee in a Church and it shall not be too near for good neighbourhood, nor yet too far off to pay a friendly visit.' After Macartan had been appointed bishop, around AD 493, St Patrick preached a mile away at Findermore to a vast congregation to whom he expounded the Gospel.

St Brigid, who happened to be St Macartan's niece, came to Clogher, and many other saints have associations with the place – St Enda of Arran, St Faenche, St Dympna, St Sinell, St Finnian, St Cillin, St Colman, St Senach, St Ultan (who was buried at Clogher) and St Tighernach, Abbot of Clones, who succeeded Macartan as second Bishop of Clogher. We had chosen to crash the microlight in a holy place.

There is evidence that before St Patrick singled out this spot, it was already holy ground to pagans. Inside the porch, among the painted bishops, stands the *Clogh-Oir*, or 'Golden Stone', from which Clogher may have derived its name. (But other authorities prefer the derivation that translates as 'stony place'.) The *Clogh-Oir* was the chief idol of the north, from which the devil used to speak until the building of the cathedral silenced him.

In the cattle mart on Station Road they were ending a busy afternoon. Cattle prices were high and no one would say if the amounts were related to smuggling on the border. From the main street you could hear the drone of the auctioneer's voice coming out of the shed, punctuated by the occasional bellow of an animal awaiting its fate. Around the little ring, the lines of dealers made their bids with winks, lifted eyebrows, a stubby finger raised above a battered felt hat and grimy coat, all noted down by the young auctioneers. There were smells of manure, straw, cattle, old boots and machines.

The grey tower of the cathedral rising into the sky is a familiar landmark for miles around, one which we would be looking out for. William Carleton, who lived in the Clogher Valley and wrote about its country folk, remembered how

> As the Bell whose distant swell
> In the grey Cathedral's tower
> With measured sweep came slow and deep
> To wake devotion's power,
> 'Twas sweet to join the village train
> And solemnize the hour.

We were following the main road to Clogher and the clouds were closing in for the last time, so that the hills had vanished. Graham decided to do the safe thing, avoid the weather and land at the first available spot. A mile west of Clogher he saw a field and made a quick investigation. First a low-level turn around a farmhouse and small church, then back to the cathedral tower before coming in for the last leg. Much of the ground was hilly, but nothing looked difficult or different from the location of other landings we had made. I noticed a farmer cutting silage in a neighbouring field with two trucks following up behind his tractor, a woman driving cattle into a shed, and a car going up the hill towards Clogher.

We turned into our final leg for landing, but instead of lightly touching down on the grassy slope, we headed straight into the ground. When you land, the ground always rushes to meet you, but this time it was doing it at the speed of gravity. Then we hit it. I could smell petrol and grass. Graham was lying below me and the wing cut a broken angle against the sky.

In the sudden silence I could hear the tractor still at work.

'Are you all right?'

Graham opened his eyes, then closed them again. 'Yes.'

It had been a good accident since we would get up and walk away. Like passengers in a plunging lift who leap up at the last moment, we had been insulated and unharmed, while the surrounding structure had taken the battering.

Microlights are less dangerous than other aircraft because of their lower speed and lighter weight. The Pegasus XL weighs 200 pounds, which is a third of the weight of the original Wrights' Kittyhawk Flyer, and a lot less than something substantial like a Cessna. The little engine in the back does not offer too much cause for worry either, and a crash and burn type of accident is unusual in a microlight which strikes the ground at only a fraction of the energy of a conventional light aircraft.

Flying in small eccentric aircraft is a relatively safe activity. In Britain, during the seven years between 1980 and 1986, twenty-two people were killed in microlights, and, eerily, exactly the same number were killed in hang gliders, and the same number again, twenty-two, in gliders and sailplanes. The safest form of recreational flying is the airship or balloon: no one at all was killed in them during that period, although, subsequently, Richard Branson gave the hot air balloon something of a bad name. Navigation error, weather hazards, carbon monoxide and ignorance will cause some accidents; others will occur because of temperament. Impatience, bad temper, urgency and over-confidence will kill you just as easily as lack of skill. An American psychologist has listed thought patterns that can affect pilot judgement – anti-authority, invulnerability, impulsiveness, out-of-control and macho. The macho condition was ascribed to 'people with the thought pattern of being under the illusion that they are superior to or better than others. Their behavior is risk-taking, and they expose themselves to unnecessary dangers.' But none of these thought patterns had been contributory to our accident. There is another factor in accidents.

Bad luck.

'What happened?'

Graham said, 'Sink.'

The field where we had crashed had seemed flat, but, unseen from the air, part of it had lifted upwards. Sink was the phenomenon engendered by this deceptive slope which had turned the field into a kill devil hill where the curl of wind, deflected against it, had caused a vacuum into which we had fallen.

Otto Lilienthal said, 'Flying is nothing more than a constant opposition to that force with which the earth attracts all creatures.'

Among the 30,000 or so people who fly in light aircraft of all types, the accident rate is relatively small compared to road accidents. Flying accidents attract publicity because they are usually spectacular and dramatic.

This one had been neither. No one took any notice. The farmer in the next field continued to cut his silage.

The Undertaker had fallen into the hill and cartwheeled over so that its nose stuck in the ground. A few hours ago we had been congratulated on the machine's pristine appearance, its gleaming metalwork, the smooth gloss of the trike, the dark mahogany of the propeller, the crisp yellow and blue of the Dacron wing. Now the front wheel had broken off, there were holes in the body as if it had been attacked with a pitchfork, bits of jagged hairy stuff had appeared as if the fibreglass was unravelling, the wing was bent at an angle, gold and alloy wires and struts were bent and broken, the propeller was smashed and the grass around was scattered with splinters of wood and pieces of metal. There were the battered cross-booms whose recommended life was 1,000 hours, the leading edges, set to last 900 hours, the bent kingpost, the snapped rigging wires, all the components programmed for a reasonable flying life now shattered after less than 100 hours.

We were fine. A few bruises, the hands shaky for a few moments. We tidied up as much as we could and piled up the bits against a wall. In the next field the man on the tractor was still mowing as we approached him.

'Can we leave it here?'

'You can, surely,' he said, and went on cutting silage.

I reminded myself that we had crashed in a border area near bandit country and he may well have wondered who we were and decided to have nothing to do with us.

I thought of the red-shirted ploughman in Brueghel's picture of *The Fall of Icarus*. The artist took the theme from Ovid who wrote that when Daedalus and his son went by, 'some fisherman, perhaps plying his quivering rod, some shepherd leaning on his staff, or a peasant bent over his plough handle caught sight of them as they flew past or stood still in astonishment, believing that these creatures who could fly through the air must be gods'. But Brueghel, the peasant,

knew better than the poet, and although the shepherd and his dog
tending sheep have time to look up at the fly past, the fisherman,
who has made a strike, and the ploughman, intent on achieving a
straight furrow, ignore poor Icarus, deceived by his wax wings as we
had been deceived by sink.

I also gave a thought to the old man who lies dead beneath the
trees on the left of that mysterious picture.

Icarus's father made the 74-mile journey from Crete to Santorini
safely. Recently a Greek cycling champion re-enacted Daedalus's
achievement in a rose-coloured, seventy-pound module made of
carbon fibre and hi-tech plastic with 112-foot wing span (the poor old
Undertaker's wing span was thirty-four feet). Far from flying too
near the sun, Kanellos Kanellopoulos pedalled along fifteen feet above
the waters of the Aegean, averaging 18.5 miles an hour. But there was
an echo of Icarus at the end, when, after completing the crossing and
achieving a record for man-powered flight, he found his machine
disintegrating just before touchdown when the wind put on a petulant
display of turbulence.

We left everything behind, shaving kits, toothbrushes, the lot,
including Pushkin and *The Rattle Bag*.

> A handsome young airman lay dying,
> And as on the tarmac he lay,
> To the mechanics who round him came sighing,
> These last dying words he did say:
> 'Take the cylinders out of my kidneys,
> Take the connecting-rod out of my brain,
> Take the cam-shaft from out of my backbone
> And assemble the engine again.'

It was about a mile up the hill to Clogher. I didn't look back as we
laboured up the winding country lane. Jackdaws were riding gusts of
wind with tattered wings, falling to earth one after another like a
tumbling house of cards. They could deal instinctively with problems
of sink. The sky was growing darker. We walked past scrappy fields
with bristling rushes, bounded by thick hedgerows, across a humped
stone bridge over a stream, past a Presbyterian chapel and lines of
gnomes leading up to a bungalow. A man on a bike raised a hand to
us.

At Clogher the black clouds that had stopped us and made us crash were spilling on to the main street. The parish priest got out of his car and hurried into MacCaughly's Food Store. Five armed RUC men emerged from their fortress and began to move up the street in the rain, followed by some soldiers wearing camouflage uniforms, also carrying stubby guns.

'Hallo sweetie!' one called out to a woman standing in a doorway on the other side of the street who didn't reply.

We walked into a bar and I ordered Irish whiskey.

The barman shook his head. 'Sorry, we don't keep it.'

Perhaps it was considered vaguely Republican? But there was a sign in the window advertising Old Bushmills. Graham ordered Irish coffee, but there was none of that either. In desperation he tried bitter, but the barman had no bitter.

Graham cried out, 'What sort of place is this?' Two men in dirty coats were watching television. One said, 'Do you know it's only twenty-three weeks to Christmas?' Five others who had come from the mart were perched around the counter drinking pints and short ones. Scotch, presumably. A man whose hat was pulled down over his ears left off discussing cattle prices and addressed Graham.

'Do you know any town where the people on one side of the street don't speak to those on the other?'

'No.'

'Here, man! Up the road. For they are facing the graveyard!'

There was a burst of laughter and then silence. Outside the rain poured down and the rush of cars and lorries made the walls tremble. My plan was to take the bus to Dublin, while Graham would get back to England as quickly as possible. I never wanted to see him again.

Later I hurried up to St Macartan's Cathedral where the evening service was beginning. Next week there would be a Festival of Flowers on the theme of Christ the King which would be opened by the Duchess of Abercorn. The great doors were swung open, the bell began to ring, and inside the porch the bishops looked out of their frames, two Leslie bishops (connections of mine), Bishop Stearne, Bishop Lord John Beresford, Bishop Spottiswood and fashionable Bishop Clayton. Mrs Delany and her dear D.D., Dean Delany, had stayed in Clogher as guests of the Claytons. She had helped to build a shell grotto and danced on Mrs Clayton's birthday.

There were eight couples of very clever dances, and madam and I divided a man between us and made up the nine couple of turns; at eleven we went to supper – a sumptuous cold collation. At twelve the fiddlers struck up again, and every lad took his lass 'To trip it on the light fantastic toe'. The Bishop always goes to bed at ten, but that night he sat up till eleven.

I went back to the bar. In the seventeenth century Clogher had been devastated by wars. 'A wild country enough to Clogher,' Sir Thomas Molyneux recorded, 'this is a borough, but a most miserable one, having not above three or four houses in it and not even the remains of any one, tho' this is certainly a very ancient See.'

The street was deserted as the rain continued to fall. I thought about my broken microlight and all those aerial adventures I had planned around Ireland. From Sligo I would have gone down to Connemara, to the Twelve Pins and Clifden where Alcock and Brown had crashed in a bog (how had they got on personally?). Those western skies with their towering peaks of clouds rising above the mountains would have contrasted with English skies. I would have joined the Shannon and flown from Limerick to Cork. There was Kerry, Killarney and its lakes to explore, the Blackwater and Lismore, Cashel and Kilkenny, familiar Mount Leinster and the Wicklow Hills. I had planned to land on Sandymount Strand.

I had flown in England and Scotland in tandem and I would never fly alone. I would have to be content with my one solo flight, and the memory of hovering over the green fields of Carlow by myself would have to be enough.

Graham had gone and so had the farmers. I went inside and ordered another drink.